Harm

Harm is first published in English the United Kingdom in 2022 by Corylus Books Ltd, and was originally published in Icelandic as *Skaði* in 2021 by Salka.

Published by arrangement with Salka, Iceland.
www.salka.is

This book has been translated with a financial support from:
ICELANDIC LITERATURE CENTER

Corylus Books Ltd

corylusbooks.com

ISBN: 978-1-9163797-8-7

Harm

Sólveig Pálsdóttir

Translated by Quentin Bates

Published by Corylus Books Ltd

HARM

1

Ríkharður felt his head spin as he stood up. He stumbled, his chair toppled and crashed against the next table, so that a grey-haired man sitting there dropped his wine. A burgundy stain spread across the pearl-white tablecloth.

'What the hell d'you think you're doing?' the man snarled, suddenly on his feet. The woman sitting opposite shushed him.

'Calm down. It was an accident,' she said, making an effort to defuse the sudden tension. A waiter abruptly left off taking an order at another table and hurried across to them.

'Really sorry, I didn't mean to spill ... Sorry ... I just needed to...' Ríkharður tried to explain, and realised that he was in no condition to say anything. A firm hand took his arm, steering him away from the table. He saw thick, dark hair, twisted into a bun. Diljá, his girlfriend. The word 'girlfriend' swam back and forth through his muddled thoughts. This was a ridiculous term to use at his age, and then he remembered that she wasn't that any longer.

'That's about enough, isn't it?'

Through the mist he registered the accusing tone of voice, and tried to give her a smile. He made a feeble attempt to stroke her back, but his hand went astray and he ended up patting her arm.

'You're so beautiful, my darling,' he mumbled. 'Let's go to sleep. I just need to nip to the...'

He barely managed to make his way between the chairs and

tables without crashing into anything or upsetting more glasses of wine, out into the passage where he found the toilets. Supporting himself with a hand against the wall, he peed as the world around him undulated. It was as well there was no nausea, not yet, at least. He staggered to the basins and let cold water gush over his wrists. An old trick from his younger days that still came in useful when he'd had a drink too many. Then he leaned down and put his head under the icy stream, scooping water in his palm to the back of his neck and behind his ears. Soaked to the shoulders, with his mind a little clearer, he cast around for towels, but all he could see were the hand dryers. Unsteady on his feet, he leaned against a basin and tried to work out how he could dry himself off. Then his head again began to swim. It would have to be toilet paper, and he reached for a roll.

'Lightweight,' he muttered to himself as he tried to pick off the scraps of toilet paper stuck to his face. 'No endurance these days, old man. And this is a bit undignified,' he told his reflection, making an effort to shake his head, but that again set the room spinning around him.

He was feeling slightly better as he pushed open the door out into the passage where Diljá waited by the coat hooks. She took his arm and supported him down the steep steps to the deserted street.

The group had arrived the day before in the Westman Islands, and were booked on the next day's ferry back. Ingi Thór, Eygló, Ásmundur and Katrín had checked into a hotel while he and Diljá were staying in the caravan he had bought a few days before in a fit of extravagance. At any rate, that was his explanation. The real reason was that he wanted Diljá all to himself and simply had no inclination to stay in the same place as her friends. Ríkharður had figured out that there was a good chance of being woken at some early hour to go and ride a bike, swim in the sea or even take an ice bath, or some such madness that he had no desire to be part of. He had already agreed to buy the caravan when Diljá announced that this trip would mainly be about enjoying the better things in life, although it went without saying that the featherweight racing bicycles would also come with them. So it didn't seem worth cancelling the caravan.

They had stayed up well into the night, and the following day had been packed. Lunch had taken two hours, with delicious seafood at the restaurant, liberally accompanied by white wine. Then they had walked out to the famous graveyard with its 'I live and you shall live' legend over the gate, which had remained clear of the ash that blanketed the island in the 1973 eruption, then they had visited the museum. After that Ríkharður had meant to refresh himself with a swim, but time was pressing and there was a table reserved for them at seven-thirty. So he and Diljá had gone up to Herjólfsdalur to get changed in the magnificent caravan that was practically as smart as any five-star hotel suite. Ríkharður smiled at the thought as he ripped the plastic from a freshly laundered shirt, slipped it on and began to button it up. Diljá was wearing the colourful silk dress he had given her for the big day, but he could also see her wearing this when he took her to gatherings with his friends or colleagues. They would stare at her in fascination and envious glances would come his way. He stopped with the shirt half-buttoned and gazed at her in admiration. Diljá was so beautiful, with her long brown hair and dark eyes. She smiled, and kissed him gently on the lips. This sent a jolt of excitement coursing through him. His Diljá, young, petite and delicate, but as powerful and lithe as a cat. Her temperament followed the same pattern, enchanting, but liable to change as suddenly as the unpredictable Westman Islands winds, and that troubled him. But she was his, his alone. It was for her that he did things that wouldn't have even crossed his mind before, such as being here with her friends, whom he found rather strange, although he was aware that she no doubt felt the same way about his friends. The difference between them in age and outlook on life made their relationship a complex one, and while she wasn't exactly talkative, he'd occasionally have to ask her to talk less.

Now he yearned to be able to forget the others and give dinner a miss. He took her in his arms, running a hand down her back to cup a buttock.

'Come to bed,' he whispered breathlessly.

'Not now,' she said, drawing out her words. 'We mustn't be late.'

'Come on. Why not?'

'Afterwards. Promise,' she said, slipping neatly from his arms, adding that she'd make them each a mojito, his favourite. She opened a cupboard to reach for a pack of cane sugar. 'Why don't you finish changing, and I'll fix the cocktails?'

He did as she asked, pulling on his trousers and fastening the last shirt button just as she handed him his drink.

'Cheers, my love,' she said, looking deep into his eyes.

'Here's to us,' he replied, leaning in for a kiss, but she had again slipped away.

'Need to get myself ready. Time flies,' she said, teasingly fluttering her eyelashes.

'Are you worried about something, my darling?' he asked, taking the opportunity as she pulled her dress over her head to put his arms around her from behind, holding her tight around her middle. 'I know you'll be with me tonight...' he crooned into one neatly sculpted ear. She wriggled herself free.

'Ach, stop it, will you, Ríkharður?' she snapped.

'That's a tune from here in the Islands, by a couple of famous...'

She cut him off sharply, saying, 'you know, I don't find anything even slightly sexy about those ancient songs of yours,' and softened her tone as he was unable to hide his disappointment. 'You need to move with the times, my lovely old man. Won't you finish your drink?'

She smiled quickly, and kissed the end of his nose.

'I suppose so,' he replied sulkily. He emptied his glass and noticed that hers had hardly been touched. These days Diljá drank little alcohol and he sometimes felt she was going through the motions to humour him. He could feel the hurt inside that her words had left behind. Why did she behave like this? He was far from being an old guy who made a habit of crooning old tunes. He was a highly-educated, well-off man with a glittering career, and Diljá should be thanking her lucky stars that she had been able to reel him in.

'Don't tell me you're going to leave it like that?' he said in irritation, waving a hand at the pile of clothes she had changed out of. 'Can't you fold these up and put them away? You're like a badly brought up teenager.' Diljá glanced at him and he saw the flash of anger in her eyes, reminding him that she was sensitive. He'd have to take care. 'Just joking, my love. That's all,' he hurried to say, blowing her a kiss.

'We're going to be late for the aperitif. They'll be waiting for us,' Diljá said, picking up the clothes. He watched her clear up, and resolved to hold back with criticism. He didn't want to upset her, but it irritated him to see how clumsily she went about this. Unbelievable, he thought, that an adult should be unable to fold clothes properly.

'You're not going to drive, are you?' he said, shrugging on his jacket. 'It's only a short walk.'

'I'll drive. I've hardly had anything to drink,' she replied. 'The police have to be pretty laid back in a small place like this.'

She was right, and Ríkharður sighed with relief. He had no need of any more problems in his life, and he had to be careful of his reputation. Diljá parked and they hurried into the hotel. Ríkharður had hoped that the other couples would have given up waiting and gone to the restaurant, but a shout of laughter greeted them the moment he and Diljá appeared in the doorway. The bar was clearly buzzing.

'About time! We were starting to think you two were dead!'

said Ásmundur, a tall man of around forty who had clearly been overdoing the weights. Like Diljá, he worked as a personal trainer, and at the same gym. His tailored white shirt was stretched over his broad shoulders and muscular biceps.

'Dead! We couldn't be more alive!' he shot back, a little too loudly and with a bark of artificial laughter, as he sighed inwardly. He was starting to feel odd.

There was an open bottle of champagne in a silver ice bucket on the table. Ríkharður found it bizarre that they were all so fond of champagne and sparkling wine. He went to the bar and ordered himself a decent whisky. It took the barman a painfully long time to deal with this simple request, and Ríkharður decided that the guy had to be a little on the slow side.

The man's waist was ridiculously narrow, he thought, as he took a breath and dropped into a seat next to Ásmundur's partner Katrín, conscious that his own belly lapped over his leather belt. He made himself comfortable, and gave Katrín a smile. Of the group, she was the one he could most easily connect with. She was the director of some organisation with an acronym for a name that he couldn't remember. Katrín was the one with the greatest passion for cycling, scrupulously documenting each excursion on social media. In fact, this was where a large part of her life was, and her social media pages never failed to reflect whatever opinions and trends were on everyone's lips at that moment. Ríkharður found her rather superficial, but liked her nevertheless, unlike her partner Ásmundur who he was certain had at some point slept with Diljá. He had seen the glances that passed between them, and noticed how she became cool towards him whenever Ásmundur was present.

Ingi Thór and Eygló appeared to be a close couple. He was a builder, as well as being prominent on social media. Until recently, Ríkharður had been certain that his popularity was due to his work, and had been surprised to find instead that this was down to some spiritual awakening he had experienced. He hadn't made any effort to find out more, but thought it hilarious that Ingi Thór could be some kind of spiritual guru. Eygló had worked for many years for an insurance company but now had become a full-time yoga instructor. They cycled with a group of people who were well known within the community, cycling more for the company than competitively.

Diljá was the youngest in the group of friends and Ríkharður had never remembered to ask how this friendship between the five of them had developed, although he was certain that they were neither school friends nor childhood neighbours. He was easily the oldest, and only partially accepted. He was increasingly aware how little he had in common with this group and the jokes about middle-age directed his way were becoming tedious.

That evening he did his best to be pleasant, but it wasn't easy, not least after they arrived at the restaurant. He became more and more tired, and increasingly muddled as the evening drew on.

He was so sleepy that he dozed off as they drove back into Herjólfsdalur, and it took a monumental effort to open his eyes when he heard the car door slam. Diljá helped him out and he felt slightly better. He tried to put his arms around her, failing miserably. He made a feeble attempt to kiss her, but she fended him off.

'You're so wonderful,' he slurred.

'And you need to sleep,' she said, not hiding the irritation in her voice. 'Go to bed and behave.'

She helped him unbutton his shirt and supported him as he undressed.

'Here, a couple of painkillers,' she said, dropping a couple of tablets into his palm. She handed him a glass of water. 'Go on. Swallow.'

He did as he was told. Then he crawled into bed and didn't wake up again.

2

Day was dawning and it was almost four o'clock when Diljá returned. Even this late in August the nights still retained some of their midsummer brightness, but it was as dark as night inside the caravan and she trod carefully to avoid waking Ríkharður. Fortunately, he was sleeping soundly and didn't move as she crawled into bed. She sighed to herself, relieved that she had got into bed without disturbing him, and wrapped the duvet around her. It had been a wonderful night, energising, tranquil and beautiful. It was a delight to close her eyes and let sleep take over, knowing that before long her life would change for good. That night they had planned to undertake the big journey again, and this time they would go together. She would look her past in the eye and shrug off the burdens that had weighed her down for far too long. She would finally be free. A bird sang in the distance and she fell asleep to its sweet song.

A few hours later, Diljá was woken by the sound of voices, a cheerful chatter disturbing her sleep. She got up, lifted the blackout curtain and looked out. The voices were from a group of tourists, young men with backpacks, sauntering past the caravan and deep in conversation. One of them held a leaflet in his hands and she automatically assumed that they had to be deciding what to look at today. Maybe they were going to try their luck on the sheer rock faces, or take a boat trip around the Islands. She let the curtain fall back into place and dropped back onto the bed. The voices faded into the distance and everything was quiet again. She thought of how powerful silence could be in nature; nothing could be heard, not a single note of birdsong or the sound of a breath being taken. She listened and heard nothing. Was this too eerily quiet? She opened her eyes and glanced over to Ríkharður, but it was too dark to see him clearly. Diljá wriggled closer to him, but he appeared to be deep asleep, so she closed her eyes and decided to force herself to go back to sleep, to think of something beautiful and pleasant. This would be about her future and how wonderful it would be to finally shake off the ghosts of her past. María Líf would be proud of her mother, and when she had grown up they would be close friends who would travel together and... and... She tried to visualise images of their travels together, but she was unable to lose herself in her dreams and fall asleep again.

There was too much silence, practically a deathly silence. Ríkharður wasn't one of those people who sleep in silence, in fact, he would shift in his sleep and snore, sometimes deafeningly. A terrible thought grew in her mind. Had she given him too much? She went over the doses. No, surely not! It hadn't been that much... but maybe he had a heart problem that he hadn't known about? Was he ... could he be ... was he maybe dead? Hell, that couldn't happen. He wasn't supposed to die, just to sleep soundly, very soundly. She felt herself struggling to breathe and fear surged through her.

She jumped to her feet, switched on the lights and looked around. Everything was exactly as it had been the night before, with Ríkharður's clothes in a heap on the floor, while he was in the bed, in more or less the same position where she had left him the night before. She went closer. He had to be breathing, had to be. She leaned over him, trying to feel his warm breath, but felt nothing. He had to breathe! She placed shaking fingers on his throat, searching for the right spot under the jaw. She could feel the clammy, cold skin, but no heartbeat.

'No!' she burst out, her hands going to her mouth. The

terror that enveloped every fibre of her was so forceful that she could barely draw breath. She stared at the man in the bed, snatched at him and shook him.

'You can't do this to me!' she howled, as she fought to draw long, gasping breaths. 'Ríkharður, my love, you weren't supposed to die.'

She let go of him, and rocked herself back and forth in confusion. Her breathing was shallow and she was close to losing control. She told herself to focus, to take deep, long breaths, to stay in control and not to give way to panic that would leave her helpless. She had to be able to think, to do what was needed.

What was she supposed to do? Call 112 and ask for an ambulance? Or a doctor? She looked in desperation at the man in the bed. There was no doubt that he was dead, and she was sure she had heard that if someone died at home, the police would always attend. Would a caravan count as well? She was certain of it. The police would come, there would be an autopsy and the drugs in Ríkharður's bloodstream would be identified. Everything would point to her, since he was a doctor and of course would know better than to take that mix of drugs. How could she explain that she hadn't meant to kill him, but had simply wanted him to fall into a deep sleep while she went out during the night? Who was going to believe that? No, she'd been down that road before, telling the truth to authority. They wouldn't believe her any more than they had believed her back then. Nobody would take any notice of a woman with a past like hers. No, society would ostracise her. Crazy Diljá would be behind bars, or else locked away in a psychiatric ward. That dreadful place! She trembled with horror at the thought, shivering as if she were standing naked on a glacier.

Being locked in was the worst thing she could imagine. Nothing could be worse. She would lose custody, and she might never get to see María Líf ever again. That couldn't be allowed to happen. No, not again! He mind was a whirl of thoughts, none of which she could bear to follow to a conclusion. All she knew was that she had to get away from here as soon as possible – get away and give herself space to think logically. The clothes she had worn the night before were in the wardrobe and she hurried to pull them on. She wiped her face with a towel, picked up her sports bag and jammed a baseball cap on her head. She was being stifled here – she had to get away, far from this nightmare.

3

Diljá watched from the ferry *Herjólfur* as the Islands faded into the distance. She wished that the last twenty-four hours could be wiped out and totally forgotten. If only she and Ríkharður had never gone on this lousy trip, and had instead stayed in to watch Netflix in his smart house in Reykjavík. They could have curled up on the grey-green corner sofa, his arms around her, guarding her and making her feel secure. But now he was dead. She could feel sobs rise in her throat, and she swallowed them back again and again. She couldn't let herself tremble like this, or do anything that would attract attention. In just one day, everything she had so painstakingly built up had collapsed. Just as she had been about to get a proper grip on life and do well. The old feelings of shame cascaded over her yet again. She was worse than useless, what had she been thinking, trying to drag herself up? Ríkharður had been good to her, yet she hadn't appreciated it and screwed everything up yet again. Diljá Sigurðardóttir was an ungrateful failure, a crazy bitch who couldn't be trusted.

She summoned what little energy she had left to stand up and spend the forty-minute crossing to the Landeyjarhöfn wandering from one place to another. The longest spell was spent on the ferry's upper deck, with the baseball cap, sunglasses and a mask obscuring her face. In the middle of a pandemic there was nothing unusual about someone wearing a mask, and right now this served her well. As soon as land was in sight, she hurried down to the car deck, squeezing between the rows of vehicles of all types and sizes, until she reached the jeep. Sitting inside, she let the seat drop back and pulled the cap down. From under the brim she could watch as *Herjólfur's* crew prepared to dock at Landeyjarhöfn while drivers made their way to their cars.

It went without saying that she should have spent the whole crossing down here, she realised that now. She could have tilted the seat back and closed her eyes. But, no, she dispelled that thought. She had probably done the right thing by going up to the passenger area, as she was sure that *Herjólfur's* crew would check every vehicle. She was sure that there was a sign somewhere stating that passengers should leave the car deck during the crossing.

Elbow against the window and one hand hiding her face, Diljá picked up her phone and scrolled through news websites. There was no mention anywhere of a fatality in the Westman Islands. Maybe the body hadn't been found yet...? But it would happen soon enough when the others started to wonder what had become of them. There was a chance that the rest of the group would think that they had decided to skip lunch, as Ríkharður would need to sleep off the effects of last night's drinking. But what about her? She had been practically completely sober and the others would think it odd if they didn't hear from her. It occurred to her to send the group a message to say that she and Ríkharður were unwell, and that they were going to stay on the Islands until Monday, thanks for a great trip and see you soon... But then she'd have to take the ferry back, and how would that look if the body had been discovered? That was also completely contrary to the other story she had been taking pains to create, something along the lines that she had needed to head back because of something that she hadn't quite figured out yet... It was getting difficult to think and she was already regretting having fled in a panic. She couldn't trust her own thoughts. Indistinct fragments of the last twenty-four hours flew through her mind. She felt the tears begin to flow down her cheeks and she struggled to think straight. She fought as hard as she could to stop herself from panicking. There was no question of losing control, but where could she go? Once the ferry had docked, she would have almost no time to decide whether to go to the nearest police station and give herself up, or to hide away somewhere until she could work out what her next step would be.

She reached for the sports bag she had taken with her and felt inside it. Apart from a swimming costume, a towel and some cosmetics, she had clean underwear, socks, a shirt and trousers. They had meant to go for a swim once everything had been squared away, leaving nothing but to hitch the caravan to the jeep. She longed for that to have been the reality, but now she was sitting here in Ríkharður's jeep and had put herself in a terrible position. Diljá unzipped the pocket on the outside of the bag. As well as her pool membership card, she found a creased 5,000 krónur note, and a faint smile spread across her worried face. On this terrible day, finally something had turned out right.

4

After detective Guðgeir Fransson became a grandfather, he found himself revelling more than ever in time off, and this Sunday had been a special pleasure. He and Inga had been swimming, taking the little boy with them, while their daughter Ólöf took the opportunity to immerse herself in her studies. She was in the third year of a law degree, determined to follow in her mother's footsteps, and had even worked at her legal practice during the summer. Guðgeir was immeasurably proud of his daughter who was so adroitly managing motherhood and a demanding course of study. He hadn't yet heard her complain, which was something he felt today's youth did too much. Or maybe that wasn't quite right, he decided, maybe the voices of complaint were simply loudest in the world of social media, amplified by the general media. There was a toughness to Ólöf and those friends of hers he knew. But what he found less easy to understand was her relationship with Smári, the little boy's father. Right from the start, Guðgeir's concern had been that he wasn't good enough for her, that he wasn't a strong enough personality, and that turned out unfortunately to be true.

By the time the baby was barely six months old, the cracks had begun to emerge, and over the ensuing months Ólöf and Smári were in an on-off relationship until they decided that it was time to go their separate ways. To begin with, he and Inga had hoped that the young parents would be able to resolve their problems, as it would be better for the lad to grow up in a home with both parents, but now he was beginning to feel that the present situation might be better for the boy. Since parting with Smári, Ólöf was blooming like never before. The energy that he had sucked from her was now going into herself and the little boy. Recently she had little to do with him, as Smári had been in Spain for a month, working remotely. So the little lad knew his father best as a voice on the phone or a face on the screen.

'Grandad, more,' little Guðgeir said, and his grandfather slipped half a rolled-up pancake onto his grandson's plate.

'No, Dad. Don't give him sugar,' Ólöf admonished.

'Sorry. Of course,' Guðgeir said, retrieving it. The little boy wailed heart-wrenchingly. 'Can he have a grape?'

'If you peel it and cut it in half.'

Guðgeir followed the instructions to the letter and the little one soon calmed down as he happily chewed the grape. The boy had been christened Guðgeir Jökull, and his grandfather found the middle name a handsome one, even though it was rarely used. On the other hand, he felt there was no need for the boy to be Smárason, and it would be more fitting for him to carry a matronymic with Ólöf's name.

Guðgeir gazed happily at his family. Their son Pétur Andri was still living at home and still at high school. The boy who had spent most of his early adolescence asleep was now finally emerging from hibernation, taller than his father, who was himself above average height. Pétur had decided to return to basketball training, and Guðgeir approved. He had been a useful player himself as a young man and had made some good friends through basketball. The phone buzzing in his pocket interrupted his thoughts. The number on the screen showed him the caller was Særós, who ran the Reykjavík CID department he was part of.

'Sorry, my darling. Work's calling,' he said, standing up from the table and going into the bedroom to take the call.

A few moments later he returned and announced that he was going to the Westman Islands, as a doctor there had called in a fatality that merited investigation, and the local force had requested support, with half of their manpower either off sick or away on holiday.

'But this is your weekend off, Dad,' Ólöf said, wiping Guðgeir Jökull's mouth with a damp flannel. The little boy scowled and backed away from the cloth.

'I know, but it doesn't look like anything big, so I shouldn't be away long.'

'You haven't even had any pancakes yet,' Inga said, sounding disappointed. 'Shall I roll a few up and put them in a bag for you?'

'It's all right, my love. I'll get something to eat on the ferry.'

He stuffed some essentials into a bag, said goodbye and drove off to Kópavogur to collect his colleague Elsa Guðrún. They would have to move fast to get to Landeyjarhöfn in time to catch the afternoon ferry to the Westman Islands.

5

Cars rolled off Herjólfur and a nose-to-tail line snaked through the black dunes. Diljá sat in the dark grey jeep, still uncertain which turning to take when she reached the junction. If she were to head eastwards she would have to sleep in the car or find a place to stay, and that certainly wouldn't be easy. The other direction led to more familiar territory, but that road was busier so there could be more chance of her being picked up. She was startled from her thoughts as the impatient driver of the car behind sounded his horn a couple of times. Decision made, Diljá took the turning to the west. She drove for a quarter of an hour along Highway 1 without having any idea of where she meant to go. Her thoughts and memories of the last two days were a whirl of confusion in her mind, until something came to her. She recalled that Eygló and Ingi Thór had travelled to the Westman Islands after spending two weeks in their summer cottage. Diljá had been there with them several times and had a rough idea of the way. The cottage was among the foothills of Mount Hekla, around an hour from the main road.

Ingi Thór and Eygló had told the group that their holiday was over and they were both due to go straight back to work the next day, and considering it would be far out of their way, it was hardly likely that they would stop off at there on their way to Reykjavík. Diljá's heart beat a little faster and she smiled to herself for the second time during this strange day. She even remembered where the key was hidden. She glanced in the mirror and saw that the car behind her was some distance away. She took a spur-of-the-moment decision, snatched up her phone and pulled the car off the road and onto the verge. She fiddled with the phone for a while, eventually managed to extract the SIM from it, and dropped it into her sports bag. Then she wound down the window and hurled the phone out.

It wasn't easy to keep to the speed limit, but she forced herself to drive carefully so as not to attract attention. Just before Hvolsvöllur she found herself rigid with fright and hardly able to breathe as a police car came hurtling towards her. Its lights flashed and the siren howled as it hurtled past. Her heart hammered in her chest and her fingers were locked so tightly on the wheel that her knuckles turned white. It took her a while to calm down, and she could feel herself shaking.

There were now more police cars to be seen, and when she reached the Landvegur junction where she would head inland, she saw the tarmac yard in front of the shop there was empty. She parked directly outside the shop and put on her mask and sunglasses. Then she went inside with the 5,000 krónur note in her hand. A teenage girl sat at the cash desk. Immersed in her phone, she didn't even look up as Diljá entered the shop. She only appeared to notice the presence of a customer when Diljá dropped bread, skyr and hot dogs on the counter.

'You don't have a card or a phone?' the girl asked in surprise at the sight of cash.

'No. Forgot both at home,' Diljá answered and glanced outside. The car park was still empty.

'All right,' the girl said and started to add up a total on her phone. It seemed to take forever. She finally opened the cash register with an exhausted look on her face. 'I'll have to give you change,' she said.

'Yes,' Diljá said and it felt like an age before the girl finally put the money on the counter. She wanted to leave the change, but knew that would look strange.

'It's best to pay by phone,' the girl called out to her as she left. 'Notes can give you diseases. They're covered in bacteria and germs.'

'I'll remember that next time,' Diljá assured her as she hurried out.

There were no more than a handful of cars coming the other way on the hour's drive from where she had turned off Highway 1. She slowed down and paid attention to her surroundings as she approached the cottage. This wasn't an area with many such summer houses, and she saw neither people nor any traffic. She had to drive along a stretch of unmade road before she turned into the drive to Eygló's and Ingi Thór's place. She parked the jeep behind a leafy birch spinney and hurried up to the green-painted house.

On the decking behind it was a large iron cool box that she quickly pulled open. At the bottom was a pack of long-life milk cartons, the plastic wrapping around them ripped. She picked up the pack to take a closer look and was relieved that her memory hadn't failed her. One of the cartons had been carefully resealed, and contained no milk. She had found the key. She put the milk cartons back in their place and shut the cool box. Then she went to the front door and opened it.

6

Elsa Guðrún felt a growing urge to push her way past people, to shove her way through and to be down the steps and off the ferry as soon as possible. A couple in front of her stopped to kiss and take selfies. It took them a minute or two to find the right look, while Elsa Guðrún felt the unease swelling inside her. She had felt odd ever since getting out of the jeep at the Landeyjarhöfn terminal. She had meant to walk the short distance to the terminal building while her boss Guðgeir sat in the queue of cars waiting to board. But she had hardly shut the car door behind her before an Arctic tern dived at her.

'Hey, take it easy!' she yelled as she cowered from the squawking bird. Further off, she could see more birds approaching. With their featherlight bodies and strong wings, they swooped to peck at the top of her head. It was past mid-August and their chicks should be long hatched, so what was wrong with them? Elsa Guðrún held her bag over her head to ward off the attacks and jogged as fast as she could over the black sand. She didn't relax her pace until she was inside the Herjólfur ferry terminal where the birds could no longer persecute her, but the discomfort stayed with her.

During the crossing she had sat outside on deck while Guðgeir had been in the cafeteria with coffee and a croissant. He hadn't taken a single bite as he was constantly on the phone, either to Leifur from forensics who was already at the scene, or going over the situation with Særós, their superior officer. Only a few years ago, Guðgeir had been in her position and for a while it had looked as if he would resume his former role. But it hadn't happened, and Elsa Guðrún was sure that he was quietly pleased. Guðgeir was a detective by nature and he was far more at home at a crime scene searching for clues and evidence than shackled to a desk writing reports and checking budgets. On the other hand, this was where the über-organised Særós and her famous knowledge wall were perfectly at home. Year-round, every Friday a new aphorism or nugget of wisdom would appear on the wall behind her desk, and every week a case of beer would be wagered on whether or not her system would fail. It hadn't happened yet.

Elsa Guðrún took a deep lungful of the fresh sea air and watched the wave-speckled sea. She was feeling better by the minute. Should she go back inside and sit with Guðgeir? No, she felt better out here, and he could inform her of any new developments to the case on the way to Herjólfsdalur. There was no land in sight; the sea stretched away as far as the eye could see. She leaned against the rail and watched the waves rise and fall. The trepidation that had filled her thoughts since the ship sailed from Landeyjarhöfn was ebbing away and completely forgotten by the time she saw the Westman Islands sparkling in the distance. It was a wonderful sight to see them rise from the ocean, with green-capped sheer cliffs and seabirds riding the breeze high above. The settlement at Heimaey came gradually closer, the houses becoming visible, and before she was aware of it, the ferry was at the dock.

Elsa Guðrún went inside where passengers were gathering into groups as they waited to step ashore. She couldn't see Guðgeir anywhere, so he was probably already down on the car deck. To kill time while she waited, she checked out her fellow passengers. There were all ages represented, some with backpacks or suitcases, others carrying no more than a shoulder bag or a shopping bag as if they had just run across to Reykjavík for the day.

She had been to the Westman Islands once before. She was

seventeen and had gone with some friends to the August Bank Holiday weekend festival. That had been before there had been a dock at Landeyjarhöfn so they had taken the four-hour sailing with the old *Herjólfur* from Thorlákshöfn. The girls had been full of energy and popped open Breezers as soon as the ferry was at sea. The weather had been fine and the party atmosphere continued all the way to Herjólfsdalur.

By the time they journeyed home three days later, they weren't quite so cheerful. They were all hung over and hoarse after singing along with the country's most popular singers at the top of their voices. They were short of sleep, with a damp tent stuffed into a sack and no groundsheet. Once they got to Reykjavík, they had to take a bus home to Akureyri. The journey had seemed endless as the bus stopped at practically every little kiosk on the way north, much to their dismay.

When she had opened the door of their house in Akureyri, her parents thought she looked rather pale. Elsa Guðrún smiled at the recollection.

Now there was no party waiting for her in the islands, but a death that was suspicious enough to require assistance from the Reykjavík force. Fifty-two-year-old doctor Ríkharður Magnússon had been found in his caravan in Herjólfsdalur. According to the reports, his girlfriend, Diljá Sigurðardóttir, had not been there when the body was discovered, and the couple had travelled to the Islands the previous day, along with two other couples. They had all been due to travel back with the afternoon ferry today.

The group had had dinner at one of the more popular restaurants last night and intended to meet up again at midday before getting ready for the return trip. The other couples began to wonder where Ríkharður and Diljá had got to, and decided to check on them. He turned out to be dead, and she had disappeared.

Elsa Guðrún's feeling of discomfort at what could be waiting for her and Guðgeir returned. More than a year had passed since she had been the victim of a brutal attack in her own home. She had received all kinds of professional support in coping with the after-effects, but in spite of all this, insomnia and panic attacks had become constant companions. She was able to hold her own at work and did her best to perform as the cheerful, smiling woman she had been before that terrible ordeal, but she wasn't always able to maintain the façade.

Finally off the ferry, she glanced around. She heard a car's horn and saw Guðgeir wave to her. She jogged across the dock and jumped into the jeep. They took the road that went through the town, past the sports ground and into Herjólfsdalur. In these few minutes he explained that the doctor who had been called to the scene with the forensics team had agreed strongly with the local doctor's opinion that there was good reason to examine this case more closely.

The valley with its ring of surrounding rocky slopes was beautiful, but smaller than she remembered. It seemed impossible to imagine that a giant stage, thousands of people and a tent city could all fit into this space during the Islands' Bank Holiday festival. Elsa Guðrún tried to imagine the place packed with tents, musicians on the stage and the slopes thronged with singing people. This was a mental image that she wasn't sure was rooted in her own memory, or simply from TV news reports.

'There's the caravan,' Guðgeir said, running fingers through his dark hair that was starting to thin. This was a mannerism of his that emerged whenever he was feeling the pressure.

The caravan stood alone under a low cliff, some distance away from several others. It was strikingly large, made even bigger by the extended awning. The area around it had been closed off with yellow tape and a police car blocked the road.

'Were there just two of them in there?' Elsa Guðrún asked, eyebrows raised. 'It's so big.'

'Yes, according to the information I have. The deceased was divorced and has grown-up children. His girlfriend's name is

Diljá and she's almost twenty years younger than he is,' Guðgeir replied as he pulled over at the side of the road and switched off the engine.

'Any idea how long they had been together?' Elsa Guðrún asked.

'Haven't a clue, but I spoke to Særós earlier and she has been in touch with Ríkharður's son, so we can assume that family members have been informed. She'll be in touch with them later today and hopefully that will give us an idea of the family circumstances.'

A police officer came towards them. He was above average height, with shoulders that were slightly hunched. The sunshine that had made unusually frequent appearances that summer had clearly failed to reach him, and his pale skin appeared stretched, as if it were a size too small for him. He introduced himself as Elías.

'Not many of us on duty right now. Some off sick, holidays and whatnot. It's unfortunate that the Commissioner is in the Faroes at the moment. Her sister lives there and turned forty yesterday,' he said, and fidgeted. Elsa Guðrún couldn't help noticing the size of the man's hands and how swollen his knuckles were. He had to be suffering badly from arthritis.

'Understood,' Guðgeir said, looking around.

'Normally we have a few quiet weeks when the Bank Holiday weekend's over,' Elías said, shifting as he spoke. 'And the forensics team is here. They turned up about two o'clock.'

'Anything new?' Guðgeir asked.

'Yes. The girlfriend, Diljá, has disappeared and seems to have taken the ferry this morning. She took the car they arrived in, and her phone. Her handbag and some clothes were left behind in the caravan. It looks like she left in a hurry. The south coast force have started to search for her, but just to make sure that she hasn't stayed behind here somewhere after all, my colleagues and I have been going door to door to see if anyone has any relevant information. Someone must have seen something.'

'I don't doubt she'll be found soon enough,' Guðgeir said. 'You've alerted the other police authorities?'

'Of course,' Elías replied. 'We did that right away and had a report just now to say that a phone that's most likely hers was found not far from the Landeyjarhöfn turnoff.'

7

Guðgeir cast his gaze over the green valley, stretching right up to the steep cliffs and the birds riding the wind between the crags. Down here at ground level a few chalets perched above the caravan, some of them built with steeply pitched roofs and others that were tub-shaped, more like giant herring barrels laid on their sides. Beyond them was another building that was undoubtedly where the campsite's toilet, kitchen and washing facilities were to be found. Downhill at the bottom of the valley were buildings that Guðgeir assumed had something to do with the annual festival, and just by the caravan was a turf cottage that looked to have been constructed within the last few years, although the building method was that of previous centuries.

'You've checked the buildings?' he asked, pointing in their direction.

'Yes. There was nobody down in the valley, but there were four tourists staying further up last night. They were in those two there,' Elías said, indicating the two barrels furthest up the slope. 'Three men and one woman, all foreigners. They all said they weren't aware of anything, but they had noticed the caravan. It's not something you could fail to notice, a monster like that with two axles,' he said with emphasis. 'They said they hadn't seen anyone about, and when we asked a few more questions it turned out that they hadn't spent much time here in the valley. Of course they're visiting around the Islands and only came up here overnight to get some sleep. I reckon it's more or less certain that nobody else has been here, hardly anyone comes up here to the camping ground once the festival is over.'

'All the same, I need to speak to them,' Guðgeir said quickly.

'Really?' Elías raised an eyebrow; his skin looked ready to rip under the strain.

'Yes. Or did you take a formal statement from them?'

'No, nothing formal. We just had a chat, and like I said, they hadn't seen anything.'

'Were these people travelling together?'

'I don't think so,' Elías said, drawing out his words and looking around uneasily. 'There were two guys around thirty, who stayed in that chalet,' he said, pointing at one of the barrels. 'And there was an older couple, in their fifties. They were in the one that's down there by the service block.'

'Where are these people now?' Elsa Guðrún asked, giving Elías an encouraging smile. The man was clearly concerned that he had got things badly wrong.

'Gone, I expect. They were packing when we got here,' he replied, now visibly uncomfortable. 'Listen, I'll run down to the dock and check. I think they were going over to the mainland today.'

'Please do. We need to speak to them,' Guðgeir said. 'What do you know about the person who found the body?'

'Ásmundur?'

'That's him.'

'Only that he was one of this party of six who came here the day before yesterday. Yesterday evening they were all together at a restaurant called Magni, and Ríkharður was pretty drunk, by all accounts. They were meant to meet up for lunch at a place down by the quay, and when Diljá and Ríkharður didn't show up, Ásmundur came up here to check on them. He turned around when he saw the car wasn't there, and assumed they had missed each other.'

'And then what?' Elsa Guðrún asked.

'He went back to the restaurant, and when they still weren't there, he came back up to the valley. This time he got out of the car and knocked on the door. There was no answer, so he tried the handle, and the door wasn't locked. He found Ríkharður dead in the bed and Diljá nowhere to be seen. There's a handbag there on the table with her papers, keys and some cosmetics, and it's weird that she didn't grab that on her way out, especially as there's medication there.' Elías coughed, and rocked on his heels. He put a hand in his trouser pocket and took out car keys. 'Well, the guys in there can tell you more,' he said, nodding towards the caravan. 'I'm going to run down to the harbour.'

'Good luck, and let me know what you find out,' Guðgeir said, raising a hand in token of farewell. 'So, Elsa Guðrún. Shall we take a look inside?'

'Yep. That's best, I reckon,' she replied in a low voice.

They walked the short distance, and Guðgeir stopped abruptly.

'Before we meet anyone else, I'd like to know what you think,' he said, directing an intense look her way.

'That handbag bugs me,' she said without hesitation. 'I mean, not so much the bag itself, but that Diljá didn't take the contents with her. Keys, documentation, medication.'

'Agreed,' Guðgeir said. 'But she took her phone.'

'And discarded it not far from the ferry terminal at Landeyjarhöfn,' Elsa Guðrún added.

'She, or someone else did,' Guðgeir said, a thoughtful look on his face as he set off. He stopped by the awning and moved the zipper upwards to open the gap wider.

'That's exactly what I was wondering,' Elsa Guðrún said as she followed him through the opening.

'She could have witnessed a murder, which means she could be in danger,' he said darkly, as he knocked at the door.

8

It was a strange feeling to put on white overalls, pull on gloves and shoe covers, and then step inside the caravan. Leifur was waiting for them inside, as his two colleagues from forensics had gone outside to make space for Guðgeir and Elsa Guðrún. The caravan's fittings were strikingly high-quality, although the layout was nothing out of the ordinary. A U-shaped sofa arrangement at one end provided six to eight seats, upholstered in a material that resembled leather, all arranged around a table that could no doubt be turned into another place to sleep. At the other end was a double bed, where Leifur stood with his back to them. A spacious kitchen area occupied the centre of the caravan, close to the door. A couple of used glasses stood by the sink, along with half a bottle of rum, a plastic tray, half a squeezed lime and a little kitchen knife with a green handle. A white towel lay on the floor and a colourful dress had been discarded on the sofa.

'Wow,' Elsa Guðrún said in admiration. 'This must have cost a bomb, fabulous design.'

Guðgeir opened a door and peered inside. In a little space that could hardly have been more than a square metre were a toilet, a cupboard and a basin with a mirror over it. Two toothbrushes and a tube of toothpaste occupied a glass fixed to the wall. There was a bottle of liquid soap by the sink, and a small towel hung from a hook next to it. An electric razor and lipstick lay on a shelf. He shut the door and turned his attention to the wide double bed that could be approached from both sides. The dead man wore underpants and socks, while a jacket, shirt and trousers lay in an untidy pile on the floor. Guðgeir took care to stay clear of the pile of clothes, in case the forensic team hadn't yet got to it. He had been a tall man, heavily built but not fat, his forehead high and wide. His carefully cut brown hair had begun to grey and thin. The eyebrows that were a striking feature of his face had clearly been trimmed. The overall impression was that Ríkharður had been a handsome man who took care of his appearance.

The three of them stood for a moment, looking at the lifeless body before them.

'Any news of the girlfriend, Diljá?' Leifur asked, adjusting his overall. The belly that had been one of his prominent features was finally on the retreat following repeated stern warnings from his doctor that he needed to change his diet, take more exercise and reduce his workload. Two years ago, Leifur had suffered a heart attack, and had narrowly survived the ordeal. He had largely followed the first two recommendations with positive physical results, but less so in other respects. While he had previously been an easy-going type, now his temper had become more volatile.

'Not yet. But she's bound to show up before long,' Guðgeir replied, speaking slowly without taking his eyes from the body. 'She won't be able to get far.'

'She's petite. All the clothes she left behind are in small sizes, as you can see,' Leifur said, opening a cupboard that was packed with clothes. A shirt hung on one hanger and a down anorak in a similar size on another. There were more clothes neatly folded away beneath, mostly for sports and outdoor activities of various kinds. Another cupboard was obviously Ríkharður's. With a gloved hand, Leifur moved aside a shirt so they could see better. It was a size 36, and on the floor below was a large pair of man's shoes.

'There's a photo of her,' Leifur said, showing them the screen of his phone.

'We've already googled her,' Elsa Guðrún said. She tried to

stifle a smile, but the dimples that formed on her cheeks gave her away.

'Diljá seems to be big on sports,' Leifur said earnestly, but moderated his tone when he saw the expression on Elsa Guðrún's face. 'That's not to say she's at peak fitness, just because she owns clothes like these. All kinds of people wear this stuff, even I have a pair of multi-coloured trousers made from Spandex that my wife bought for me in the hope that I might get more exercise. But enough of that,' he said, shutting the cupboard. 'The police here in the Islands have reports that Ríkharður was very drunk last night. They went for a meal at Magni, which is the smartest place in town, and Ríkharður was so unsteady on his feet that he crashed into someone's table and sent their drinks flying.'

'Ach. That's lousy,' Elsa Guðrún said, glancing at the lifeless man.

'OK to open the fridge?' Guðgeir asked.

'Help yourself. We've finished with it,' Leifur said, hands on his hips. 'Y'know, somehow I think it's unlikely that the booze finished him off, and why did the girlfriend disappear?'

'That's something...' Elsa Guðrún muttered just to say something.

'What?''

'Nothing.'

The fridge contained an unopened bottle of white wine, long-life milk, strawberries, blueberries, one lemon, two limes and a bundle of mint.

'They didn't forget to bring mint for the cocktails,' she said. 'Or the brown sugar,' she added, pointing at a shelf that held a row of jars. 'Was there anything in the toilet?'

'A sponge bag, obviously his. We've sealed that, although there was nothing unusual to be seen in it, at least, not at first sight. Apart from the usual deodorant and stuff, just painkillers and blood pressure tablets,' Leifur replied.

'OK. Elsa Guðrún and I are going to go over to the hotel to take statements from their friends,' Guðgeir said.

On the way, they saw a police car coming the other way. They recognised a doctor sitting in the passenger seat who had often worked with the police in the last few years. She had been involved in a number of Guðgeir's investigations, and he leaned gently on the horn and waved as the cars passed each other, but she didn't notice them.

'That was Ísgerður. Remember her?' he asked, even though he knew the answer.

'Of course I do. She examined me after the assault,' Elsa Guðrún said in a subdued tone, and Guðgeir glanced at her in concern. Just the sight of Ísgerður seemed to have upset her, bringing painful memories back into sharp focus.

'You're sure you're ready for this?' he asked cautiously.

Elsa Guðrún said nothing. She stared out through the windscreen, her bag clasped tight in her arms. Her long brown hair was pulled back in a ponytail and her broad face was serious. He stopped the car and turned to her.

'If you don't trust yourself to take this case on, then you'll have to tell me now.' Elsa Guðrún didn't reply, and sat as still as if turned to stone. He saw her draw a deep breath, but said nothing. 'One call to Særós, and you're free. Is that what you want to do?'

'No.' She shook her head and her gaze remained fixedly ahead.

'You have to be honest with me, Elsa Guðrún. Anything less doesn't help anyone, you, me or anyone else,' he said firmly.

She seemed to shake a weight from her shoulders and in a few seconds pulled herself out of the trance. She looked towards him and her wide blue eyes caught his.

'I'll be fine, Guðgeir. You can rely on me a hundred per cent,' she said hurriedly.

'Sure?'

'Absolutely.'

'That's good,' Guðgeir said, and pulled away. 'Now we need to squeeze everything we can out of this bunch of friends of theirs.'

'You think this amounts to a criminal case?' Elsa Guðrún asked.

'It's impossible to say, but as long as we can't be sure, then we have to assume that it does, and that gives us a more secure basis for an investigation,' he replied.

'I know that. But what's your gut feeling?'

Guðgeir said nothing for a moment, staring at the road ahead.

'To tell the truth, I have a very odd feeling about all this. It feels like we're jumping into something that stinks,' he said, finally bringing the car to a halt and reversing into a space outside the hotel. 'I can't explain exactly, but it feels like there's something very fishy about this affair.'

'Agreed,' Elsa Guðrún said.

Guðgeir switched off the engine and reached for his folder on the back seat. Then he again caught her eye, a serious look on his face.

'Whatever happens, I'd like you to promise me you'll do one thing if you feel that this investigation is too much for you.'

'What's that? Meditation? Mindfulness?' she asked, the fatigue plain in her voice.

'I'm sure both of those are great, but that's not what I had in mind,' Guðgeir said.

'Well? What, then?' she asked in the same resigned tone of voice. 'I've tried all the conventional things,' she said, counting them off on her fingers. 'I've been to a psychiatrist, taken part in workshops for people who have been through trauma where they're taught new ways to sleep properly again, been through panic management...' She stopped counting, a note of scorn in her voice. 'Now I just need to start on the unconventional stuff. Are you going to suggest laughter yoga, or sound baths?'

'I see what you mean,' Guðgeir said and decided not to go further down this slippery slope, but to try and lighten the mood instead. It was clear that Elsa Guðrún had already had more than enough well-meaning but uninvited advice from other people.

'Or you could just summon up a mental image of Leifur exercising in his multi-colour Spandex leggings,' he said with a twinkle in his eye.

The tension vanished from Elsa Guðrún's face and she burst into a shout of laughter. Guðgeir was relieved to see the humour return to those deep blue eyes, and the familiar smile again spread across her tired face. While time wouldn't heal every hurt, Guðgeir hoped that it would at least soften the worst of the pain.

9

A middle-aged man greeted them courteously in the lobby, introducing himself as Höskuldur. While he was nominally the manager, in a small place like the Westman Islands there were few jobs around the hotel he didn't do. Despite the polite reception, Guðgeir couldn't help noticing that this reserved man found the experience uncomfortable, and that he considered all this turmoil would do little for the hotel's reputation. Höskuldur took them down to a small meeting room in the hotel's basement where they could be comfortable and undisturbed.

'At your request we asked everyone to remain in their rooms, and then a man arrived and took away everyone's phone,' he said, gently rubbing his palms together.

'That was Leifur,' Guðgeir said. 'He's leading the forensics team.'

'Of course. But people were extremely unhappy with this, I can tell you,' the manager said, his brow furrowed with concern.

'Understandably, but they won't be without their phones for long. If they need to contact family or workplaces, then we can arrange for that to be done,' Guðgeir assured him.

Höskuldur nodded.

'I'll let people know, and if there's anything you need, give me a shout. I arranged the furniture for you,' he said, gesturing to a table in the middle of the room. Two chairs had been placed on one side of it, and a single chair on the other.

'Move things around to suit yourselves, and there's a bigger table if you want to swap. If you need more chairs, there are plenty.'

Höskuldur gestured in the other direction to where chairs were stacked in one corner.

'No, it's absolutely fine the way it is,' Guðgeir said and smiled courteously to indicate that they had talked long enough. 'Thanks.'

'In that case, I'll leave you to it,' Höskuldur said, but he didn't make a move. He ran his fingers over one closely shaved cheek and then through his fair but tousled hair.

'We'll keep ourselves out of sight,' Guðgeir assured him. 'You can be sure that your other guests won't notice anything unusual.'

'Well, good. That's good,' Höskuldur said, visibly relieved.

'Who shall we take first?' Elsa Guðrún asked when the door had shut behind the departing hotel manager. She pulled the band free from her thick hair, shook it out, combed it loosely back with her fingers and again secured it. 'Look, there's even coffee here, water, biscuits,' she added as she went over to a small table in one corner. 'Shall I get you some?'

Guðgeir nodded his head.

'Yes, please. Y'know, I don't think it matters about the order. There are two couples, Ásmundur and Katrín, and Ingi Thór and Eygló.' He took the coffee and a biscuit from Elsa Guðrún. 'We ought to concentrate on gathering information about Diljá and her relationship with Ríkharður. Then we need to work on what they have been doing and whom they met, whether anything unusual happened, and yes, whether they have any idea of where Diljá might be.'

'I'll go, then,' Elsa Guðrún said, popping the last piece of biscuit into her mouth. 'Let's stick to alphabetical order and fetch Ásmundur first. We may as well start with the one who found the body.'

Guðgeir took the opportunity while she was out of the room to call Særós, but she had nothing new to tell him of Diljá.

They knew for certain that she had taken that morning's ferry to the mainland, and used her phone to pay the fare.

'I'll let you know as soon as there's anything,' Særós said. 'Otherwise, I'll speak to you when the statements have been taken.'

He had just ended the call when Elsa Guðrún appeared with a man in obviously outstanding physical form, with brush-cut fair hair. Guðgeir got to his feet and shook the man's hand. He was a head taller than the man, who was around average height.

'Hello. I'm Guðgeir Fransson. My condolences... Won't you take a seat?' he said, showing him to a chair.

'Thanks, well... We didn't know each other well,' Ásmundur muttered as he sat down. He sat with his legs splayed and the back of the lightweight chair looked ready to give way under his weight.

'Really?' Guðgeir said in surprise.

'Only met him a few times,' Ásmundur said, running a hand over a muscular bicep. He wore a black short-sleeved shirt and grey jeans. Part of a colourful snake could be seen appearing from under a sleeve and red-gold flames could be glimpsed at the open neck of his shirt. Guðgeir decided that the image as a whole had to cover half of an arm and his whole shoulder. He had always failed to understand why people wanted to be tattooed, even covering their whole bodies, but took care to keep this opinion to himself.

'Would you start the recording, Elsa Guðrún?' he said, watching the man with interest. He seemed ill at ease, although that needn't indicate that he might have something on his conscience. The morning's events must naturally have had a deep effect on him and the others.

'Is this some kind of interrogation? Look, I don't know anything and didn't see Ríkharður after they left the restaurant last night.'

Ásmundur's voice was hoarse and Guðgeir noticed that beads of perspiration had formed on his upper lip.

'No, nothing like that. But we have to take statements from everyone who interacted with Ríkharður during the last hours of his life. We're trying to work out how his death occurred, and there's no certainty that there's anything illegal connected to this,' Guðgeir said slowly, and glanced at Elsa Guðrún to assure himself that the recording was in progress. He kept to his measured tone until the formalities were over, then stepped up a gear, with more determination behind his questions.

'Where were you between eleven last night and seven this morning?'

'Me?' Ásmundur asked, clearly taken aback by the directness of the question.

'Yes. You.' Guðgeir took his glasses from his jacket pocket and gently polished the lenses. 'Where were you?'

'I was just here at the hotel, and then at Magni, the restaurant we all went to. We stayed there until they were about to close, and then walked straight back here.'

'Who was that?'

'My partner Katrín, me, Ingi Thór and Eygló.'

'And then what?'

'Katrín and I went to our room. We were both tired after a long day and we didn't come down until this morning... Just before ten, probably, because we almost missed breakfast.' Ásmundur fell silent, as if he had just remembered something. 'Well... I remember now that Ingi Thór and I had a drink at the bar here in the hotel. It was about to close, so we sat there for a while. Maybe half an hour.'

'When did you arrive in the Westman Islands?' Guðgeir asked, leaning back in his chair.

'Friday afternoon,' Ásmundur said, folding his arms, stretching out the tattooed snake. 'We checked in at the hotel and took it easy up to dinner time. Diljá and Ríkharður had come with that caravan of his, and they had to spend some time getting it sorted out. They put up the awning and it seems there was more to it than they had expected.'

'Did you notice anything unusual on Friday?' Guðgeir asked, switching to an encouraging tone.

'What do you mean?' Ásmundur asked, glancing from one to the other and back, while Elsa Guðrún gave him a warm smile.

'Was there anything unusual about Diljá's and Ríkharður's behaviour?' Guðgeir probed.

'No. They were maybe tired at the end of the week, and they hadn't worked out everything about how things in the caravan worked. There was some trouble to do with the gas. Oh, and of course Ríkharður's work is very demanding, that has an effect...' Ásmundur fell silent. 'Was, I mean.'

'And Diljá. Where does she work?' Guðgeir asked, carefully folding a neat white cloth before putting his glasses on.

'She works at the same centre as me.'

'Centre?'

'Fitness Centre. It's a gym. We're both personal trainers,' Ásmundur replied, and the impatience in his voice broke through. 'Have you found her?'

'Unfortunately not. We need assistance to build up a picture of what actually happened,' Guðgeir said, leaning forward. 'I want you to go over the whole of yesterday, morning to evening, choose your words carefully and don't leave anything out.'

Guðgeir placed his elbows on the table, hands clasped together and caught Ásmundur's eye as he thought for a moment before speaking.

'Well, the four of us who stayed at the hotel went for a cycling tour around the island, did some yoga up there among the rocks, dipped our toes in the water, and so on. We left around nine and didn't get back here until eleven-thirty. Stopped off at the hotel for a shower and a change of clothes... ' Ásmundur's narrative was interrupted as Guðgeir's phone began to vibrate.

'Excuse me. I have to take this call,' he said, getting to his feet and moving away so that he could talk to Leifur.

'Anything new?' he said in a low voice.

'Yes. Ísgerður has done a preliminary examination and she's in agreement with the local doctor that this deserves further examination. At least, until we know more,' Leifur said. 'So keep at it on your side.'

'We'll do that,' Guðgeir said, glancing meaningfully at Elsa Guðrún. 'It'll be as well to not screw anything up, if that turns out to be correct.'

'The body will be flown to Reykjavík and the pathologist, the German guy, will do the autopsy. He's been on holiday and will be back tomorrow or Tuesday.'

'Understood.'

'How's it looking?'

'We're going through things with the first of the four,' Guðgeir replied. 'Then we'll take a closer look at the scene and try to talk to a few more people.'

He ended the call and put his phone in his pocket before taking his seat again opposite Ásmundur, who clearly felt that the atmosphere had changed, as he appeared even more agitated than before.

'Let's pick up where we left off, shall we?' Guðgeir said with a shadow of a smile. 'We were talking about the bikes. Where do you keep them?'

'They let us keep them in the basement here.' Ásmundur waved a hand in the direction of the wall to the right, as if showing them where the storage area was. 'These are really expensive bikes, so we don't want to take any risks. There could be thieves here, just like there are in Reykjavík.'

'Understood. Then what?' Guðgeir asked, steering the man back to the question.

'We went over to the restaurant, and Diljá and Ríkharður were already there. It must have been gone two by the time we finished, and then we went up to the Landa Church. Ríkharður really wanted to take a picture of the gate, because of the eruption, you see... Back then everything was deep in ash, only the gate wasn't covered, and then we went up to Eldheimar.

That's a museum all about the eruption, and we spent a while looking around.'

'Was there anything noticeable about Diljá's or Ríkharður's behaviour?' Guðgeir asked, scratching at the dark stubble on his chin.

'No... Such as what?' Ásmundur asked, running his fingertips over his forehead. His nails had been bitten to the quick.

'How was their behaviour to each other, for instance?' Guðgeir explained.

'Yes, I see. They were just the way they usually are. I think Ríkharður was relieved to miss out on the bike ride, as he's more inclined to take things easy. Maybe Diljá would have preferred to come with us, y'know. But he was older, and a different type,' Ásmundur said.

'In what respect?' Guðgeir asked, eyes narrowed. 'Did he hold her back?'

'Not exactly. He just wasn't as into sports in the same way as Diljá is...' Ásmundur said and paused, as if he had decided against saying what he had in mind. 'She told me that Ríkharður would have preferred to have not come over to the Westman Islands, but he also wasn't happy with the idea of her going with the rest of us and without him.'

'What's the nature of your relationship with Diljá?' Guðgeir asked quickly, watching him carefully.

'What do you mean?' Ásmundur asked, in a tone of voice that indicated he took this as an insult.

Guðgeir didn't reply, but waited patiently for the answer that came after a few moments.

'We're just good friends and we have similar interests,' he said, and shrugged. 'We're in the same business and we both work at Fitness Centre. If you're implying anything else, then there isn't anything between us and never has been. I mean, nothing beyond a good friendship.'

'All right,' Guðgeir said, leaning forward. He sensed that this was the moment to change tack and to push the man further. 'What's your explanation of Diljá's disappearance?'

Ásmundur shrugged and spread his hands in a theatrical gesture.

'I don't have an explanation for that, or for any of this. I don't understand what's going on... Why are you asking me? Ríkharður didn't mean anything to me beyond being my friend's boyfriend, and I hardly knew him,' he said, his voice rising. 'I mean, the man's dead and it's one of those things that happens.'

'Then why did Diljá make herself scarce?' Guðgeir asked, glaring at him. 'Why isn't she here?'

'How on earth should I know?' Ásmundur shot back, raising his voice a little too much, and appearing to be about to continue, before pulling himself back.

'Where is she?' Guðgeir asked without dropping his gaze. 'Where's Diljá?'

'I don't know. Maybe she had a nervous breakdown and ran for it, or someone could have kidnapped her. Maybe the murderer... What would I know?'

'You think that Ríkharður was murdered?' Guðgeir asked in a dark tone and watched as reddish flecks appeared between the red-gold flames on the man's chest.

'Yes... I mean, no...What the hell? I don't know anything about this! You're getting me confused!' Ásmundur looked beseechingly at Elsa Guðrún, who had taken a seat opposite and sat in silence. He seemed to be asking for help from that direction, and when none came, he muttered apologetically, 'I mean, isn't that what you were on about?' His eyes flickered from one to the other.

'No,' Guðgeir said slowly, after a pause. He took off his glasses and looked directly into Ásmundur's eyes. 'Nobody's mentioned murder.'

10

While Ásmundur's nervousness had been on clear display, that certainly wasn't the case with the woman who now faced them. Considering the circumstances, Eygló seemed too calm and collected, sitting straight-backed, legs crossed, dressed in a co-ordinated sports outfit from a well-known designer. Short red hair softened her square face and prominent glasses perching on her freckled nose framed green eyes. Elsa Guðrún and Guðgeir had swapped seats, leaving her to take the statement while he kept quiet. So far Eygló had given a full answer to every question, after a moment's thought. Her description of the previous day tallied perfectly with Ásmundur's.

'Ingi Thór and I live in Reykjavík. We have two children, a boy of fourteen and a girl of three,' she said in response to Elsa Guðrún's question.

'Let's go back to yesterday evening,' Elsa Guðrún continued. 'You said that Ríkharður had been pretty drunk at the restaurant.'

'To tell you the unvarnished truth, he was completely hammered,' Eygló said with a disapproving look on her face.

'How did that manifest itself?' Elsa Guðrún said.

'I saw pretty quickly that he had been putting it away, but didn't think too much of it until he tried to stand up and crashed into the next table. He knocked over a glass and there was an embarrassing scene. Shortly after that Diljá took him home... I mean, to their caravan,' Eygló said, arms folded.

'Do you have any idea how much he'd had to drink?'

The question appeared to take Eygló by surprise and she rubbed the tip of her freckled nose as she thought.

'I don't know... Maybe a glass at lunchtime, and I didn't notice anything more, he might have had a drink at the hotel bar, I remember that. He and Diljá were late getting to the hotel and we went over to Magni for dinner. We ordered one or two bottles of wine with dinner, so there wasn't much for each of us. I certainly didn't notice any effects and was wide awake. Why do you ask?'

'We need to put together as clear a picture as we can of Ríkharður's last twenty-four hours. There's no evidence that there's anything suspicious about his death, but we have to assume there is until we can be certain.'

'Do you think it was alcoholic poisoning?' Eygló asked, eyes wide.

There was a greenish tinge to the whites of her eyes. Elsa Guðrún decided that she must have used strong eye drops that morning to hide signs of fatigue.

'That's unlikely,' Guðgeir said.

'Have you found Diljá?' Eygló asked, concern appearing in her voice for the first time.

'No. And we don't know where she is,' Elsa Guðrún said. 'Do you have any idea where she could have gone?'

Eygló gazed out of the room's only window and appeared to be thinking carefully, before shaking her head.

'Where would Diljá go if she was in trouble? Who would she ask for help?' Elsa Guðrún asked, encouraging her to continue, but Eygló said nothing. 'You, maybe?'

'I wouldn't know,' she said sharply. 'I can't understand all this, to be honest. It's all so weird.'

'And that's why we're asking you to help us understand,' Elsa Guðrún said amiably.

'I get that,' Eygló muttered.

'How would you describe Diljá?'

'She's... She's a lively, fun sort of girl,' Eygló said after pausing for thought and shrugging her shoulders. 'We have similar interests. We both see the importance of cultivating our personalities.'

'Have you been friends for long?' Elsa Guðrún asked.

'Yes... A few years. We connect well through our work in holistic health.'

'So you know her family?' Elsa Guðrún asked. This time she didn't need to wait for an answer as Eygló seemed to finally open up.

'A little. She has a daughter, María Líf, who has just turned thirteen. Diljá's parents split up when she was a child and her father disappeared from her life, and she has an older brother and a younger sister. They...' Eygló fell silent and her attention went to Guðgeir who was clearly sending a text message.

'Thanks,' Elsa Guðrún said, catching his eye. There was every likelihood that he was messaging Særós to ask her to contact the siblings.

'I don't know if they are close. I don't think so...'

'And Ríkharður? What can you tell me about him?'

'I was shocked when I heard he died during the night, but to tell the truth I hardly knew him,' Eygló replied.

'Your friend was living with him, and you travelled together,' Elsa Guðrún said in a relaxed tone, and Eygló shook her head.

'I hardly recall ever having much of a conversation with him. He was older, and his interests were different to ours,' she said.

'What did you make of him?'

'I didn't have an opinion about him,' she said, and there was a chill in her voice.

'You surely couldn't be completely indifferent to your friend's boyfriend?' Elsa Guðrún probed, her gaze intensifying. 'Be honest. Tell us what you thought. It won't be used against you.'

Eygló shifted in her chair.

'Could I have some coffee?' she asked, nodding towards the tray on the corner table.

'Of course,' Guðgeir said as he got to his feet. 'Milk?'

'Do you have almond milk?'

'Unfortunately they don't offer much choice here,' Guðgeir said with a ghost of a smile.

'Black is fine,' Eygló said, demonstrating her disappointment with a frown.

'Here you go,' he said, handing her a cup.

'Thanks.'

She smiled at Guðgeir and Elsa Guðrún cleared her throat loudly.

'Eygló,' she said. 'It makes a significant difference if you can give us the most accurate information possible. Your friend Diljá hasn't been accused of anything, but for whatever reason, she's disappeared. There's no certainty that she has run for it, she may have been abducted by someone who has an interest in her not being here.'

'What?' Eygló's face turned pale beneath her tan. 'What do you mean?' she demanded, clearly horrified.

'Just that time may not be on our side, and of course that we know nothing. She could have fled, she could have been abducted, or she might be caught up in something with other people. The only thing we know is that she's disappeared.'

'I know nothing about that,' Eygló said quickly. 'All I'm concerned about now is getting home, because our little girl is being looked after and we have to get ho...'

'So it's vital that you answer our questions promptly and fully,' Guðgeir broke in.

'Were you aware of anything unusual in the behaviour of Diljá or Ríkharður yesterday or in the previous few days?' Elsa Guðrún asked, her usually soft voice hardening.

'No...' Eygló hesitated for a moment, and continued. 'Not as such, but I had the impression that Diljá was tired of him, and she was noticeably irritated yesterday. I have wondered sometimes if she was with him purely for the money. Diljá can be impulsive... Ríkharður isn't the first older guy she's been with, but he's certainly the oldest. She has nothing against living well and allowing herself all sorts of luxuries, but...' Eygló bit her lip, as if frightened that she had let slip more than she had intended.

'Was she in financial difficulties?' Elsa Guðrún asked.

'Well, she's sometimes barged into stupid situations. Like I said, she can be impulsive. She's a spur-of-the-moment type. The darling girl needs to build up some inner peace, even though she's worked hard on herself and has been doing really well,' Eygló said, and for the first time there was a little warmth in her voice.

'How long has their relationship been going on?' Elsa Guðrún asked.

'Maybe a year, or a year and a half. It wouldn't have come as a surprise to me if she had ended it,' Eygló said. 'Right after this trip.'

11

Diljá was startled from sleep a noise from somewhere. It took her a moment to realise where she was as she stared at the pile of mattresses at her side. Before long she recalled that she was in the upstairs space of the summer house owned by Ingi Thór and Eygló. She rolled over onto her front and crawled to the small window, taking care not to be seen. There was nothing to be seen outside and she wriggled closer, peering out and listening. She was sure she could hear the sound of a car in the distance, and she watched as a small jeep drove down the track from one of the other summer houses. Someone was leaving. She pulled back from the window and hoped that she hadn't been spotted. Now she needed a little more time to think things over and look for a way out of this predicament.

She had no idea what the time was, or how long she had been asleep. There was a television downstairs and she switched it on, quickly scanning the news media.

Man found dead in Herjólfsdalur.

It was just a short news item, but she read it again and again. There was no more information in the full text than the headline had provided. There was no mention of her disappearance, or anything referring to the group's trip to the Westman Islands, other than that the deceased was a fifty-two-year-old man from Reykjavík.

What options were now open to her? Give herself up and try to explain, in the forlorn hope that she would get away with it?

No. Nobody would believe her. Was she prepared to be remanded in custody, to be shut away in a cramped, windowless cell? Her claustrophobia was so severe that even taking the lift from one floor to the next was too much for her. A stream of thoughts whirled through her mind, one after another, and it was difficult to keep them under some kind of control. Occasionally María Líf appeared in her thoughts, and that magnified her misery. Her stomach made a strange sound, and she realised that she hadn't eaten since the night before. Something to eat would help her think straight. She found the bag of goods she had picked up at the shop by the Landvegur crossroads. Two of the hotdogs went into a pot and she rooted around for ketchup and mustard in one of the cupboards, and smeared both onto some bread. The aroma sharpened her hunger and she wolfed down the two sausages. It was years since she had last eaten processed food of this kind, but her stomach didn't rebel and she felt better for it.

She took a quick shower and washed her hair. The green towel on a hook must have been hung up wet, as it was stiff to the touch. Diljá dried herself vigorously, hard enough to leave her skin red and tender. The steam from the shower had left a mist on the mirror, and when she looked at her reflection she saw the raw skin, eyes puffed with tears and the worry on her face.

'You always fuck everything up, you idiot,' she snarled angrily at her own reflection.

12

There was nothing unusual about Særós being at work on a Sunday. Since she'd taken over Guðgeir Fransson's role this had become the rule rather than the exception. Crime pays no more respect than illness does to the days of the week. Even when there were no serious cases that demanded her attention, as often as not her time was spent in front of a screen while she tidied up loose ends. Særós was simply not the type to leave work unfinished. Organised and precise by nature, she wanted to see investigations completed quickly and properly. Consequently, her days were much the same. She lived in a roomy, tastefully decorated apartment that she had worked hard to be able to call her own, was always awake early and started the day with a green smoothie of some kind before running at least six kilometres or a going to the gym to work out. She always tried to find time for an hour's cycling after work, normally alone, but occasionally she would join a group that met outside the swimming pool near where she lived. A ride with them was fine, but she was less excited at the prospect of joining them at a coffee house or even a bar afterwards.

This Sunday she had just come in from a ten-kilometre run when the call came from the police in the Westman Islands. Since then she had been busy. Less than an hour had passed before the forensics team were headed there in a small aircraft, while her closest colleagues, Guðgeir and Elsa Guðrún, were on their way to the Landeyjarhöfn ferry terminal. Shortly afterwards, a search was being co-ordinated across the south of the country for the deceased's girlfriend, Diljá Sigurðardóttir. Reports were coming in at intervals from the forensic team who were at work at the scene, and now there was a confirmation from the ferry operator that Diljá had paid for the crossing at 10.20 that morning, and a full passenger list was expected at any moment. The ferry hadn't been fully booked, which increased the likelihood that someone might have noticed Diljá. Unless she had jumped overboard? The thought occurred to Særós, but she immediately dismissed it. This had to be out of the question, considering her phone had been found not far from the terminal.

Now Særós would have to pay a couple of difficult visits – first Ríkharður's family, and then Diljá's. She would have much preferred to have had Guðgeir with her for this. He was much more adroit with this kind of thing as somehow he had a delicate touch of his own when it came to people and sensed exactly when were the right moments to keep quiet, while she often came across with an impatience that manifested itself in asking questions too quickly, or else her questions were too intrusive, discouraging people from expressing themselves. Guðgeir had a natural intuition for timing, something that she still had to learn from others. Særós had forgotten to put up a new aphorism before the weekend, and now she quickly googled for something that would help her cope with this reality. She printed it out in bold lettering, and pinned ***patience is bitter, but the fruits of patience are sweet*** to the wall behind her desk.

She pulled on her jacket and picked up her briefcase. Then she stood still for a moment, shut her eyes and allowed the meaning of the words to sink into her consciousness. This was a nugget of wisdom that she was determined to keep at the forefront of her mind.

An hour later, after stopping off at home for a quick shower, she parked outside an imposing detached house in one of the sprawling estates on the outskirts of Reykjavík. She adjusted the starched collar of her shirt and ran her fingers through hair that was still damp from the shower. She applied a touch of pale pink lip gloss, and got out of the car. Each house in this district was more magnificent than the next, but the angular, boxy shape of Ríkharður's house was exceptionally simple and understated, and she liked that. The garden was bordered by green concrete walls, and only the hefty front door of dark hardwood stood out. Særós went up the wide, tiled steps, applied a finger to the buzzer and admired the cast cement tubs filled with white and pink summer flowers. She had hardly removed her finger from the button when the door swung open. A tall young man with hair gathered in a bun looked at her inquiringly.

'Hello. My name's Særós... I'm from Reykjavik CID.'

'Vilhjálmur,' the young man replied in a dull voice. 'Ríkharður's son.'

'My condolences.'

'Thanks.'

He quickly wiped damp eyes.

'Could I come inside and ask a few questions?'

'Of course. We have been expecting a visit from you,' Vilhjálmur replied. 'My sister Lára is here and so is my father's sister Ingibjörg. The priest is here, but he's about to leave. Please, come in.'

She followed him through the lobby and into a large living space. There was a gleaming kitchen at one end, behind a heavy marble island unit. Next was a large dining table, around which Særós guessed twelve or fourteen people could sit. At the far end was a green corner sofa stretched along two walls. Two women sat on it. One looked to be between twenty and thirty, and Særós guessed this had to be Vilhjálmur's sister. They had strikingly similar features, both with dark blonde hair, big-boned but slim. The older woman had to be the deceased's sister. Her long hair was as black as night, her face was broad and Særós felt sure there were signs of plastic surgery. Her face had a look of permanent surprise, and her plump and gleaming lips appeared to have been recently filled. Ingibjörg was clearly in shock and cautiously brushing away tears with heavily ringed fingers with lacquered sharp nails. The bearded man at the far end of the sofa was presumably the priest, and Særós was sure she had met him before.

The three sat apart from each other like islands on the sea-green sofa. A green glass jug of water stood on the table before them, but no glasses were to be seen. Særós introduced herself, offering her condolences.

'Have you caught her?' Ingibjörg asked, her voice a blast of cold.

'Who?' Særós asked, although she could guess who she meant.

'Well, Diljá of course!'

'No, she hasn't been located,' Særós said, sitting down without being invited on a matching green chair facing the sofa.

'Do you think Dad was murdered?' The question came from Lára. Her voice was neutral, as if frozen, and her eyes were glazed.

'It is possible that his death could be due to a criminal act,' Særós replied cautiously. 'But until we have clear evidence to that effect, we have to take every precaution. It's urgent that we locate Diljá. Do you have any idea where she might have gone?'

The priest coughed politely, and got to his feet.

'I think it's time for me to be on my way. Please don't hesitate to get in touch if there's anything I can do for you,' he said to the family with a look of priestly concern on his face.

'I'll show you out,' said Vilhjálmur, who seemed always ready to be of service.

'Could I have some water?' Særós asked, pointing to the green jug. She was still thirsty after that morning's run.

'Ach. No glasses,' Lára said, hauling herself to her feet and making her unhurried way to the kitchen. They watched as she opened one cupboard after another without success. 'Do you know where they are?' she asked her aunt. 'I'm so dazed that I don't remember a thing.'

'Me? How should I know?' Ingibjörg demanded. 'I don't come here that often, and certainly not to go through the kitchen cupboards.'

'What are you looking for?' Vilhjálmur asked as he came back in.

'Glasses.'

'In there,' he said, pointing to a drawer. Clearly he was more familiar than his sister or aunt were with the layout.

'I was asking about Diljá. Do you have any idea where she might be?' Særós asked again.

Lára shook her head as she handed her a glass.

'Not a clue,' Ingibjörg shrilled. 'I hardly know her.'

'Have they been living together for long, Diljá and your father?' Særós asked, her question intended for the brother and sister.

'She moved in about a year ago,' Vilhjálmur said. He seemed more worried than upset.

'How was your relationship with her?'

'As far as I'm concerned, as good as non-existent,' Lára said in the same neutral tone as before. 'I didn't get the feeling of being exactly welcome here after she moved in. But you got on all right with her, didn't you, Villi?'

'Yes. It was OK. Diljá isn't as terrible as you think,' he said, and Særós wondered if he was the family's shock absorber, the one who would always go the extra distance to keep everyone happy.

'Even though she might have murdered Dad,' Lára snapped. She was clearly about to continue, but fell silent when she saw Ingibjörg and Vilhjálmur staring at her. 'What's the matter with you? I'm just saying what we're all thinking. We've only just found out that they went to the County Sheriff and got married a month ago.'

'Without your knowledge?' Særós said in surprise.

'Yes,' Vilhjálmur said. He flushed, and glanced at his aunt who sat with her lips tightly pursed. 'We found the marriage certificate in their bedroom, just now. It's come as a shock.'

'So as his next of kin, Diljá stands to inherit everything,' Lára said with a bitterness that she didn't try to hide. She was clearly distressed, and Særós felt that sorrow had given way remarkably rapidly to concerns over inheritance. This was obviously a family riven by deep tensions. She watched them without saying anything, conscious that patience could bear fruit.

'I get the impression that you weren't happy about your father's relationship with Diljá. Why's that?' she asked, when silence hadn't prompted an explanation.

'Ach. She was much younger than him, always skint, and endlessly in some sort of trouble,' the dead man's sister answered for them.

'Really? Doesn't she work as a personal trainer?' Særós asked.

'Yes. Something like that,' Vilhjálmur replied. 'But because of Covid everything has been more or less shut down for a whole year, and even before that she wasn't doing well financially. My own feeling is that she has made a few unfortunate decisions...'

He flushed again, and his eyes went to the floor.

'Diljá, unfortunate!' Lára snarled with a snort of exasperation. 'Maybe, right up to when Dad paid off all her debts.'

'Did they have a turbulent relationship? Would you know about that?' Særós asked, pretending she hadn't heard what Lára had said.

'Only that she spent money like water,' said Ingibjörg, who seemed to share her niece's opinion of Diljá.

'And they were so unalike. No shared interests or anything. This was the old man having a mid-life crisis, and Diljá wasn't the first to get her hooks into him, but she had a stronger grip on him than the ones before.'

Tears streamed down Lára's cheeks and Særós wondered if this was anger, jealousy or sorrow, or a mixture of all three.

'We don't know anything about their relationship, Lára,' Vilhjálmur said. 'It's not as if we spent a lot of time with them.'

'I saw practically nothing of her, but I know you liked her company well enough,' Lára shot back angrily.

Ingibjörg was on her feet.

'Stop it, both of you,' she hissed at them as if scolding small children. 'I don't expect to hear that kind of talk!'

Then she turned to Særós, who could see how the sharp, deep red nails were cutting deep into her palms as she fought to maintain control.

'It's best that you go now. There's a lot of grief in this house and it manifests itself in all kinds of ways, as I'm sure you understand.'

13

Guðgeir went to the hotel lobby with the coffee flask to ask for a refill, while Elsa Guðrún went to fetch Ingi Thór. He had just put the refilled flask in its place on the corner table and poured himself a cup when he turned to see Ingi Thór standing before him, wearing blue jeans and a thin long-sleeved sweater. He looked vigorous, tanned and physically fit, without being quite as buff as his friend Ásmundur. His full beard was neatly trimmed and the long hair that reached almost to his shoulders was maybe supposed to give him a more macho look, in a way that Guðgeir failed to understand.

'Can Eygló and I leave when we've given our statements?' he asked. There was an undertone of impatience in his voice. 'Our daughter is with relatives, and it's a working day tomorrow.'

'Unfortunately, I can't tell you right away, but we'll do everything we can not to delay you without good reason,' Guðgeir said, and put on his glasses. He sized the man up thoughtfully. There was no escaping the fact that he was agitated, his blue eyes flickering this way and that.

'We'd really like to catch the evening ferry. Our car is at the Landeyjarhöfn terminal, and it'll take some time to get home.' Ingi Thór put a hand in his pocket and pulled out a car key that he rolled back and forth in his palm, clearly concerned. 'Our little girl had a bad night so we really don't want her to have another night away from us, and the same goes for our relatives. They have to go to work tomorrow as well, and it's important for our son...'

Elsa Guðrún broke into his monologue.

'We understand that perfectly and we'll do what we can to accommodate you, so the best thing to do is to get on with it,' she said, sitting in the chair that Guðgeir had vacated and switching on the recorder. 'Please, take a seat.'

'Full name?' Guðgeir began.

'Ingi Thór Bjarnleifsson.'

'Age?'

'I'm thirty-eight.'

'What's your job?'

'I'm a builder, self-employed.'

'Marital status?'

'I'm married to Eygló Benediktsdóttir. We have two children, a teenage boy and a girl of three,' Ingi Thór said, supplying more information than had been asked for. He had a pleasant voice, spoke clearly, and answered without hesitation. He clearly wanted to get this over with as soon as possible. One leg jerked constantly up and down, and the table shook slightly.

'Would you go through the sequence of events since you arrived in the Westman Islands, as precisely as possible?' Guðgeir said, pushing his glasses higher up his nose. Ingi Thór nodded and produced a narrative that was virtually identical to those already provided by his wife and by Ásmundur.

'Was there anything in particular about Diljá's and Ríkharður's behaviour that caught your attention?' Guðgeir asked.

'No, nothing that I noticed,' Ingi Thór replied. 'Except that Ríkharður was pretty drunk last night. He must have had more to drink than just the wine we had with the meal.'

'Was he already drunk when he turned up for an aperitif at the hotel bar?' Guðgeir asked.

'Well...' Ingi Thór hesitated, as if weighing up what he should say. 'Well, not that I noticed. Although he could have been.'

'How was their interaction yesterday?' Guðgeir asked, taking off his glasses to massage the bridge of his nose, but without taking his eyes off Ingi Thór.

'Y'know, I didn't take much notice of them, I was concentrating on enjoying myself. But Diljá was a bit sulky with him.'

'In what way?' Guðgeir asked, narrowing his eyes as he stared at him, at the same time polishing his glasses before putting them on again.

'Ach. You could see it on her face last night, and there was a bit of tension between them earlier in the day when we were at the Eldheimar museum.'

Ingi Thór ran his fingers quickly through his long hair and cast a longing look at the window.

'What was that about?'

'I have no idea. I didn't hear their conversation. I just saw that they were disagreeing about something or other. Have you found Diljá?'

'Unfortunately not. Do you have any idea where she could have got to?' Guðgeir asked, leaning forward on the table and looking at him intently.

'Me? How should I know?' Ingi Thór asked in reply, slumping against the back of the chair and fiddling with his beard, pulling at the short hairs and then patting them down.

'Are you and Diljá good friends?'

'Yes, of course,' he replied quickly.

'How did you get to know each other?'

Ingi Thór didn't answer right away. He shrugged his shoulders and the look on his face indicated that he was trying to retrieve old memories.

'I don't recall exactly when I met her first, but we've known each other for a few years. We've knocked about together quite a bit, as we have interests in common,' he said after a pause.

'Can you imagine where she would seek refuge if she were in trouble?' Guðgeir asked. He folded his arms and gazed at Ingi Thór with a serious look on his face. 'Where would she feel safe?'

'I wouldn't know,' Ingi Thór replied right away. 'Diljá can be impulsive. You never know what she'll do next.'

'You don't need to answer straight away. Give yourself time to think. Where would she go?' Guðgeir said, encouraging him, and watching the man's right foot as it bounced up and down. He wondered if this was a tic, or a manifestation of stress that appeared under such conditions.

'Well, probably her family,' Ingi Thór said after having weighed up the options. 'Most likely to her mother. As far as I know, they get on well, but her father disappeared from her life a long time ago. I think he's dead. She also has siblings and she might go to them.'

'Anyone else who might be a possibility?'

'I don't know...' Ingi Thór said and fell silent. His eyes flashed around the room, and he again began to fidget with the car key. It was clear that he was struggling with a dilemma. After a pause, it came out. 'Look, Diljá was a long way from being a perfect teenager and she told me she'd tried all sorts of stuff... but only for short periods. People have varying tolerance levels, and Diljá's one of those who can't take that kind of thing well. She was off her head at one point. She was in a psychotic state... I think that's what it's called... At any rate, she was highly disturbed and did all kinds of stuff that she doesn't remember. Later on she was diagnosed with a mental illness. That was after her daughter was born.'

Ingi Thór fell silent and waited for their reactions. His knee bounced even faster than before.

'Ah, well. We weren't aware of this,' Guðgeir said slowly, focusing on Ingi Thór as he now seemed to regret what he had told them, and began making efforts to trivialise it.

'That was all a long time ago and everything's changed since then. More than that... Diljá is highly health-conscious, deeply into yoga, and she coaches other people as well. She eats healthily, hardly drinks at all. I mean, all that mental stuff is just my own prejudices coming out. Can you take that out of my statement?' He was again noticeably agitated, tugging at his beard, his feet constantly shifting. 'Can you do that?'

'No, we can't do that, but we naturally respect your confidence,' Guðgeir explained quietly. 'Diljá has experienced mental health problems, so do you recall her at any time exhibiting violent behaviour?'

The question clearly took Ingi Thór off guard, and he shook his head.

'No... I don't think so... It's so hard to believe but...'

He hesitated, and glanced at them each in turn, clearly in doubt about whether or not to say anything.

'Let's hear it,' said Elsa Guðrún, who had so far listened in silence.

'I can see that there's something that's troubling you, and can only remind you of the importance of telling us everything you know,' Guðgeir said, his tone encouraging.

'Well, y'see...' He ran his fingers quickly through his hair several times, allowing himself time to think. 'You see, Diljá's mother really wanted the little girl to be with her permanently. I don't know exactly why, but that tells me she didn't trust her daughter to look after the child. Something bad happened when she was tiny.'

14

There was a delay before they could speak to Katrín. Guðgeir took the opportunity to call Særós and they decided that it was best to put out an alert for Diljá. They both had the feeling that the case was looking increasingly serious as the day progressed.

'It's at the point where we can't justify any other course of action,' Særós said, sounding concerned. 'We have to bear in mind that she could be mentally very unstable after everything that has happened.'

'Yes, and if there's any truth in what we've been told about her daughter, then things must have gone badly wrong for her,' Guðgeir said.

'I'm on the way up to Grafarholt to meet her mother,' Særós said. 'I've just come from Ríkharður's house. I had a meeting with his son and daughter, and his sister as well. There was no mistaking that the two women can't stand Diljá, and they don't bother to hide it. They said straight out that she was a gold digger, although I felt that the sister was more adamant about that than the daughter.'

'And the son?' Guðgeir asked.

'He was more positive about her, and he seems to be more balanced than the other two,' Særós replied.

'What's the situation there?'

'The priest was with them. I don't know if he was asked to call on them, or if they called him themselves, but I wasn't aware of a lot of sorrow in that house. The sister was in tears, but I can't tell if that was solely because of her brother's death.'

'Some people are numbed by shock, shut themselves off somehow,' Guðgeir said. 'The reactions to a bereavement can appear in all kinds of ways.'

'There was no sign of anyone being numb, and I got the impression very strongly that Ríkharður hadn't been in much contact with his closest relatives. The daughter, Lára, is very bitter towards him, but especially towards Diljá. She's deeply upset and practically accused her brother of being smitten with his father's girlfriend. Sorry, I mean his wife. They got married a month ago.'

'They were married! That's interesting,' Guðgeir said, unable to keep the surprise out of his voice. 'I'm not certain at all that their friends here know anything about that. That's an interesting angle in itself, but how about the other side of all this?'

'Forensics are still at work in the caravan in Herjólfsdalur, and Ríkharður's body has been brought to Reykjavík by air,' Særós said.

A medley of car horns could be heard in the distance and Særós groaned.

'What's up?' Guðgeir asked.

'Ach. Road works and a contraflow,' she muttered, irritated. 'It's a problem I guarantee you won't encounter in the Westman Islands.'

'I'm a hundred per cent sure of that. It's a pretty laid back sort of place,' Guðgeir chuckled. 'Elsa Guðrún and I will stay here overnight and be here until sometime tomorrow. There are things we need check out at the scene, and it's too late in the day to do that now.'

'Sounds good. Hope it goes well and speak to you later,' Særós said, and ended the call.

15

The blinds were closed in every window and the way things had been left indicated that the owners had no plans to be back any time soon. Now it was close to the end of August and the evenings were getting dark as the bright nights of summer receded further into the past. It was ten o'clock and it was dark already. Diljá didn't dare switch on a light, and wondered if she could chance turning on the television. A passing neighbour might be able to see a narrow strip of light along the edge of one of the curtains, which would arouse suspicion that someone could have broken in.

She went from one window to the next, cautiously peering out. There was nobody to be seen, so she gave in to the temptation and fast-forwarded through the news until she found what she was looking for.

Police are looking for Diljá Sigurðardóttir, age 33, from Reykjavík. Height one metre, sixty-three centimetres, slim build, with medium-length dark hair and brown eyes. She is believed to be driving a dark grey Land Cruiser and caught the ferry from the Westman Islands this morning. Anyone with information regarding her whereabouts is asked to contact the police urgently.

Diljá stared at the screen. Everything that had happened over the last twenty-four hours had just jumped into sharp focus. She tried to swallow but found that her throat was completely dry. An old photo of her appeared on the screen, one taken by a colleague at Fitness Centre, then another of her leading María Líf by the hand, but with the little girl's face blurred out.

This picture had been taken on Easter Sunday three years ago. The two of them were on their way to have dinner with her aunt. Diljá was sure that she could see the trust in her daughter's eyes and her clear voice asking if there would be other children there with whom she could play.

Her hands shook as she switched off the television.

16

Katrín appeared in the doorway, blonde, dressed in sports gear and with a water bottle in one hand. Like her husband Ásmundur, she was in peak physical condition. She took a seat and crossed her muscular legs. Silver rings adorned practically every one of her fingers, but even more noticeable were the long, dark blue nails that she ran through her long, straight hair. A tiny diamond sparkled as it nestled against her right nostril. Katrín's dark eyebrows lifted and she sighed.

'This is just such a mess.'

'A mess?' Guðgeir repeated in surprise. 'What do you mean by that?'

'Ach, I mean all the inconvenience...'

'What's so inconvenient?' Elsa Guðrún asked.

'I mean, it's really tragic about Ríkharður, but it's completely ridiculous if you think that one of us murdered him.'

'Nobody has made any such suggestion,' Guðgeir said, speaking slowly and emphasising every word.

'Really? Then why do you need to question us all separately and take our phones off us?' Katrín smiled coldly and tapped one sandalled foot. 'I would like to make it clear that we are all peaceable people who wouldn't hurt a fly.'

'The circumstances of his death are still unclear,' Guðgeir said, raising one eyebrow. 'We are keeping every option open until we have more information. So let's get on with this. Yes, and this is an informal statement, not an interrogation, just so that's completely clear.'

Katrín was thirty-seven years old, childless and said that she worked for the Association of Driving Instructors. In fact, she was practically its managing director.

'Practically?' Guðgeir asked. 'What do you mean by that?'

'Well, you see. Someone else has that title. But I do all the work. There's only two of us at the office,' she said, sliding a blue nail through her hair.

'I see. Have you worked for this organisation long?'

'Almost two years,' she replied. 'Before that I was at the same centre as Ásmundur.'

'And Diljá,' Guðgeir said. He folded his arms and looked at her with interest.

'Yes, but not as a trainer. I looked after the accounts. That needs attention, just the same as muscles. Have you found her?'

Guðgeir acted as if he hadn't heard her question, but Katrín wasn't going to give up easily.

'Well? I asked if you've found Diljá?' she said, transferring her attention to her hair on the other side. Her nails rasped lightly over her skin and left a trail of pink behind them.

'We don't have any reports so far,' Guðgeir replied. 'Do you have any idea where she might be?'

'No, haven't a clue.'

The reply came so quickly that Guðgeir stared at Katrín in amazement.

'Think it over. We have plenty of time. There's no rush,' Elsa Guðrún said.

Silent, Katrín shrugged.

'No. I don't know where Diljá is,' she said after a pause.

'How about friends and relatives?' Elsa Guðrún prompted, but Katrín shook her head.

'Have you checked on her mother?' she said suddenly, eyes wide. Black lashes swooped majestically upwards to meet her eyebrows, but her mascara had smeared in a couple of places, ruining the overall picture.

'Yes. And she's not there,' Guðgeir said, sizing her up. There was something intriguing about Katrín, who came across as impulsive and not clear in her thinking, and he wasn't sure that was the reality.

'Can you give us the names of any friends of hers?' Guðgeir asked.

'The four of us are her friends. Apart from us, she doesn't associate with many other people other than her clients at the gym and Ríkharður. Or she did, at any rate.'

'How did those two get to know each other?'

'He trained with her,' Katrín replied. 'Then he was smitten with her, like so many other people have been.'

'I see. How long have they been together?'

'Around a year, or a year and a half,' Katrín said, replying as promptly as before.

'And how were they towards each other yesterday?' Guðgeir asked.

'I didn't pay much attention, but I reckon he was getting on Diljá's nerves.'

'In what way?'

'Ach. There was a bit of tension between them when we went to Eldheimar earlier in the day. I saw they were squabbling and there was some unpleasantness in the evening. At the restaurant Ríkharður was so drunk that he knocked a glass off the next table. It was embarrassing and I can understand Diljá being irritated.'

'Do you know what they disagreed about earlier in the day?' Elsa Guðrún asked.

'I've no idea. I just went over to the next exhibit. Their personal affairs are no concern of mine,' Katrín said, shrugging again as if all the day's events had passed her by.

'It's sad to hear that they were arguing, since they had only just tied the knot,' Guðgeir said.

The uninterested expression vanished instantly from Katrín's face. She had clearly been taken completely by surprise.

'What?' They were married?' she gasped.

17

Guðgeir and Elsa Guðrún ordered a meal at a restaurant at the cheaper end of the scale. The two couples were about to leave the Islands on the evening ferry, and had done nothing to disguise their relief at being allowed to go. All the same, Guðgeir had stressed to them that they could expect to be called in to give more detailed statements. He also did his best to impress on them that they shouldn't hesitate to contact him if anything were to come to mind that would help with the investigation.

Elsa Guðrún stepped outside to make a call to the father of her twins to ask him to have them a little longer. Her former husband lived in Akureyri, in the north of Iceland, where she had also grown up and where they had spent most of their marriage. After the divorce she had moved back to Reykjavík and returned to her old job with the police, while the boys took a flight once a month to Akureyri to spent time with their father.

'How did it go?' Guðgeir asked as she came back in. 'Everything OK?'

'No problem. He's happy to have them for another week. They love it in Akureyri, with both sets of grandparents close by to spoil them rotten.' Elsa Guðrún dropped into a chair and sighed. 'A shame we have to put up with a cheap place to stay here. I could have done with staying in a smart place like those fitness freaks did. I like the idea of a hot bubble bath and a full night's sleep.'

A dreamy expression appeared on Elsa Guðrún's face at the thought of it.

'We can also be thankful that we don't have to sleep in a tent. The department is always looking to make economies,' he said ruefully. 'Are you still sleeping badly?' he asked, catching her eye, but she quickly looked away.

'Yes, but only at home,' she said, and he saw her face harden. 'It's worst when the twins are in the north and I'm in the flat on my own. That's when all the memories return. They aren't pleasant, to say the least.'

'You haven't thought about a change? I mean, selling up and moving elsewhere?' Guðgeir asked.

'Actually, no. The boys are happy at school and I have good friends nearby. The flat is fine, and I had already put a lot of effort into painting it and getting it fixed up. In reality, I was delighted with it as our new home, until...' she said and her voice faded away. A flash of pain appeared in her eyes and when she spoke again, there was a hard edge to her voice. 'If I sell the flat and we move out of the area, then I'll feel that I've given that revolting man free rein over my life and I certainly don't want that. He's done enough harm! Do you know what I mean?'

Guðgeir felt a deep respect for Elsa Guðrún as he looked back at her, with her bright, open face. He nodded slowly. Elsa Guðrún was about to say more, but just then a middle-aged man in an apron bustled up to them with a plate in each hand. There was a generous portion on each and the porcelain beneath the food could hardly be seen.

'Cutlets in breadcrumbs?' he said, holding out one of the plates.

'That's me,' Guðgeir said, and he rejoiced at the sight of golden cutlets, potatoes, a blob of jam, and peas that came out of a can. This was food that he never had at home, and he couldn't resist texting Inga a picture with a 'once a year' message. Elsa Guðrún had ordered fish, although deep fried was the only option here. They set to in silence for a few minutes. Both of them were hungry and each wrapped up in their own thoughts after the events of the day.

'That was wonderful,' Guðgeir sighed as he swallowed the final morsel. 'Just like Mum used to cook at home in the west. Poor Leifur can never again allow himself anything like that. The thought of it would be too much for him.'

'The poor guy. All those vegetables are making him bad-tempered,' Elsa Guðrún said, still busy with her meal. 'The fish is really good,' she added. She dabbed at her mouth with a serviette, and gestured for Guðgeir to do the same. 'There's a bit of cutlets-in-breadcrumbs-artery-blocking-grease on your face,' she said.

'Oops. Better out than in,' Guðgeir said, dabbing at the corner of his mouth carefully, as the paper absorbed the yellow fluid. 'But, now... What are your thoughts on all of today's business?'

'Mainly how unlike they are,' Elsa Guðrún replied without hesitation. 'On the one hand the group of friends, and Ríkharður on the other. At least, going by the information we have. It's not just the difference in age. It seems to be everything else about their lives as well. Interests, education, experience... I don't quite see why Ríkharður was with these people. I mean, apart from his mid-life crisis with Diljá.'

'Men will go to all sorts of lengths for young, beautiful women,' Guðgeir said. 'But I agree it's difficult to understand this. Maybe he got drunk as a way of being companionable?'

'And you. What's your take on it all?' Elsa Guðrún asked.

'It's noticeable that they all told the same tale,' he said. 'They all described yesterday more or less the same.'

'Well, they were all together and doing stuff together,' Elsa Guðrún said. She reached for a little jar on the table and took a toothpick.

'Of course. But that's not what I mean. The narratives were almost identical, especially those of Ásmundur, who was first, and his girlfriend Katrín, who was the last one. Like the other couple, they went to their room as soon as the news arrived of Ríkharður's death ... and they naturally went through the same experiences, but it's noticeable that they all noticed the same things and even used the same forms of words to describe them, such as saying that Diljá had been irritated and that there had been tension between them at Eldheimar, instead of saying that they argued, or quarrelled...'

'Couple who have been together a long time will often use much the same vocabulary,' Elsa Guðrún cut in to say.

'Certainly, but all the same ... Ásmundur's and Katrín's narrative was almost identical to the other couple's recollections. At least, it looks that way.'

'You mean the four of them agreed what they would say?' she said.

'Ásmundur found the body and waited there until the police arrived at the scene. He had enough time to call the others, easily. No precautions were taken until it was clear that Diljá had made herself scarce, and it was assumed that there was no particular reason for any such measures. Or he could easily have met the other three at the hotel before they were put in separate rooms,' Guðgeir said.

'Of course. I have to say, there's something about this group of friends that I find deeply troubling,' Elsa Guðrún said, snapping the toothpick in two.

'I agree with you a hundred per cent,' Guðgeir said, and let his hand fall to the table so that the empty plates and glasses tinkled.

'Eygló has much more self-confidence than Katrín, who is obviously uncertain of her ground but hides it behind her attitude,' Elsa Guðrún said. 'But what about Diljá and this illness of hers? Has that been confirmed?'

'Særós is checking up on that,' Guðgeir replied and paused for a moment before continuing. 'What bugs me about these people is that they're not displaying any emotion about all of this, concerning either Ríkharður's death or Diljá's disappearance. They're practically stone cold.'

18

The only one she could trust was Ásmundur. She'd have to get in touch with him and work out what would be the best thing to do. But how? She had no phone and the usual methods of communication were out of the question. The police would be watching her social media. She again regretted not having picked up her medication, as with that everything would be so much easier. But now she would have to do everything in her power to keep the fear at bay and to think logically. She sat down and concentrated on gaining control of her breathing. When she felt her heartbeat slow to a normal rate, she stood up and looked around, but could not see what she was searching for anywhere, so she made for Ingi Thór's and Eygló's bedroom. The wardrobe was unusually large and Diljá went systematically through every shelf. She cautiously felt under, over and around sweaters, shirts, trousers and underwear, but without success. It wasn't until she moved aside the clothes on hangers that she found a cloth bag that had been looped over a hanger. It contained an iPad and a charging cable. Tears of relief coursed down her cheeks and the weight in her chest lifted. At last, something positive. Now all she needed was the password to get into it, and then she could send Ásmundur a message via a confidential messaging app. This was something they had used a lot between them during the trip. Sooner or later he must check it.

19

Særós adjusted her suit jacket and the collar of her shirt, and pressed the button marked 802. The paint on the window frames in the lobby of the stairwell was either flaking or bubbled. She dug a nail into the woodwork and the soft paint gave way under the pressure. There had been a leak here at some time, and the damp had been given ample opportunity to do its work. She pressed the buzzer button a second time. The automatic door opened almost immediately. The narrow lift was of the older variety and the journey to the eighth floor took its time, and was accompanied by vibration along the way. As the lift door squealed as it opened, Diljá's mother was waiting in the doorway of her flat. She was a petite woman with dark hair cut short, streaked with grey. The look on her face was tired and there was clear concern in her eyes.

'Hello. I'm Pálína, Diljá's mother,' she said in a low voice. 'Her daughter, María Líf, is here with me and I'd like to ask you to take care what you say around her. That's to say, if she comes out of her room. She's extremely sensitive about her mother, the poor little thing.'

'I'll bear that in mind,' Særós promised, following along a narrow corridor. An aroma of fried fish met them. The living room was wide and had a beautiful view over much of the city, with an open kitchen area at one end, and three doors set back in an alcove. The furniture was colourful and Pálína bundled a duvet that lay on the deep blue corner sofa into a utility room.

'I sleep here when María Líf is with me, and she has my room,' she said apologetically, gesturing to the closed doors. A faint rumble could be heard, and Særós decided this had to come from a computer game. 'Please take a seat. Can I get you something to drink? Coffee or tea?'

'Just water is fine, thank you,' she said, and sank down into the soft sofa.

While the woman filled a glass, Særós looked around and saw that it was hardly likely that Diljá could be hidden away in this little apartment. There was probably just one bedroom, considering that Pálína had to sleep on the sofa when her granddaughter came to stay. Unless Diljá and María Líf shared a room. Pálína brought her a glass and watched intently as Særós drank, but made no move to take a seat herself.

'It was on the evening news that you're already asking people to report sightings of Diljá, and I have to say it's unpleasant,' she said as she wrung her hands. 'I mean, it's not even been a whole day...' She fell silent, took a deep breath and glared at Særós. 'And I want you to be aware that I know my daughter and she doesn't do people any harm.'

'Maybe not,' Særós retorted. 'In that case, why is she on the run?'

'Diljá has always struggled to cope with reality and I'm sure that she just wasn't able to deal with what was happening, and was stupid enough to run for it. That's the story of her life,' she said, speaking through pursed lips and in a tone of resignation.

'Do you have any idea where she could be?' Særós asked, wishing that the woman would take a seat, instead of standing in the middle of the room with her hands on her hips and a glare of accusation on her face, as if she, or rather the entire police force, were to blame for the whole affair. But Pálína stood resolutely still, and made no reply.

'I've no idea where she's taken herself off to,' she said finally, her voice softer. 'My daughter has always struggled with responsibility, ever since she was little. If something's tough, she disappears. She got a Christmas job in a shop when she was about twenty, and as soon as the place filled up with people, she sneaked out. Can you imagine? Her siblings are completely different ... It's so weird how much of a difference there is between my children.'

She again fell silent, went closer to the window and looked out. Bearing in mind Guðgeir's strategy that worked so well to get people to open up and say more than they had meant to, Særós waited for her to speak. Sometimes Guðgeir's approach resulted in what Særós felt were painfully long silences, and now, after an uncomfortably long time, she gave up. Pálína gave no indication that she was going to say anything more unprompted. She stood by the window, wringing her hands, fingers twisted together as if working lotion into them.

'We have to find her,' Særós repeated, and got up from the uncomfortably soft sofa. 'As I told you on the phone earlier this evening, we know very little at present and are trying to figure out the key events, so I'm hoping you can give me some more insight into Diljá's personality. Is it possible that she simply had a nervous breakdown when she found her husband was dead?'

Pálína's astonishment was obviously no pretence, and she turned pale. There was no mistaking that this had taken her completely by surprise and she struggled to find words.

'What did you say?' she gasped finally, shaking her head.

'I asked if she could have...'

Særós got no further before Pálína interrupted.

'You said husband. They weren't married.'

'They were. The ceremony took place at the Sheriff's office a couple of weeks ago,' Særós said. 'I've just had conformation that Ríkharður's son Vilhjálmur and Diljá's colleague Ásmundur were the witnesses.'

'Him? That's impossible. Those two were a couple only a few years ago,' Pálína said in disbelief. 'I knew Diljá was impulsive, but this is too much.'

'Diljá and Ásmundur had a relationship?' Særós asked to make certain.

'Yes, but that was over a long time ago,' Pálína confirmed. 'These days they're colleagues and good friends.'

'And how was Diljá's relationship with Ríkharður?'

'I don't really know ... I only met him once. Not for long, at a restaurant. They invited me to come out for a meal. Yes, and María Líf was with us.'

'So he hasn't been here?' Særós asked.

'No. Never. Actually Diljá doesn't come often after I moved here a few years ago. She suffers from claustrophobia and never uses a lift. She says she can't be bothered to walk up to the eighth floor, which seems ridiculous coming from someone who's supposed to be in such great physical condition and is at the gym every day.' Pálína again lapsed into silence and stared out of the window over the roofs and cars that looked tiny from this distance. 'She gets married, and her own mother and daughter aren't told about it.'

She said no more, but her attitude had changed and she seemed about to collapse.

Særós felt sympathy for her. This last piece of news had hurt her deeply, but it was probably no more than the straw that broke the camel's back on this strange and difficult day.

'How did he come across, the time you met him at a restaurant?' Særós asked, making an effort to be sympathetic.

'Hell, I don't know. Of course he's really clever, or supposed to be. Not everyone gets to be a specialist doctor, but to tell you the truth I had the feeling that I was totally out of my depth with him,' Pálína admitted, as if ashamed of her own feelings.

'Understandably. It can be a nervous experience meeting a new member of the family for the first time,' Særós said. She sounded sympathetic, but inwardly she was pleased that she had got through the woman's armour.

'It's not that. What freaked me out was the way he watched every movement. He was somehow so critical.' Pálína placed the flat of her hand on her chest and patted a few times so that it generated a dull thump. 'Ach, I'm sorry,' she apologised. 'It's wrong to speak like that of someone who's dead.'

'You're simply recounting your experience,' Særós said. 'There's nothing wrong with that.'

'You know, I didn't hold the glass properly, and I got a quarter of an hour's lecture on French wine, and why you should hold a glass one way and not another,' Pálína said, and for the first time there was a glitter of humour in her eye. 'It seemed very weird to me, but then I'm probably just someone who doesn't have a habit of making a big thing out of something trivial.'

'Were they in love?' Særós asked.

Pálína shrugged.

'I have no idea. He was all over her at the restaurant, but she ... I don't know ... She's hardly said a word about him. But as I've told you already, my daughter is easily infatuated and she's impetuous.'

'Ríkharður was a wealthy man and we have evidence that he paid off debts for her some time ago. This was a substantial amount.'

'He did? Before they were married?'

There was no mistaking the surprise in Pálína's voice.

'Yes, and again after the marriage. Do you know why she was so heavily in debt?' Særós asked.

There was an immediate change to Pálína's expression. Særós saw her lips purse, and she again began to wring her hands. This was a subject that was clearly painful, but she made herself reply.

'Diljá has been through all kinds of things, including an expensive custody battle over the little girl that has gone on for years. The parents fight constantly. They don't seem to be able to agree on a single thing, and the poor little thing is mostly here with me. But there's more to it than that. Diljá can be a spendthrift. This is her impulsive nature, you understand. She's certainly no criminal. We're all feeling our way through life and everyone makes mistakes.'

'We understand that she had to deal with mental problems in the past,' Særós said, trying to choose her words with care. 'Can you tell me more about that?'

Pálína's face hardened and she folded her arms.

'Actually, no. Some people suffer badly, others get away with it. That's all there is to say about it,' she said drily, and had hardly finished speaking when a door opened and a petite, slim girl with large, intelligent eyes stood before them.

'Are you here because of my mum?' she asked in a low voice, looking Særós up and down.

'No, of course not, my love. She's just come to talk to me,' her grandmother said quickly. 'Go back to your room for a while. Aren't you playing a fun game?'

'Don't try to lie to me. I know perfectly well that Mum has disappeared and Ríkharður is dead,' María Líf said, looking at Særós with childlike sincerity. 'Do you think Mum killed him?'

20

They were sitting in the Islands Bakery with cheese rolls and coffee in paper cups on Monday morning when Leifur called with the news that the initial findings of the autopsy had identified unusual medication levels in the deceased's body.

'So that's confirmed. Is this going to be a tale of drug misuse?' Guðgeir said.

'Not according to the information we have, but you can never tell. That kind of thing doesn't get noticed, especially when a doctor is concerned,' Leifur said. 'I spoke to Elías just now, and he agreed that the investigation should be entirely in your hands, even though our colleagues there in the Westman Islands will help with whatever's needed.'

'That's fine. Any reports of Diljá?'

'No. Nothing.'

'How's everything else?' Guðgeir asked, sipping his coffee.

'We took samples from around the caravan yesterday and now we're working through everything. The caravan itself will be brought across on the midday ferry today,' Leifur said. 'Have you interviewed anyone other than those four?'

'Not yet. We're on our way to meet the tourists and the man who runs the camp site. We hope to be finished today,' he said.

'Fine. Then we'll be in touch later,' Leifur said, and ended the call.

The tourists were German lads of around twenty and a middle-aged American couple, who had stayed in chalets in

Herjólfsdalur. They had all noticed the caravan, but hadn't been aware of any movement other than the couple thought they had seen the jeep drive away from the caravan around dinner time on Saturday evening. They had been cooking pasta for themselves in the utility block at that time. After their meal they had played cards and gone early to bed, tired after the day's sightseeing. The German boys had been down in town until after ten o'clock that evening, had a few beers and then headed back to the valley to go to sleep. They had been asleep by eleven, as their plan had been to make an early start in the morning to get round all the sights they wanted to see. No, they hadn't noticed anything more than the couple or the camp site warden had seen.

The next stop was Magni, the restaurant where they had arranged to meet the staff who had been on duty on Saturday evening. It was on the first floor of a former factory, a stone's throw from the quay, and the place had been tastefully decorated. Two youngish men and two women who turned out to be mother and daughter were waiting for them. They sat around a table in the restaurant.

'Aren't you expecting lunchtime customers?' Elsa Guðrún asked.

'No,' the older woman replied. 'We're closed from Monday to Wednesday.'

'Good to know we're not interrupting business,' Guðgeir said, and went on to explain why they were all there.

'I didn't notice anything unusual until he bumped into a table and a glass of wine went flying,' one of the two men said. 'I was at the other side of the room when it happened and I went over because Siggi was fetching plates. The man was clearly very drunk and was having trouble staying on his feet. He lurched out to the toilets and left soon afterwards with one of the women. The rest of them stayed longer. That's all I saw.'

'And you, Siggi? This was your table?' Guðgeir asked.

'Yes, that's right. And I have to say that he seemed strange from the moment they came in.'

'In what way?' Elsa Guðrún asked.

'He was dazed. He couldn't see the menu properly, even when he put his glasses on. He was pretty confused and slurred. He ended up saying that he'd have the same as the others, even though they had all ordered different things. The woman who was next to him ordered for him.'

'This was the one who left with him?' Guðgeir asked.

'No, this was one of the others who ordered for him. She was trying to help him.'

'Do you remember her appearance?'

'I think this was the one with long, fair hair.' Siggi paused in thought, as if concentrating as he tried to recall something. 'I think she had extremely long nails. You know, way over the top. It's fashionable at the moment.'

'Yes, I know what you mean,' Guðgeir said, recalling Katrín's nails.

'Did he eat his food?' Elsa Guðrún asked.

'I really don't remember. We were insanely busy. But he must have eaten something, otherwise I would have asked him if there had been something about it he didn't like.'

'I see,' Guðgeir said. 'Has all the crockery used on Saturday been washed?'

'Of course it has,' the older woman said, shocked at the thought. 'Everything is washed right away and all surfaces are sterilised because of Covid. We do everything by the book!'

Elsa Guðrún and Guðgeir exchanged glances. As far as they were concerned, this was no help.

'So you weren't aware of anything other than Ríkharður slurring early in the evening, and then the incident with the glass?' Elsa Guðrún asked.

'I noticed something,' the younger woman said. 'I saw to the bread that night, and they asked for more a couple of times, and I also refilled the water jug for them several times.'

'What did you notice?'

'I saw that the man wasn't all right, that Ríkharður,' she said.

'Exactly, we see that,' Elsa Guðrún said, getting to her feet. They would have to be quick to finish everything here in the Westman Islands if they were going to catch the afternoon ferry. Otherwise they would be into a second day's subsistence allowance, and they had no permission for that.

'I thought it was weird that the others didn't seem to care. I mean, this kind of thing rarely happens here, but when it does, people look out for each other, if you know what I mean, that the person in question doesn't cause a scene or anything like that,' the woman continued.

'Of course,' Guðgeir said. 'And what about this group?'

'They simply acted as if they couldn't see him. As if he wasn't there. I remember thinking that he might be the alcoholic in the group and the others had already had enough. But I noticed that he hardly touched his glass and drank a lot of water.'

'Thanks for the information,' Guðgeir said. 'This could all have a bearing on the case, but one more thing. Was there any sign that he had vomited in the toilets?'

'No, none,' the younger woman replied immediately. 'I went in there to check on just that, and everything was as it should be. Even if he had thrown up straight into the toilet, there would still have been a smell. I've worked in plenty of restaurants and have often had to clean up that kind of thing.'

Having declined the fish soup that the Magni staff offered them, they left before Elsa Guðrún could say what was on her mind.

'This Siggi. He was referring to Katrín,' she said as soon as they were in the car and heading for Eldheimar.

'That's for sure. The nails and the hair don't tally with either Diljá or Eygló,' Guðgeir agreed.

'Exactly. But I would definitely have gone for the fish soup. It wouldn't have held us up for long, and Magni is supposed to be one of the best restaurants in the country.'

'Really?' Guðgeir said in surprise. 'Why didn't you say something?'

'Aren't you the boss? The one who takes the decisions?' she said with a grin.

'Sure. But no reason to take things too seriously and turn down a meal at a smart restaurant.'

'You were so quick that I didn't have the heart to protest. That would have looked bad,' Elsa Guðrún said with a regretful sigh.

They had made an appointment to be at Eldheimar, as the museum was closed on Mondays and Tuesdays. The eye-catching building stood on the outskirts of the town and part of it could be seen from the car park, emerging from the lava. The sight was too remarkable to hurry past, and they stood for a while in silence to take in the concrete wall and two broken windows. They had both heard accounts of the eruption in the Westman Islands and this was a moment that demanded few words.

'Imagine watching the lava flowing over your home,' Elsa Guðrún said with a shudder. 'Swallowing up all your earthly possessions in no time at all, and not a thing you can do about it.'

'Your house, your street, your whole district. It was terrible and there was no warning. Nobody had even imagined that Heimaey could be a live volcano,' Guðgeir said. 'The whole of Reykjanes shuddered and shook for weeks before the Fagradalsfjall eruption, but fortunately that one wasn't right on top of people's homes like this one in the Westman Islands was...' His words faded away as he gazed mutely at the ruins. 'Well, we had better go inside,' he said at last.

The museum's manager, a vivacious middle-aged woman, was there to meet them. Sigríður Sigmundsdóttir turned out to be exceptionally efficient and well-prepared. The staff who had been on duty at the weekend were unfortunately not available, having gone to the mainland, but she had spent the morning going through the CCTV recordings.

'Let's use my office,' she said briskly, leading the way through the museum's darkened exhibits hall, where the fury of the eruption and the destruction left behind were on display. 'I've been through everything, and I'll let you see the sequences that caught my attention.'

'That's fine, but it would be even better if you could send all of the recordings from Saturday to the forensic unit,' Guðgeir said, taking his glasses from the inside pocket of his jacket.

'Already done. It's Leifur who handles this case for them, isn't it?' Sigríður said. She spoke rapidly, and there was a slight rasp to her voice.

'That's him. And I see you don't hang around,' Guðgeir said with obvious satisfaction, polishing his glasses before putting them on.

'Nope. Never. Let's look at this,' she said, pressing the play button.

The footage was in black and white, and the quality was poor, but they were still able to see a tall man and a petite woman who seemed to be deep in an animated conversation. The body language indicated strongly that this was an argument. The sequence passed quickly by, and Sigríður replayed it. The man was clearly agitated and took hold of the woman's arm, but she wrenched herself free, turning away from him. She said something and the man stepped closer, his stance threatening.

'Looks to me like something more than a little friction between them,' Guðgeir muttered to Elsa Guðrún.

'Agreed,' she replied. 'But there are more people than just those two.'

'I was only watching them and didn't notice anyone else,' Guðgeir said.

'Would you play it again?' she asked, and Sigríður replayed the sequence. 'There. Look.'

'Where?' Guðgeir asked, peering at the screen.

'There's another man there. The shadow in the corner,' Elsa Guðrún said, pointing.

'Can we enlarge it?' Guðgeir asked, getting close to the screen.

'No problem,' Sigríður said, zooming in.

'The man's build looks like Ásmundur's, doesn't it?' Elsa Guðrún said. 'What do you think, Guðgeir?'

He squinted and peered at the image.

'It looks likely,' he said, reaching for his phone. 'Leifur? I'm going to send you some CCTV material from Eldheimar that you need to look at very carefully.'

'We received it this morning,' Leifur replied. 'From the museum director.'

'I know. I mean the short sequence I'll send now. It's a couple arguing and we're sure it's Diljá and Ríkharður, but there's a shadow of someone else there as well. We need to find out who that is. The sequence ends with more people coming into the room.'

'I'll get right to it,' Leifur said. 'And I was just about to call you. Did you notice a bag of brown sugar in the caravan?'

'Yes, I saw that,' Guðgeir said.

'It had been laced with drugs.'

'That's something new!' Guðgeir said, immediately excited. 'What's in there?'

'We're not certain yet, but the indications to begin with are both a sedative and a hallucinogenic,' Leifur said. 'It looks like Ríkharður had been doped, which led to his death.'

21

Diljá watched the snake as it slithered forward. It came towards her slowly, steadily. It left behind it a trail of flattened grass and patches of slime. It came closer and closer. To begin with she felt no terror, just awe that triggered a delightful dread that shivered through her. She waited for inspiration and knew that she must not fight it, that she should welcome her master and accept his wisdom. The snake writhed as it approached, with frequent sparks of rainbow brightness from its new skin as the old one lay colourless and tattered. Its glittering beauty was overwhelming and she knew that this vision marked a new beginning, the past would have no more meaning than a useless cast-off snakeskin and Diljá Sigurðardóttir would rise up, reborn to begin her new life. Now he had almost reached her and the wonderful dread gave way to respect tinged with fear. The snake raised itself up high, jaws wide, its thin forked tongue darting out. She stumbled back. What was that growing from its head? She could hardly believe her eyes. This was a two-headed snake! Hell! Diljá called out and struggled. Her heart hammered in her chest and she could hardly catch her breath. Was she still herself, or was she part of him? Terror-struck, she opened her eyes and looked around. There was nothing to be seen but the stillness. Reality gradually returned to her thoughts. She remembered that Ríkharður was dead and she had a vision of him lying still in the bed. She recalled the terror that had gripped her when she realised that he had stopped breathing a long time ago.

22

They could hardly have cut it any finer. Guðgeir's car was the last one on board and the gate clanged shut behind it. As they were making their way up to the passenger area, Særós called to inform them that the investigation into Ríkharður's death was now officially a criminal case.

'I want you to run this, Guðgeir, with Elsa Guðrún,' she said. 'We'll have a status meeting as soon as you're back.'

Guðgeir felt a shiver run through him, a familiar feeling that always came to him when he faced a case that was yet to be solved. It was all at once anticipation and excitement, like a traveller heading out into dangerous uncharted terrain.

Three hours later they were at the station. It was a sparse meeting, just the two of them, Særós and Leifur. Guðgeir took a seat at the end of the table and fumbled for his spectacle case in the inside pocket of his jacket. He opened it, took out his glasses and a little cloth to clean them. He carefully polished the lenses and noticed Særós and Elsa Guðrún as each caught the other's eye. They knew his mannerisms well and he wasn't going to disappoint them. They knew that once his glasses were securely on his nose, his fingers would lightly drum the table a couple of times before he said anything. He went through his familiar routine, and saw how they quietly shared a smile.

'What we know now is that traces were found in Ríkharður's body of drugs that probably led to his death, and his wife fled from the scene. The last sighting of her was leaving the ferry at Landeyjarhöfn. She was driving a dark grey Land Cruiser with the registration YE-B29. A mobile phone believed to be hers was found at the junction with Highway 1, but the SIM had been removed from it,' Guðgeir said, and turned to Leifur. 'Has the phone been shown to her mother and daughter?'

'Yes. It's locked, but the case is unusual and it's the right brand, so they were fairly sure it's her phone.'

'Good,' Guðgeir said, shifting in the uncomfortable seat. The chairs in the room were long overdue replacement.

'We also have the CCTV sequence from Eldheimar,' Leifur continued. 'There's no doubt that the couple are arguing and the person watching them is Ásmundur. This wasn't something he said much about when he was questioned in the Westman Islands, so I feel we need to call him in to give a further statement.'

Guðgeir nodded his agreement.

'We know that he and Diljá were a couple at one point,' Særós added.

'Then we get him in as soon as possible,' Guðgeir said firmly. 'Can we get into the group's activity online?'

'Let's see what we can do. We'll need permits and stuff for that,' Leifur said, with a meaningful glance at Særós.

'I'll do what I can,' she sighed.

'The drugs have been analysed and it's a mixture of medication for sleeping and a sedative, plus there's some other stuff that's still being checked out,' Leifur said, and finished by clasping his hands over his stomach.

'Were the doses enough to kill such a heavily built man?' Elsa Guðrún asked, her northern accent unusually noticeable.

'We have yet to find out, but it was a hefty dose, and don't forget the booze. There was quite a high alcohol level in his blood.'

'Then there's the marriage that nobody knew about except for his son Vilhjálmur and her friend Ásmundur. They both kept it secret,' Særós said. 'We need to work out why they did that.'

'Yes, and we also need to examine the long legal battle between Diljá and the father of her child,' Guðgeir said. 'There could be something in that.'

'His name's Ævar Brjánsson and he works at the Met Office,' Særós said. 'To begin with, Diljá had the child alone and it wasn't until the girl was two or three that he claimed joint custody, and sometime after that he went for full custody of the child. A lot has happened over the last few years, according to the information we have, and all attempts to engineer a settlement between them have come to nothing.'

'I'll get in touch with him,' Guðgeir said, and glanced in Særós's direction. 'What more do we know about Ríkharður?'

'A little more than earlier, as I did some digging while you were on the way,' she replied. 'I have a few points to go over with you.'

Særós stood up and went to the screen that hung at one end of the meeting room. Her tailored dark blue suit, cream silk blouse and heels put Guðgeir more in mind of a bank executive or a minister than a senior police officer.

'Look,' she said, indicating the bullet points she had put next to Ríkharður Magnússon's name. 'He was an orthopaedic surgeon, trained in the US. He was an exceptional student and as far as I can find out, he was highly respected professionally. He has been at the National Hospital since graduating from his specialist studies, as well as owning a private practice. His parents are deceased, and he has one sister, Ingibjörg. I met her at his home yesterday. He had been married three times. The first marriage was the one that lasted the longest, eleven years. His former wife's name is Erna Daníelsdóttir and she is the mother of Lára and Vilhjálmur. I understand from her that their marriage had been a good one until she suffered a severe shock.'

'Which was?' Elsa Guðrún asked.

'To tell the truth, I wasn't comfortable asking her about it over the phone,' Særós said with an apologetic glance at Elsa Guðrún, who acted as if she hadn't noticed.

'Shocks can come in all shapes and sizes,' Guðgeir said. 'Then what?'

'He got married again pretty quickly, to an American engineer who specialises in medical buildings. That marriage lasted three years, and the woman, Ashley Davis, returned to the US soon after the divorce. He was single for some years until Diljá appeared on the scene and of course we don't know what went on in between but I understand he was something of a womaniser. I've trained a few times at the gym where Diljá and Ásmundur work as personal trainers and I know someone who works there. Her name's Birna and I spoke to her earlier.'

Særós paused, adjusted her jacket and ran the palm of her hand over her immaculate hair. It was noticeable that she was relishing bringing information from an unexpected angle into the investigation, as there was a satisfied look on her face, as if she were about to share with them a wonderful secret that would be theirs alone. Guðgeir wondered if she was missing the active side of being part of an investigation, and he recalled clearly how it felt to stand alone and bear a heavy responsibility, as he had done back when he had been in the role Særós now occupied.

'Good stuff,' he said, sounding appreciative and giving her a smile. 'What did Birna have to say?'

Særós took a deep breath.

'Birna said that Ríkharður had started training with her, but Diljá had pestered her to let her be his personal trainer. Birna said that she hadn't been prepared to let him go, but Diljá kept on at her until she finally gave way, saying that at the time she had too much on her plate anyway. So she spoke to Ríkharður and offered him the opportunity to switch. He was happy to do that, and Birna said that she found it amusing to see Diljá flirting with him every time he turned up to train. It was as clear as day what she was up to.'

'She led the poor man by the nose,' Leifur said scornfully.

'By the what?' Elsa Guðrún asked, and seeing that Leifur

was about to explain at length, she quickly added that it didn't matter.

'Thank you, Særós. Some very interesting information there,' Guðgeir said. 'Let's continue with Diljá. The rescue squads along the southern region are organising a search starting tomorrow morning. They are bringing dogs, so they should be able to sniff out a trail. And they're using drones as well. At the moment there isn't much to add to her profile, except that she was admitted to a psychiatric ward suffering from a psychotic disorder as a teenager, and was admitted again about ten years ago. As far as we can ascertain, she has been healthy since, so I suggest we don't focus too closely on possible mental disorders.'

'What exactly was wrong with her the second time?' Elsa Guðrún asked.

'We haven't been able to get that confirmed,' Særós said with chagrin. 'You know, patient confidentiality and all that.'

'There was packaging from medication that's often prescribed for bipolar disorders, and tablets for panic attacks,' Leifur said. 'It seems like every second person these days is suffering from stress or depression. It's completely out of proportion! People don't have enough to keep themselves occupied, spend all their time glued to the internet and think that's the be-all and end-all of everything. People need to have something to do, something useful, instead of getting caught up in their own thoughts and navel-gazing.'

'You're a fount of wisdom, aren't you?' Elsa Guðrún said, unusually sharply, her accent again noticeable. Her origins always showed through when she was under tension or something upset her. 'It's beyond belief that the National Hospital's psychiatric department hasn't noticed your talents for diagnosis, my dear Leifur.'

What little remained of the belly of the would-be expert on the state of the nation's mental health wobbled.

'You're getting better, Elsa Guðrún! That's more like you!'

'I never lost my sense of humour or my ability to say what I think,' she said, and smiled just enough for the dimples in her cheeks to appear. Guðgeir noticed that the smile didn't reach her eyes.

'That's enough for now,' he said, getting to his feet. 'Let's leave it at that. The search for Diljá gets underway tomorrow. Elsa Guðrún, will you make sure Ásmundur is here to give another statement tomorrow?'

'You're finished for today?' Særós asked in surprise.

'Not quite. I'm going to track down the two we haven't heard from yet.'

23

The father of Diljá's daughter was answering neither calls nor messages, so Guðgeir decided to call in at the Met Office in case he might be on duty. He had somehow come to the assumption that staff there must work shifts, but when he thought about it, he realised that he had no idea what the working arrangements there were. Eruptions, earthquakes and natural disasters resulting from extreme weather had given him the impression that the Met Office had to be manned around the clock, every day of the year. Maybe that was a complete misconception on his part, but it would do no harm to drop by and find out.

Guðgeir took the opportunity while he was driving to call Inga and let her know that he wouldn't be home in time for dinner, and found out that she wasn't overly concerned as she was on the way out to something she called Hatha yoga, and hadn't even given a thought to dinner. Their lives had changed in so many ways in recent years and what had been fixed points in their home life had become far more elastic. Inga said that she was looking forward to seeing him that evening, and he was relieved to hear it as deep inside he sometimes felt that the freedom that came with fewer household responsibilities could drive them apart. Guðgeir shook his head at his own ridiculous concerns, and switched on the radio. The news bulletin had begun, including an item about Diljá and the request for anyone who might have information concerning her disappearance to contact the police immediately.

'Where the hell are you?' he muttered to himself as he took the turn up the slope to what is normally known as Met Office Hill. The low building spread over a wide area and was surrounded by lush greenery that would be gone in a few weeks, leaving just bare branches to struggle through the long, dark winter. Getting out of the car, he paused and looked around, gazing over the street to Öskjuhlíð and the landmark of Perlan, the strangely shaped building that always put him in mind of a spacecraft, and over the graveyard that was now mostly hidden behind a packed district of terraced and detached houses. This was the resting place of many people to whom Guðgeir had been close, but now only memories of them remained.

The thought came suddenly to him that Diljá might be dead, and at the same time it also occurred to him that it was odd this possibility hadn't been mentioned at the meeting. He shook these thoughts off and walked over to the Met Office's main entrance. An elderly man leaving the building almost walked into him.

'Sorry! Didn't mean to bump into you,' Guðgeir apologised.

'Likewise,' the man said. 'It looks like we both have other things on our minds, a proper pair of absentminded professors.'

Guðgeir laughed, and took the opportunity to ask where he might find Ævar. The man pointed him in the right direction, adding that even though it was a Sunday, it would be worth checking his office.

'He's the hardest worker north of the Alps, I'm pretty sure of that. Go along the corridor and then to the right. I've a feeling you'll find him there.'

The door to Ævar's office stood open and Guðgeir sensed from his reaction that he had been expecting a visit from the police. He stood up and stepped around the desk to meet Guðgeir, who had the impression that the man appeared older than the date of birth embedded in his ID number would indicate. He was stocky, with unruly brownish hair, wearing baggy trousers and a zipped outdoor sweater that was too thick for the time of year.

'Hello. I'm Guðgeir Fransson and I'm from the police.'

'Hello,' he replied and Guðgeir wasn't sure if he habitually whispered or if he had a naturally low voice. 'I expect you're here because of the search for Diljá.'

'Quite right.'

'I haven't the faintest idea where she is, otherwise I would have been in touch with you right away. We keep contact to an absolute minimum, and that's only because we need to communicate about our daughter. If it wasn't for María Líf, I wouldn't want to have anything to do with her.'

Ævar ran a hand over his thinning hair and glanced out of the window. This uneven hill, here in the middle of the city, remained mostly untouched by the determination of humans to organise their surroundings. Yet more than likely it was just a question of time until buildings would sprout there.

'I understand you don't find it easy to co-operate as parents. Can I ask why?' Guðgeir said, looking at him intently as he waited for a reply.

Ævar's expression showed his exasperation. He folded his arms and sighed.

'Well, I hardly know where to start. But to cut a long story short, the simple answer is that we can't agree on even the simplest thing. We have very different ideas of how to bring up a child. For instance, it's impossible to organise anything with Diljá, and you never know what she'll do next. Regardless of anything that's been decided, she can make a hundred-and-eighty degree turn at a moment's notice. It makes life difficult.'

'I understand that you applied for full custody of María Líf. Will you tell me why you did that?'

'I was studying overseas, and when I returned to Iceland I became aware of the girl's confused circumstances. Then Diljá was taken ill and was admitted to hospital for a while. I felt that the little girl was emotionally damaged and nervous, and it didn't look good. Small children need stability. Routine is important.'

'But you hadn't spent time with her up to then?' Guðgeir said.

'No, like I said, I had been studying. I had neither the time nor the money to be travelling from one country to another in the middle of demanding studies,' he said, and Ævar's tone made it plain that the thought itself was ridiculous.

'Exactly. So Diljá was alone with the child for the first few years?' Guðgeir asked, keeping his voice neutral. He could sense his own lack of sympathy for Ævar, and knew that he mustn't allow that feeling to grow. Personal feelings shouldn't be allowed to affect him at a professional level. That had happened once, and it had cost him dearly.

'Well...' he hesitated. 'Her grandmother Pálína was there as well.'

'Really? Wasn't she at work?' Guðgeir asked, realising as he spoke that his tone was sharper than necessary.

'Yes,' Ævar said, taking a seat at his desk. 'Of course.' He put his hand on the mouse and clicked, as if telling Guðgeir that he was interrupting his work.

'You said it's impossible to know what Diljá will do next?' he asked, pretending not to notice the man's body language.

'Well, she's pretty unpredictable ... mental problems...' Ævar muttered, eyes on the screen in front of him.

'Dangerous?' Guðgeir asked.

There was nothing but coldness in Ævar's laughter.

'If you mean the doctor guy of hers who died, then you can be fairly sure that Diljá didn't kill him. Except maybe with her endless bother and trouble. That could finish off any man.'

'Have you spoken to Pálína or your daughter?'

'No,' Ævar said. 'Not yet.'

'You haven't even heard from María Líf?' Guðgeir shook his head and raised an eyebrow in surprise. It was strange that the man hadn't been in touch with his daughter. Clearly noticing his reaction, Ævar made haste to explain.

'I've been drowning in work. There's a big report that has to be delivered this week. It's been crazy.' He sighed and lifted both hands in the air. He obviously saw himself as important, Guðgeir decided.

'How did you hear about Ríkharður's death? His name hasn't yet been released to the media,' Guðgeir asked, his voice soft.

'It's all over social media and it's buzzing with gossip. Diljá is well known in certain circles,' he replied, finally taking his eyes from the screen.

'Such as where?' Guðgeir asked, and didn't point out that a man drowning in work would hardly have time for social media.

'Ach. Fitness groups, and places where that spiritual wellness crowd hang out,' Ævar said, his lip curling and in a tone of obvious disgust.

'Which you're also part of?'

'No, of course not,' he retorted resentfully. 'Not in that way. I'm a scientist, not a nutcase.'

'So how do you know about these groups?'

'Well, it goes without saying that I have to have some idea of what the mother of my child gets up to, who she associates with and so on,' Ævar said.

'That's how you know...' Guðgeir began, until Ævar cut him off.

'Well, anything less would be completely irresponsible, because of María Líf. Surely you understand that!'

24

She constantly tossed and turned, unable to make herself comfortable, forced her eyes shut but was unable to unwind enough to get to sleep. It was getting cool in the summer house's low attic room, which seemed to be hemming her in on all sides, but she didn't dare sleep in any of the beds downstairs. There were duvets and sleeping bags up here, and she had tried to disturb as little as possible, in case she might need to hide quickly. The thought had come to her that maybe Ingi Thór and Eygló might need to pay an unexpected visit to their summer house. Maybe they would need to set up mouse traps for the winter, or they might have forgotten something important, such as the iPad. If that were to happen, she would lie here, completely silent, until they disappeared again. She would hear the stairs creaking if anyone were to come upstairs and that would give her a moment's warning so she could hide herself behind the storage boxes that had been stacked in one corner.

Being slightly built would be to her advantage. Ingi Thór and Eygló would never stay long on a weekday, and it was actually unlikely that they would come here. Then there was the jeep, and that wouldn't be hard to find, even though it was hidden behind the birches.

But if they were to take her by surprise... Would they understand... Would they help her? No, probably not.

Her illness would be blamed, the fact that she was completely crazy.

Anyone who had at some time been mentally ill was branded for life, that's the way it is, regardless of what anyone says.

Diljá curled into a ball on the thin mattress and pulled the patchwork quilt up over her head, trying to not think, to not think of Ríkharður, of María Líf, or the search for her. All these problems. She tried and tried, but couldn't forget.

25

The visit to the Met Office hadn't yielded much, but Guðgeir felt there was something about it that troubled him, Ævar's frosty attitude towards the mother of his child and his lack of involvement with his daughter. Why on earth had the man gone to court for custody of a child for whom he had little time? What was driving him? Could it be straightforward self-centredness, a need for attention or a simple thirst for getting back at her? If he had strong feelings for his daughter, why hadn't he been in touch with her? The girl's mother had disappeared, her face was all over the media and Ævar meant to get in touch when he had time, when he had finished writing some report!

Guðgeir had felt his dislike for the man grow the longer he spoke to him, and thinking it over now, there were a number of questions that still demanded answers. But which one was most important?

He sat unmoving in the car, staring out through the windscreen, startled as heavy raindrops smacked against it. He noticed that a few leaves had settled on the bonnet while he had been inside the Met Office. Some of them had begun to change colour. September wasn't far away and soon it would be winter. The thought made him shiver. He switched on first the heater and then the wipers, at the fastest setting. The rain became heavier as he took the road to the western side of the city. He was hot by the time he parked outside a four-storey block built in the shape of a horseshoe.

Ríkharður's former wife lived on the ground floor and he had called in advance, so she was expecting him. There were three outside doors under the house number, and Erna Daníelsdóttir's name was next to the third buzzer. He applied a finger to the button and waited.

'Come on in,' a voice called out to him, and he opened the door. 'Don't take your shoes off... I'm in here.'

He stepped through a short corridor and into a large open living room. A beautiful blonde woman in a wheelchair came towards him. He was immediately struck by her looks, and her bright countenance. Her pale trousers and a colourful top were another reminder that summer was on the way out.

'Hello, Erna. Thanks for taking the time to meet. I promise I won't keep you long,' Guðgeir said apologetically as he looked around. There was a piano against one wall and next to it a stack of sheet music. The other walls were packed with paintings, photographs and shelves filled with books of all shapes and sizes. Practically the whole of one wall was a single large window with a view over a communal garden with a children's playground. Thriving plants filled pots on the windowsills.

'You don't need to worry about that. This evening's choir practice has been cancelled, so I have plenty of time. You want to talk to me about Ríkharður? You must know that we split up years ago, but I've always tried to maintain some contact with him because of the children, even though they're grown up now,' Erna said. She spoke with animation, her face lively and expressive.

'My condolences,' Guðgeir said quickly.

'Thanks for that. Sit down, please. It's always awkward having people looking down at me.' She pointed to a round coffee table next to the semi-open kitchen, with one chair next to it. 'What do you think? It's a lovely place, isn't it?'

'Yes. Very pleasant,' Guðgeir agreed, taking a seat. Erna placed herself opposite him and there was a familiar fragrance about her. Maybe Inga had used the same perfume at some point?

'A lot of fuss going on,' she said, and there was a hint of sarcasm in her voice. 'Poor Ríkharður. I don't doubt he would have preferred a more dignified way to go, if I knew him right. What was he doing in a caravan? It's not exactly his style to be slumming it on some campsite with the great unwashed.' Erna looked at him enquiringly, shaking her head to express her surprise. 'People never cease to take you by surprise.'

'It wasn't at the cheaper end of the range and it's pretty smart. A man with a young wife sometimes needs to step outside his own comfort zones,' Guðgeir said, and immediately wondered why he was justifying the actions of a dead man he had never met.

'Wife, that's it,' Erna said abstractedly, fiddling with a delicate gold pendant.

'You knew they were married?' he asked curiously.

'Yes. The children told me, and to tell the truth it didn't come as a surprise. Ríkharður would have wanted to have her carefully tied down so that he could mould her to his wishes,' she replied quickly.

'What do you mean by that?'

'Ríkharður was a teacher by nature,' Erna said. 'He was always giving instructions,' she added and the sarcastic tone was again noticeable.

'What are you implying?' he asked, and although he was watching her closely, he wasn't able to fathom the look on her face.

'Ach. Nothing,' she replied and looked out at the clipped hedge and green grass. In the middle of the area was a playground, and raindrops pattered on the glistening slide.

'Was Ríkharður violent?'

This time Erna made no immediate reply, her gaze fixed on the window. Using both hands, she lifted one leg to cross it over the other, without saying a word, and then looked Guðgeir straight in the eye.

'I don't know exactly where the boundaries lie these days, but the Ríkharður I knew would never have used physical violence. Never. But he liked to have everything just right, and he could become angry if things weren't exactly as he wanted them. He was someone who felt that he always knew best.' Erna fell silent, her gaze unwavering from Guðgeir until she broke the silence and her eyes went back to the window. 'Maybe the poor girl ran out of patience? It happens.'

'We still don't know the circumstances,' Guðgeir said.

'If Diljá did him harm, which is what the opinion seems to be, then she can hardly inherit. I mean, it ought to be relatively straightforward to have her right to inherit annulled in court, shouldn't it? Then she could also be dead, and the marriage with it. I don't imagine her daughter would inherit on an equal basis with my children. I don't believe that for a moment.'

'You don't hold back, do you?' Guðgeir said, making no attempt to hide his astonishment at how she made no pretence of hiding what was on her mind,

'No, of course not. I've long given up on that kind of crap. I feel that our children deserve to receive their full inheritance,' she said, and for the first time Guðgeir felt that there was a touch of pain in her voice.

'I'm looking for a profile of Ríkharður, and don't want to be troubling your children with questions so soon after the loss of their father. Can you help?' Guðgeir asked gently.

'We hadn't had much happiness together for a very long time, but we were high school sweethearts. After that I went to teacher training college, specialising in physical education, and he studied medicine. Later on we moved to America where he specialised, and I stayed at home with the children. We took care to get married so that we wouldn't shock the Yanks. After we came home I taught PE at secondary school for a few years. Then there was the accident, and that was a job I wasn't able to return to.' Erna dropped her hands to the wheels either side of her. 'I don't need to explain why.'

Guðgeir nodded.

'May I ask what happened?'

'I lost my footing up in the mountains, fell many metres and ended up on a sharp rock ledge. I was in hospital for around a year.'

'It's shocking how life can change direction completely and so suddenly,' Guðgeir said. 'The whole basis for everything gone in a matter of moments.'

'Yes,' Erna said shortly. 'That's the way it is.'

'Had you already parted company by this time?'

'No. We divorced roughly a year after the accident.'

'Ríkharður was an orthopaedic surgeon, wasn't he? I imagine he could have been a great support at such a difficult time?' Guðgeir suggested.

'No doubt he could have been...' she said and fell silent as her eyes again strayed to the window. 'Was there anything specific you wanted to ask me about?'

'Nothing specific. I always try to produce a profile of those whom I come across,' he explained.

'Why do you do that?'

'To understand people better and to see an overall picture,' Guðgeir replied.

'I don't know that I can be much help to you in doing that,' Erna said in a low voice and looked straight into his eyes. She slipped the brake and moved her wheelchair closer to him. 'What I can tell you is that Ríkharður was most certainly an orthopaedic surgeon, but there was no room whatever in his own life for any kind of disability. He expected perfection, in everything, even if it was just on the surface.'

26

The rain was still coming down hard when Guðgeir went to work the next morning. He had come home late in the evening after the visit to Erna, to find an unexpected guest in his and Inga's bedroom. His little namesake slept soundly in the cot they always had ready, and Guðgeir sat for some time and admired his beautiful grandson.

'I offered to have him overnight so Ólöf can get some rest before her exam,' Inga said, and Guðgeir was more than satisfied with that arrangement.

But on the way to the police station now, he felt as if he had a raging hangover. Guðgeir Jökull had crawled into their bed after midnight and refused to sleep in the cot. He had slept and woken at intervals through the night, stretched out sideways over his grandfather's head or poked a finger in his eye. This restless night appeared to have no ill effects on the little man, who woke early, cheerful and with a song on his lips, while his grandparents struggled to open their eyes. Inga had a court appearance, so it fell to Guðgeir to change the little boy and feed him his morning porridge so she could sleep a little longer.

As soon as he arrived at the station, he made a direct line for the coffee machine. He gulped down a cup of strong coffee and was brewing a second one when Særós breezed in. Her cheeks were rosy after the morning's exercise, and as usual she was perfectly turned out. She was immaculate, not a hair out of place, and dressed as if she had just stepped out of a shop.

'Good morning!' she said cheerfully, noticing the cup of coffee and adding a word of advice.

'Be careful not to overdo the coffee, Guðgeir. It could give you heartburn. I recommend a glass of water between cups of coffee, preferably with some fresh squeezed lemon juice,' she said, and gave him a fond smile.

Guðgeir normally was able to tolerate her need to put people right with his usual good humour, but this time he felt a stab of irritation. All the same, he forced a smile and nodded. Særós didn't return the smile, but frowned and looked him up and down.

'There's something on your trousers, and one sleeve. What is that?' she continued and he followed her gaze to the blob on his trouser leg.

'That's porridge. Ólöf's little one was with us last night and I fed him this morning,' he explained happily.

'Ach. Children. So much mess. Come and see me when you've cleaned it up,' Særós said, oblivious to how inappropriate it could be seen to be for her to tell a grown man, who was also her former superior officer, to clean himself up. 'But be quick. We're about to make a start.' She meaningfully tapped her watch, which was of the type that was no doubt a multi-faceted technical marvel stuffed with every feature under the sun except the ability to tell its user the time. She strode to her office.

Guðgeir allowed himself a sigh and shook his head. Særós was a one-off, a complete one-off. He snatched a couple of biscuits from the pack, ate them quickly and washed them down with coffee. He knew that he needed doses of sugar and caffeine to get through the day.

'Hæ, did you hear that Katrín had been in touch?'

Elsa Guðrún was at his side.

'No. When?'

'She called about half an hour ago, asked if Diljá had been found yet and when I said no, she said she was coming in to talk to us. She's on the way.'

'And Ásmundur? When's he expected?'

'Eleven. She made it clear that they mustn't meet. She absolutely didn't want him to know that she was coming here.'

The status meeting in Særós's office was cut short as the reception desk called, announcing Katrín's arrival.

'We'll take her to my office and try to keep things as informal as possible,' Guðgeir said to Elsa Guðrún as they hurried along the passage. Katrín waited by the door, wrapped in a dark raincoat, the hood still up even though she was indoors.

'When are you expecting Ásmundur?' she asked, looking nervously around. There was no mistaking her discomfort.

'He's due to give a statement at eleven,' Elsa Guðrún said. 'He didn't mention this to you?'

'No. He thinks I don't know anything and he absolutely mustn't know I've been here. Promise me that.'

'You have my word on that,' Guðgeir said in his deep, measured voice, opening the door for her. 'We'll go to my office so there's no chance of you bumping into each other. Do you want to take that off?'

Katrín dropped the hood to her shoulders, unzipped her damp coat and handed it to Guðgeir. Under it she wore jeans and a thin short-sleeved sweater. She was clearly cold, as the goose pimples on her arms demonstrated. The ends of her long fair hair were wet, and her face, this time completely free of cosmetics, was wet and flushed. Elsa Guðrún sat down while Guðgeir hung up Katrín's coat.

'Would you like a towel to dry off?' she asked, but Katrín shook her head.

'No. Thank you. I want to get this done as quickly as possible... Look, I didn't tell you the truth on Sunday over in the Westman Islands,' she said with palpable awkwardness, fiddling with one of her silver rings. She spun it a few more turns around her finger before moving on to the next one.

'Is that so?' Guðgeir said in a tone of exaggerated surprise.

'You are maybe not aware, but there are laws relating to hindering a police investigation with deception.' Katrín's eyes widened, and he immediately regretted his words when he saw the fear on her face. 'Don't worry. I won't make a big deal of it, but please tell us the truth this time.'

She nodded.

'I can't stay long. I have to get to work, and Ásmundur mustn't see me. So...' she hesitated. 'I hope ... I'm doing the right thing.'

'No doubt about it,' Elsa Guðrún said. 'What's troubling you?'

Katrín took a deep breath, wrapping her arms around herself to catch hold of them, as if hugging herself. Her dark blue nails lay like claws against her skin.

'Look... Ásmundur said that on Saturday evening he had one drink at the bar with Ingi Thór, and I went up to the room go to sleep.'

'That's correct. He told us he had been at the bar until close to midnight,' Guðgeir said. 'Then he went up.'

Katrín shook her head.

'No. That's not right. The truth is that he didn't come back to our room until almost six in the morning,' she muttered disconsolately.

'Did you ask where he had been?' Guðgeir asked, keeping his voice quiet. He had a feeling that Katrín needed some extra delicate handling.

'No. I pretended to be asleep.'

'Why?' Elsa Guðrún asked.

'I was frightened of what his answer would be.'

'What were you frightened of?' Guðgeir asked.

'I've suspected for a while that there has been something going on between him and Diljá. Maybe I just didn't want to have that confirmed,' Katrín murmured. Her face twitched, and she incessantly twisted the rings on her fingers.

'And Diljá had just got married,' Guðgeir said.

'I just don't get that at all. That marriage is just completely crazy,' she said, her voice rising as she shifted to sit straighter in her chair.

'And Ingi Thór? Do you know when he came up?' Guðgeir asked.

'I was feeling bad about this and asked Eygló, without telling her anything, and she said that Ingi Thór had come up to the room before she fell asleep,' Katrín said.

'So you think that Ásmundur was with Diljá?' Elsa Guðrún said.

'Yes. I'm pretty sure of that,' Katrín said, the bitterness clear in her voice.

'You said that you didn't want to confront the possibility of there being a possible relationship between them. Why not?' Guðgeir asked, trying to be tactful.

'Because I'm scared that they have something special between them that I'll never understand. There's something going on but I can't put my finger on what it is. I feel like I'm completely excluded.' Katrín slowly got to her feet, took her raincoat from its hook and put it on. 'I have to go. And I don't have anything more to tell you.'

She pushed the door open and they sat in silence until the sound of her footsteps in the corridor had faded away.

27

The Ásmundur who arrived to give a statement at the police station in Reykjavík was noticeably different to the man they had spoken to at the hotel in the Westman Islands. His appearance was naturally the same, with short-cropped hair and muscles that nobody could avoid noticing, but his demeanour was somehow very different, more in keeping with his appearance.

In the Westman Islands he had been tense and on the defensive, but now he was supremely self-confident. He adroitly answered every question, until they came to the night when Ríkharður died. At this point he became cautious. He glanced repeatedly in the direction of the lawyer whose presence was required by law when a formal statement was taken, and constantly rolled his phone in his hands, until he saw that this fidgeting was attracting Guðgeir's and Elsa Guðrún's attention, and then he placed it on the table in front of him.

'We have CCTV footage from Eldheimar that shows Ríkharður and Diljá arguing. You are seen standing close to them, so maybe you can tell me what they disagreed about?' Guðgeir suggested, taking out his glasses.

'Me? No, I don't remember noticing anything,' Ásmundur replied with a look of amazement on his face which Guðgeir wasn't sure was a pretence or not.

'You're quite sure about that?' Elsa Guðrún asked, without taking her eyes from his face.

'I mean, I was just checking out the museum. It's a fantastic place.'

'So you don't have any idea of what was going on there?' Guðgeir asked, and glared at Ásmundur, who gripped his own arm, kneading it so that the brightly coloured snake writhed.

'No,' he said, hesitating. 'I sometimes found him tiring to be around. He was so stiff and tense.' Ásmundur formed his hands into a rectangle to demonstrate what he thought of the deceased's outlook on life. 'A total square!'

'Let's get back to Saturday evening,' Guðgeir said. 'Diljá went back to the caravan with Ríkharður and the four of you remained at the restaurant?'

'Yeah, we paid the bill and strolled back to the hotel. It's no distance at all,' Ásmundur said, putting one hand in his pocket.

'And what then?'

'We went to sleep,' he said offhandedly, and took out a pack of chewing gum. He popped two pieces of gum into his mouth and offered the packet around, and everyone declined.

Guðgeir leaned forward, elbows on the table, and looked deep into the man's eyes.

'When we spoke to you in the Westman Islands, you said that you and Ingi Thór went to the bar.'

'Ah, yes. Of course. That's right. Look, I get forgetful when I'm under pressure. I have ADHD, and sitting here is stressful. But, yes. That's correct that Ingi Thór and I had one drink at the bar, chatted for a bit, and then went up to bed,' Ásmundur replied, chewing fast.

'Do you recall what time it was when you went to your room?' Guðgeir asked.

'I reckon it must have been close to midnight. That's more or less when the bar closes.'

'I see, and Katrín had gone up ahead of you?' Elsa Guðrún asked. The question was phrased to sound as if she was seeking a straightforward confirmation of a fact. This was Ásmundur's opportunity to tell the truth.

'Yes.'

The reply was instant. Elsa Guðrún was careful to keep her expression remain unchanged, and Guðgeir was stony-faced.

'So she can corroborate your testimony?' he asked in the same neutral tone.

'Well, she was asleep when I came in. It had been a long day, but of course she was aware of me in bed. Do you want me to call her?' he asked, reaching for his phone.

'No, that's not necessary. We'll contact her ourselves for confirmation if that's seen as being necessary,' Guðgeir replied.

'OK, cool,' he sighed, and his relief was obvious.

'Have you been diagnosed as hyperactive or with attention deficit disorder?'

Elsa Guðrún's question took Ásmundur by surprise.

'Diagnosed, and not diagnosed. I have all the symptoms.'

'I see. What symptoms are those?'

'Am I here for some kind of psychiatric assessment?' Ásmundur asked, laughing awkwardly.

'No, far from it,' she said, smiling.

There was a pause, until Guðgeir broke the silence.

'Do you suffer from memory loss?'

'It happens, like just now,' Ásmundur said, now less certain of his ground.

'Do you fail to notice things?' Guðgeir continued, as calm and measured as ever.

'Yes. Sometimes.'

'Doesn't that present problems in your work as a personal trainer?'

'Well, no. Not exactly. I keep detailed notes of every client,' Ásmundur replied, patting the phone he had placed on the table before him. 'I have a fantastic app that keeps track of everything.'

'We have a witness who has stated that you were not in your room that night. The witness states that you went out somewhere,' Guðgeir said, maintaining his gaze on the man opposite him, who was clearly taken by surprise.

'Who was that?' he asked in a sharp voice.

'That's immaterial,' Elsa Guðrún replied.

'The guy at the bar?' Ásmundur asked, the suspicion clear on his face.

'We aren't mentioning any names at this point, but we have a reliable witness,' Guðgeir said. 'Where did you go that night?'

'I didn't go anywhere! I already told you that!'

Ásmundur's voice rose in volume, and his fingers furiously kneaded the tattoo.

'Could you have forgotten?' Elsa Guðrún suggested.

'No! What is this crap?'

Ásmundur was becoming highly agitated and his voice grew louder.

'Quite sure?'

'Yes! What is all this?' he snapped in irritation.

'All right. That'll do for now. We'll be in touch,' Guðgeir said gently, switching off the recorder.

He escorted Ásmundur out of the room, while Elsa Guðrún stayed behind and made a call to the hotel in the Westman Islands. He saw him out, went back inside and stopped at the first window, where he looked out over the street. The rain had finally stopped and an imposing rainbow rose in the blue sky over the city. The beauty of the sky had no effect on Ásmundur, and there was no mistaking his discomfort, even from a distance. He went over to a red Tesla, opened the door, and instead of getting in he took out his phone and made a call. Then he went back and forth along the pavement, looking agitated, punching the air with his free hand as if to add emphasis to his words.

'The hotel manager confirmed that Ingi Thór and Ásmundur were in the bar until midnight, but unfortunately nobody noticed whether either or both of them went out or to their rooms,' Elsa Guðrún said, appearing at Guðgeir's side.

'Wasn't there someone at reception?'

'No. The doors are open around the clock and there's no night shift.'

'They don't have much to worry about in these small places, do they?' Guðgeir said with a grin.

'I'd love to know who he's talking to,' Elsa Guðrún said, her attention on Ásmundur as he paced the pavement. 'He has something on his conscience. I can smell it.'

'At any rate, he's as nervous as hell,' Guðgeir said, eyes on Ásmundur, who was now getting into his car.

'I thought you'd ask him about the stealth wedding. He was one of the very few who knew about it,' she said, as the Tesla drove away.

'No. That's enough for the moment,' Guðgeir said. 'Let's let him sweat and see what effect it has.'

28

Time passed slowly, and the day was only half over. Diljá tried to settle her nerves with meditation, but was unable to calm herself down. What was she going to do? Give herself up and try to explain? She knew she wouldn't be believed, any more than she had been in the past. No, no chance. Diljá Sigurðardóttir would be sentenced to spend time in prison, locked away, and she wouldn't survive.

She logged into the email app again and sighed with relief when she saw a message waiting for her.

'Where are you? I'll come and get you,' it read.

The words merged and parted before her eyes like waves on the shore. At last, something positive. He was going to support her, and not leave her alone in desperation. It was a wonderful feeling. She put the tablet to one side and buried her face in her hands.

29

The evening TV news bulletin murmured comfortingly in the background. Inga lay on the sofa, absorbed in a book, while Guðgeir was busy in the kitchen. He had browned beef mince and fried the onions, and Særós called just as he finished slicing mushrooms.

'Where does this information come from?' he asked, the phone at his ear as he dropped mushrooms into the hot pan.

'A call from an unregistered phone. Half an hour ago. We reckon it's a man's voice.'

'I see,' Guðgeir said, and felt that the news disturbed him. 'Why wasn't I told?'

'Some time went into trying to locate the caller, but without any success,' Særós explained.

'All right. What did he say?' Guðgeir asked earnestly.

'That Diljá is in a summer house close to Hekla, in an area known as Fjallaland. The summer houses are supposed to be quite far apart there.'

'Where are you now?' Guðgeir asked.

'On the way out east,' she replied. 'Just set off.'

'Shouldn't I be coming as well?'

'Let's see. The Commissioner wanted to send the Special Unit, and their vehicles are some way ahead of me.'

'What on earth do they want the Special Unit for?' Do they think she's armed?' Guðgeir demanded, amazed and sensing the anger welling up inside him.

'We don't know,' Særós replied. 'At any rate, her actions up to now haven't done her any favours, and according to the information we have she's both unpredictable and impetuous.'

'She's suspected of murder using drugs, not weapons,' Guðgeir said.

'We all know that,' Særós said shortly.

'So why wasn't I informed earlier? I'm supposed to be running this investigation,' Guðgeir said, aware of how harsh his voice sounded. Of course, he knew exactly why nobody had spoken to him. The Commissioner must have known that he would have been completely against bringing in the heavily armed Special Unit to apprehend Diljá. The anger surged inside him, and he knew that if he didn't take care, it wouldn't take much for it to boil over.

'You need to take that up with someone other than me,' Særós replied firmly, and he could hear that she was dissatisfied with the way this had developed, but was wary of treading on too many toes.

'I'll speak to you later.'

It was difficult to concentrate on cooking after the call had ended. He put the meat in a saucepan, added canned tomatoes, threw in a handful of olives, and sprinkled it all with herbs. Then he stood still and stared out of the window. He felt a deep concern. What if bringing in the Special Unit were to end badly? This was unacceptable behaviour by the Commissioner, who had no business interfering in the way he ran his investigation. They had found a lead but this development could wreck everything.

The food sizzled vigorously on the stove and he quickly turned down the heat. He peeled garlic and used the flat of the knife to crush one clove after another. The Commissioner's ill-thought-out decision was no doubt because three days had passed since Diljá's disappearance. All the same, the Special Unit was taking things too far. He battered the garlic, crushing and chopping as if his life depended on it.

'Are you making a garlic stew with some meat in it?' Inga asked, putting the book aside. She stood up and went over to him. 'How much did you put in there?'

'Oops! Sorry, I was miles away.' He took a spoon and began to fish garlic out of the saucepan. 'There, that's better. But I think we can be certain that there won't be any colds in this house in the near future.'

'Or vampires,' Inga said. She wrapped her arms around him and squeezed. 'At least, we have each other, and mouthwash... ' she laughed.

He kissed the top of her dark head, and she went back to the sofa, where she reached for the remote control and turned the TV up while Guðgeir made an effort to concentrate on food and forget work.

He was doing well until he heard a voice from the TV.

'The newsroom has reliable information to the effect that the Commissioner of Police's Special Unit has been seen not far from Ytri-Rangá, heading for the Leirubakki district near Hekla. Their movements are believed to be connected to the search for Diljá Sigurðardóttir, who has been the subject of police attention over the last few days.'

Guðgeir felt himself stiffen.

'What kind of fucking idiots are they?' he snarled to himself, stirring the pot so energetically that the contents splashed over the stove.

'Who?' Inga asked.

'The ones who had the bright idea of sending the Special Unit out to do a simple job! Darling, would you watch the pot? I need to make a call.'

He hurried to the hall, where his phone lay on a little dresser.

'Have you heard the news?' he asked as soon as Særós answered.

'No. What?'

'The whole country has been informed that the Special Unit is heading out east to arrest Diljá,' he said.

'What? How did that happen?'

Særós sounded understandably concerned.

'Isn't it obvious?' Guðgeir said, sarcasm dripping from every word. 'When there are four or five black Range Rovers hurtling along some remote country road, isn't it obvious who's on the move? Someone must have recognised their cars and called in to give the newsroom a tip-off. You know what, I don't like the look of this.'

30

She didn't trust him completely and could feel her own inner restlessness growing. She needed her medication and with every passing minute her fear increased, her attention homing in on minor details that she couldn't stop herself overthinking. She tried to eat, nibbling at greasy pasta she had boiled for too long. She had no appetite, but knew that she had to have the energy and the strength to get through the next few hours before he arrived to collect her during the night.

She opened the iPad once more and read his message over and over. She used all the willpower she could summon to convince herself that everything would turn out well. When she had gained better control of herself, she turned to the latest news, hoping that something new had come up, maybe even something positive. She turned up the volume, but the newsreader's words and the images associated with it failed to register until she heard the Special Unit mentioned, quickly followed by her own name.

No, it couldn't be true! What the hell was going on? Did the police think she was dangerous? Diljá dropped the tablet and scrambled to her feet. She cautiously lifted the blind and looked along the road. There was nothing to be seen, but she felt the fear gnawing at every nerve in her body and a heavy weight settled in her chest.

What could she do now? These people considered her dangerous enough that an armed response team had been sent to track her down. She had been branded a murderer, a crazy killer! Had someone given her away? She tried to put together all the pieces, and gradually it became clear to her that it had to be him. There was no other possibility: the Special Unit wasn't coming to search for her as there was no need. The police knew exactly where to find her. They were coming to get her. Diljá fought for breath and her whole body trembled. What were the options? She'd be thrown to the floor, tasered, handcuffed where she lay and hauled to a police car. A series of images flashed through her mind as she paced to and fro in the limited space. Yet again she would cause her mother endless disappointment and shame. Someone would record the arrest and it would be all over social media, and it would be shown on the news. She had done everything to deal with her challenges, pay her debts and live a normal life.

Her head in her hands, Diljá howled. Everything was wrecked, her humiliation would be absolute and María Líf would be branded for life. In a whirl of desperation, she screamed. Her last spark of hope had been extinguished and there was only one way out. In despair, she wrenched the door open and ran out, in the direction of the Ráng River.

She made her way as quickly as she could, but soon realised that she would be exhausted before long. The coarse lava underfoot was heavy going, and her thin-soled trainers weren't made for this kind of terrain. Diljá came to a halt in a patch of greenery between the lava outcrops. She was panting so hard that she could barely catch her breath, and she could hear her heart pounding in her ears. She looked around once she had calmed down. There was no sign of life to be seen anywhere, and she allowed herself to collapse onto the mossy ground for a moment. There were a few clouds high in the sky and her thoughts went to her childhood when she would spend hours lying on her back, watching the changing sky overhead. Back then she had imagined all kinds of wonderful adventures, but now she was here, alone, a grown woman fleeing armed police. That had become her reality. She longed to be able to go back to being the little girl she once had been, so that she could start all over again. Diljá forced herself to her feet, and continued to run towards the river. It was further, much further than she had thought. What was she supposed to do? She didn't want to die, but it would be easier for María Líf to have a mother who was dead than a mother in prison for murder – a mother who would be a mere shadow of her former self by the time she was released from behind bars. Diljá summoned all her energy to increase her pace. The river was in sight and there were no more than a few dozen metres to go.

There was a buzzing in her ears and she felt a sudden fear that her heart was about to give out. Then the buzzing became insistently louder, like a giant wasp behind her. Diljá quickly looked up and around. The sound came from a drone that hovered in the air above her. She glanced over her shoulder. There were black jeeps driving up the track. The Special Unit was on her tail. She ran even faster and the Ráng River approached. She didn't slow her pace until she was on the brink of a cliff over the river, and saw to her horror that she would have to clamber down the practically sheer rocks to reach the water. Now the drone buzzed like a whole swarm of wasps around her head as she cautiously slipped over the edge.

31

The case meeting started at nine the next morning. Elsa Guðrún was the last to arrive, cheeks glowing and her hair damp as she dropped her bag on the table.

'Well, Særós, I deserve a pat on the back from you because I've been for a swim and a run this morning. Only four kilometres, didn't have time for more than that,' she said proudly, hands on her hips. 'I'll go again tomorrow... Hey, what's going on?' She hesitated as she saw the serious expressions on the faces in the room and that there was no response to her cheerful chatter. 'Something serious? What's new?' she asked, looking curiously at them in turn.

'You haven't seen the news?' The question came from Særós, who for once appeared to be immune to hearing about sporting prowess from those who followed her advice on healthy living. 'Last night we had an anonymous tip-off that Diljá was in a summer house in the countryside and before we knew it, the Commissioner had dispatched the Special Unit to go and collect her. The media found out, and Diljá tried to drown herself in the Ráng River.'

'Good grief!'

Elsa Guðrún fell silent. The superficial good cheer she had made an effort to display after an uncomfortably restless night evaporated.

'Yes, and it was a pretty narrow escape. She was closer to hypothermia than drowning when she was pulled out, but fortunately she's all right,' Guðgeir said, running his fingers through his dark hair. 'She'll be discharged from hospital shortly and our request for custody is already with the court.'

'Who gave her away?' Elsa Guðrún said, a sudden gloom catching hold of her.

'We don't know, but we're working on it. The call to the anonymous tip-off number was from an unregistered phone,' Leifur said with a frown, obviously less than satisfied with the success shown by his department. 'But Diljá had hidden herself away in a summer house owned by her friends Ingi Thór and Eygló. She had been there before and knew where the key was hidden.'

By now Elsa Guðrún knew Guðgeir well enough to know that despite the placid façade he maintained, there was a raging fury inside him. She wondered what had prompted the Commissioner to take this decision. She pulled out a chair, sat down and waited to hear more. But nothing happened for a few minutes, with Guðgeir and Særós absorbed in their laptops, while Elsa Guðrún and Leifur waited for more news. A tiny stain on Særós's impeccably ironed shirt caught Elsa Guðrún's attention, as this was something she had never seen before. She noticed that the other woman looked tired and had clearly slept badly. The same could be said of Guðgeir as he held his glasses in one hand and rubbed his eyes with the other at the same time as he peered at the screen before him. The Commissioner's initiative, whatever his reasons had been for intervening in the case, had worked out badly for both of them. Leifur was the one who was closest to his usual self, sitting with the ankle of his right leg hooked over his left knee as he leaned back in his chair. The top button of his shirt was unfastened and his red-patterned tie lay at an angle over his belly. He held a mug that had been glazed with a faded picture of himself, something that had been a gift from colleagues in the forensics department many years previously. Beneath the picture was the legend Leifur will find the solution.

'Let's hope so,' Elsa Guðrún muttered to herself.

'What's that?' Leifur asked, sitting up straight in the chair and paying attention. 'Hope what?'

'That you'll find the solution,' Elsa Guðrún said, pointing a finger at his mug. 'Or you and your guys in forensics.'

'Oh, that?' Leifur said, lifting up the mug. 'The guys gave me this...'

'Right. Let's make a start,' Guðgeir interrupted, a grim look on his face. 'Særós and I have been busy half the night and after yesterday's events it has become easier to pull together information. So I'll go over what we know right now, and will send you all a memo afterwards with the main points.' He stood up, put his hands to his lower back and stiffly paced the small floor space in the room as he spoke. 'We now know that Diljá has suffered from mental health problems. She dropped out of college, got into all kinds of trouble and messed about with drugs. She was diagnosed with a psychotic disorder at seventeen and was admitted to hospital. She appeared to make a good recovery, went back to college and graduated. After that she went out to work, and there were a lot of workplaces...'

'Why was that?' Elsa Guðrún broke in, unable to contain her curiosity.

'We don't have an explanation for that, but we'll check it out if it looks to be relevant,' Guðgeir replied before continuing. 'Diljá's daughter María Líf was born when she was twenty-one and the father is Ævar Brjánsson, who now works at the Met Office. After speaking to him, I checked whether he had any history of threatening Diljá one way or other, but there's nothing that has come to our attention. All the same, we'll keep an eye on the man. So, when María Líf was two, Diljá caused an accident in which she was the party in the wrong, but the worst part of it was that the child wasn't secured properly in the child seat. In the relevant statements she confirmed that she had secured the little girl properly, and had heard the click clearly as the belt was fastened. But the child seat turned out to have been worn out, didn't meet the safety criteria, and the child was thrown clear of the vehicle in the crash.'

Guðgeir fell silent, which added weight to his words.

'That's awful,' Elsa Guðrún said, shuddering.

'Bloody careless,' Leifur muttered. 'Was she off the dope when this happened?'

'Yes. She said so at the time and there were no traces of alcohol or anything else when she was tested. Her excuse was that she was hard up, said that she hadn't been able to afford a new child seat and that one had been given to her. Her car was also a proper rust bucket, worn out and...'

'And the child?' Elsa Guðrún broke in, as she felt that the conversation had become bogged down.

'María Líf had some minor injuries, and that was pretty much a miracle in itself. It could have been so much worse if they had been travelling faster or if circumstances had been different. But the whole thing naturally went to the Child Protection Board. María Líf's father Ævar was just about finishing his studies overseas at that time and he embarked straight away on a custody battle that became very bitter. He wanted to remove all of Diljá's rights concerning the child. This went on for a year or two and during that time she regressed significantly. She suffered from anxiety and depression, and became increasingly impetuous. It seems that she finally suffered a nervous breakdown and was admitted again for treatment. She was diagnosed with a psychotic disorder, but according to what her mother told me during a conversation yesterday evening, her doctor is keen to re-examine that diagnosis. She has been fine for the last few years. She has been heavily into all kinds of healthy living, and not long ago qualified as a personal trainer. Now she's training to teach yoga, some specialised variety that I can't remember the name of, and she has been conscientious in seeking out help with all sorts of therapies. So, pretty good, but her mother said that she had been hooked up with a few too many men, and Ríkharður was the third wealthy, older man she had been in a relationship with. The other two both ended their relationships with her after a few months.'

'She'd had enough of all that trouble,' Elsa Guðrún said.

'That's possible, but these therapies you mention, Guðgeir. They don't come cheap. You know how much a psychiatrist charges?' Særós asked, her words directed at Elsa Guðrún, who sighed inwardly.

Why on earth did Særós have to make a link between her personal life and this case, she wondered, put out by her words, but she nodded in agreement. In her case, the union had paid for a few sessions, but no more. Medication had helped her sleep for a few weeks after the rape, but she felt that it had a bad effect on her and she stopped using it. Now the struggle was with insomnia while the twins were in the north with their father and she was alone at home. This was when insecurity and fear descended on her with their full weight.

'Elsa Guðrún. Elsa Guðrún!'

She was startled from her thoughts as Guðgeir repeated her name.

'What?' she asked, trying to appear as if she had been paying attention.

'We're going over the situation,' Guðgeir said thoughtfully, his eyes on her. 'What motive could Diljá have had for murdering Ríkharður? That's to say, if that's what she did.'

'Insanity,' Leifur declared, and Elsa Guðrún glared at him, her expression making her annoyance plain. 'I mean, she'd been responsible for almost killing her own child,' he said, hands theatrically in the air as if justifying his opinion.

'That'll do for now,' Guðgeir said quickly, picking up the documents he had brought. 'I hope that when we interview Diljá we'll get an idea of the sequence of events.'

'Hold on,' Elsa Guðrún said. 'Sorry, I dropped out for a second because I was wondering why Ingi Thór and Eygló hadn't mentioned the summer cottage.' It was a white lie, but she felt that her point was no less valid for that. 'That's to say, they must have known that Diljá could get in and hide herself away there.'

32

Tiny and fragile. That was Guðgeir's first thought when he went into the interview room later in the day and saw Diljá. She had only just been discharged from hospital, her dark hair in disarray, and brown eyes above deep dark shadows looked at him in fear.

She wore a thin beige sweater that was too big for her, while her black tracksuit bottoms clung to her legs. She had pulled her sleeves down over her hands, delicate fingers clutching the bunched cloth. A lawyer had been appointed for Diljá, an older man who had been in this position many times before and who was, as far as Guðgeir was aware, fairly conscientious. The lawyer gestured to Diljá to take a seat. She sat down with one leg folded beneath her, and immediately leaned on her elbows, placing them on the table between her and Guðgeir. Then she buried her face in her hands and her shoulders shook. The lawyer gave her an encouraging pat on the back before he took a seat himself.

'How are you feeling, Diljá?' Guðgeir asked. 'Were you able to sleep?'

She nodded and sniffed, but remained otherwise still.

'It's really important that you are able to rest. You have been remanded in custody for a week, but if you answer truthfully and accurately, then the likelihood of it being extended becomes substantially reduced,' he continued in his usual gentle tone as he tried to make eye contact with the terrified woman. 'Now, tell me about Saturday evening and the night.'

He fell silent and waited for a reply, but none came.
The lawyer handed Diljá a packet of tissues.
'Here,' he said, lightly tapping her shoulder.
'Thanks,' she mumbled, and blew her nose without looking up.
'Diljá.'
'Yes?'
This time she lifted her head, blew her nose again, but said no more.
'You have to understand that it's vital that you tell the truth, and the sooner you do so, the better,' Guðgeir said, again trying and failing to make eye contact.
'Yes.'
'Tell me what happened,' he said gently.
She sniffed again, and swallowed with an effort, as if her throat pained her. It occurred to Guðgeir that she could be ill following her dousing in the Ráng River. Both overwhelming exhaustion and despair flickered in her brown eyes.
'I gave Ríkharður medication to make him sleep, and a sedative,' she said at last in a weak voice. 'I told him it was a painkiller.'
'Why did you do that?'
'To make sure he slept soundly. I wanted to get away... to get a little peace...'
'And to meet Ásmundur,' Guðgeir added in a dark voice. He dropped his chin to rest on his hand, his eyes fixed on her.
Diljá started, and there was a flash of fear in her eyes.
'How do you know that?' she whispered.
'We have a witness,' Guðgeir replied. 'Other witnesses, staff at the restaurant, described how Ríkharður had been heavily intoxicated earlier in the evening.'
'He drank a lot,' Diljá said. 'Both at lunchtime and before we went out to dinner, and then he drank more.'
'When did you give him the medication?' Guðgeir asked, taking off his glasses and intently watching her expression. This was her opportunity to tell the whole truth. 'Diljá?'

She hung her head and muttered something unintelligible.

'I can't hear you. Please speak up.'

'I don't quite remember,' she mumbled, raising her voice slightly.

Guðgeir picked up the cloth from his glasses case and began carefully polishing the lenses. He took his time, aware that she was still in shock and would probably need some minutes to think of what to say, but she made no move to volunteer any more information. Instead, she coughed several times and sniffed again.

'Diljá, I hope you understand the seriousness of your position,' he said after a pause, and cleared his throat. 'This is a murder investigation.' His eyes unsuccessfully sought out hers before he continued. 'If you're found guilty, you'll face many years in prison. It must be a very difficult prospect...' Guðgeir refrained from mentioning María Líf, and again fell silent to give Diljá an opportunity to respond, but she sat motionless, not saying a word. 'You'll have to wait for a verdict to be given, then there could be a long wait before you begin your sentence. You'll be well over forty by the time your sentence ends, and it won't be easy to find work ... Your past will follow you...'

'Stop! Stop it!' she whined, huddling in her chair and clapping her hands over her ears.

The lawyer put a hand on her shoulder.

'Stay in control, Diljá,' he reminded her. 'Please try to calm down and give us your side of the story. Tell us what happened.'

Diljá stared at him in confusion, as if trying to work out whether he was on her side or Guðgeir's. She reached for the box of tissues, and loudly blew her nose. Her hands shook noticeably as she let the tissue drop into a bin that stood nearby on the floor.

'I'll tell you the truth and you have to believe me,' she said, tugging at her sleeves so that her fingers gripped the cloth even more securely.

'Good. Please go ahead,' Guðgeir said, his expression serious and his arms folded. 'I'm sure you'll feel better for it. We know that you got married a little while ago, but not why you decided to keep it a secret.'

Diljá took a deep breath, and for the first time she looked Guðgeir in the face. There was still fear in her eyes and her lips trembled as she began her account in a low voice.

'We felt that it was simply nobody's business but ours. His son Vilhjálmur knew about it but Ríkharður didn't want to have an argument with his daughter. For me the marriage was all about money and I always had it in mind that I'd divorce him, right from the start, but of course I hoped that married life would be all right. That I'd learn to love him, or at least be fond of him. But as soon as we were married he became even more domineering. He was constantly telling me what to do, how I should behave, what I should think, what I ought to wear. He said that I was a poorly-informed bundle of nerves, and he broke down everything that I had spent years building up.'

'Did he treat you like this right from the start?' Guðgeir asked.

'Of course not, no. I'd never have married him. The first month he couldn't do enough for me, always giving me presents and helping me with my finances.' Diljá looked up, as if to convince herself that Guðgeir would understand what she was telling him. 'But he got more bossy by the day. Looking back, it all happened unbelievably fast. It was so subtle that I hardly even noticed to begin with, thought that he was just being thoughtful, and to be truthful, he could be really lovely, in between. But there were more and more comments and I started to doubt myself,' Diljá said quietly. 'I was starting to feel bad and was being cut off from my friends. That's why I was so pleased when the trip to the Westman Islands came up.'

'I see,' Guðgeir said, sounding both sympathetic and encouraging. 'Are you saying that you were subjected to mental cruelty by Ríkharður?'

'He was a very clever man, and that meant that he found it very difficult to tolerate weakness in other people,' Diljá explained, tugging at her sleeves.

'So to your mind that justified drugging him?' Guðgeir asked, his tone hardening.

'I didn't mean to harm him. He was a doctor and so I didn't dare give him much, just two strong painkillers and two sleeping pills. He wasn't supposed to die! You have to believe me!' Diljá croaked in desperation. 'It was an accident!'

'So, is that all?' Guðgeir said shortly. 'How about you tell me about the brown sugar?'

Diljá gasped and her face turned as white as chalk. She glanced in terror at her lawyer.

'Tell the truth. What did you put in the sugar? There's no use denying it, as we've had it analysed already,' Guðgeir continued, his voice now ice cold.

'I just put in there some of the medication I had,' she stammered, holding her head in her hands.

'Which was?'

'Tranquillisers, some sleeping pills and...'

'And what else?'

'Nothing, really!' Diljá said. 'I was just so totally tired of him and didn't want him groping me,' she said, looking beseechingly at Guðgeir as if she were asking him to understand. 'He was so pushy.'

'There were substances in there that cause hallucinations,' Guðgeir went on, taking no notice of her words. 'Don't think you can fool us.'

'I put some tiny amounts of other stuff in there. Nothing dangerous, and not that much that he could die from it. You have to believe me. I know I did wrong by giving him this stuff, but he wasn't supposed to die. Never! I mean, nobody dies from tiny amounts like that. I know loads of people who have taken way bigger doses, and Ríkharður was a tall guy, more than a hundred kilos.'

'Are you trained as a chemist?'

'Me? No.'

The question took her by surprise and she was instantly on the defensive.

'Doctor? Nurse? Any other medical training?'

She shook her head, and muttered in such a low voice that her 'no' could hardly be heard. Beads of sweat had formed on her forehead and upper lip.

'Exactly. It's important to be clear about this. You admit that you had no idea of the chemical composition of these drugs, or the effects they could have when mixed together?'

Diljá made no reply, but glared at Guðgeir in defiance. He could see that she was at the end of her tether and completely confused.

'Diljá? Do you admit it?'

'Yes.'

Her voice was so low that it could hardly be made out.

'Would you please repeat your answer for the benefit of the recording?' Guðgeir asked.

'Yes.'

'And you admit that you married Ríkharður Magnússon for money and had already decided to divorce him after some time had passed?'

'Yes,' Diljá sighed. Her face was bathed in sweat and her eyes were bloodshot.

'Thank you. That's all for now,' Guðgeir said as he stood up. 'I'll request that our doctor checks up on you. I hope that the hospital didn't discharge you too early.'

He nodded to the lawyer, and it was clear from the look on the man's face that he didn't like the look of his client's prospects.

33

Guðgeir just made it into the fish shop seconds before the doors were about to be locked. While he waited in the queue, he allowed his eyes to wander over the different varieties on display. He felt tired, but this wasn't the satisfying fatigue that came at the end of a good day's work. That was a long way from how he felt right now. He wasn't able to relax mentally as his thoughts constantly went back over the events of the last few days. Everything had happened so rapidly, and following Diljá's confession, Særós had let it be known that the case was as good as closed. There were just a few loose ends to be tied up, witnesses to be called in and such details. It was more than likely that she was right, and he was keenly aware that he must not allow the sympathy he felt for Diljá to cloud his judgement. After decades as a police officer, Guðgeir had seen everything, including much that was dismal or distressing. People's lives could often lead them in unexpected directions, and by now there was little that could take him by surprise. As far as he could see, Diljá's life had been made up of peaceful interludes between traumatic events. She had certainly lied and done bad things, but he had encountered many people devoid of any conscience, and he was sure Diljá wasn't one of those. Could he be wrong? Despite having seen the worst of human behaviour, he still managed to maintain a belief in people's goodness, or so Særós said. Now Diljá's life had been plunged into yet another disaster, the deepest and worst so far. He was fairly sure that she would be found guilty of manslaughter. If she were lucky, the court would rule it as inadvertent manslaughter.

'What can I get you?' asked a cheerful voice. 'Have you decided?'

'What?' Guðgeir asked, startled from his thoughts. 'Are you speaking to me?'

'What do you fancy for dinner tonight?' the fishmonger asked. 'Looks like you were miles away? Something bothering you? I mean fish...' he said and laughed as he patted his aproned belly. Guðgeir was a regular customer, and they had got to know each other.

'Ach, sorry. Had something else on my mind. I reckon I'll go for the cod dish, the one with pistachios. Around a kilo, please.'

He listened and sang along to music on Spotify on the way home to keep his mind from wandering as he drove. He parked in the basement garage and decided to take his sports bag upstairs with him. He knew perfectly well that he wouldn't go to the gym tonight. He was simply too tired after such a long day. He bypassed the lift, taking the stairs to convince himself that he had at least made some effort. Once home, he put some soothing music on and began to potter around the kitchen. The fish was in the oven and a pot of rice was almost cooked when Inga appeared in the doorway.

'What's this? There's just the two of us tonight,' she said, gesturing at the five places laid at the table, including a plastic Moomin plate.

'Really? I thought it would be all of us,' Guðgeir said in surprise.

'Who told you that?' Inga asked, peering into the oven. 'Looks good, though.'

'Well, nobody. I just thought...' Guðgeir muttered, wondering what had come over him.

'Ólöf and Guðgeir Jökull are eating at home tonight. She's expecting a visitor, and Pétur Andri is going out somewhere with the boys.'

'I see,' Guðgeir said, eyeing the saucepan full of rice.

'At any rate, we won't be going hungry with all that fish,' Inga said cheerfully. She opened the fridge and took out a bottle of white wine. 'Isn't it worth celebrating your closing the case so quickly and neatly?' She smiled, opened the bottle and poured wine into two glasses. 'Cheers, and well done!'

'Thanks, sweetheart,' he said, but there was a hollow edge to his voice. He had the nagging feeling that this case was still far from closed.

During the evening he relaxed and became more cheerful, and they sat for a long time over the fish as they talked. They finished more than half of the fish and all of the bottle. Guðgeir saw it as a privilege to be married to a lawyer and often allowed himself to discuss work with her. This evening was no exception and he considered it a relief to be able to talk through the Heimaey case with her. He felt that he was a fortunate man to have such a partner in life, and his thoughts went to how unfortunate Diljá had been in this respect. Or was this something more than simple bad luck? And what was Ásmundur's part in all this?

His conversation about this with Inga had long moved on and she was in the middle of recounting something Guðgeir Jökull had got up to, now that he was in the midst of what she referred to as 'the terrible twos' when he interrupted.

'Imagine a man and a woman in a secret relationship. He's in a childless marriage, and she's single. They're roughly the same age, similar interests, and in much the same line of work. They're also part of the same group of friends. The woman gets married, all of a sudden, to a wealthy middle-aged man for whom she has no fondness, and she continues the affair with her friend, who is, as I said, already in a relationship.'

Guðgeir fell silent, eyes expectantly on his wife.

'And what?' Inga asked. 'What do you have in mind?'

'What do you think of that?'

'Me?' Inga said. 'I think that's completely crazy.'

'Exactly,' Guðgeir said triumphantly. 'It's suspiciously crazy!'

34

He felt better after a pleasant evening and a good night's sleep, telling himself that yesterday's restlessness had to be down to his weariness. It had been a busy week, and he hadn't slept enough. He hadn't slept well at the guest house in the Westman Islands, and then there had been a disturbed night with little Guðgeir in bed with them. It was time to accept that with age his capacity to cope with a lack of sleep wasn't what it had once been. Guðgeir closed his eyes and tried to doze off again, but the aroma of coffee stealing through the apartment made that difficult, and before long he was on his feet. He made the most of this extra time, spent longer than usual in the shower, and shaved carefully before sitting down to coffee and two slices of buttered toast. One was spread with cheese and the other with slices of smoked lamb. This had been his breakfast for as long as he cared to remember, and he had no desire to change this habit, especially on a bright Saturday morning when neither of them needed to hurry off to work.

'More?' Inga asked, standing up to reach for the coffee pot. Her thin dressing gown was tied around her waist and he could sense her faint fragrance.

'Yes, please.'

He pushed his cup towards her and smiled.

'You know, I was thinking over what you said last night,' she said.

'And what did you come up with?'

'After all these years in the legal profession, I've come to the conclusion that everyone has some shit they want to keep secret. Everyone, no exceptions. Even people who come across as being perfect on the outside have something they'd prefer to keep quiet. But how tightly this stuff is guarded varies. Sometimes it's just below the surface. Other people have it buried deep, and with some people it becomes a part of their existence.'

'Quite true,' Guðgeir said. 'That's quite true. I've had the same experience.'

'Some people have some small shit they're worried about, others have stacks. But how much of a burden this is doesn't depend so much on how big the secret is, but on that individual's personality,' Inga said and was about to continue when Guðgeir's phone rang. He gestured to her to indicate that it was a work call, and went to the bedroom to take it. He was gone for some time, and when he returned, he was visibly disturbed.

'Who was that?' Inga asked curiously.

'Særós,' Guðgeir said, scrolling rapidly through his phone.

'And?' Inga said. 'What did she say?'

'She was asking if I had seen the email she sent last night. Which I haven't... But what she said was that there's a new report from the forensic pathologist. Some of the samples taken during the autopsy indicate that the cause of Ríkharður's death was suffocation.'

'Really?' Inga said, the surprise in her voice clear. 'So that means the drugs Diljá gave him weren't what killed him.'

'That's the way it looks,' Guðgeir said. 'And there were no signs of him having thrown up, so it's not as if he choked on his own vomit.'

'Which means that...' Inga began.

'That someone suffocated him,' Guðgeir said, finishing her sentence.

'Could Diljá have done it?'

'Well, I don't know. But what's clear is that this case is far from concluded.'

Guðgeir silently ran his fingertips over his freshly shaven cheeks. All kinds of ideas were beginning to pop up in his mind. Had Ríkharður been sufficiently sedated for the petite Diljá to be able to suffocate him? Closing off someone's airways could trigger unbelievably powerful instinctive responses. Guðgeir sipped his coffee, which was already cold, and gazed out of the window. His concern now was that the basis for extending Diljá's custody was no longer there, and that wouldn't be a good thing.

'Aren't you going to call Elsa Guðrún? Are you going to be working this weekend?' Inga asked, and he realised that she had been trying to get his attention, but he had been too absorbed in his own thoughts to answer.

'No, she's out of town and out of contact. We'll talk things over on Monday,' he replied.

'Has she turned into a mountain goat and gone up into the highlands?' Inga joked. She began to clear the table. 'With a backpack and a lot of corn plasters?'

'No. Far from it. Særós said she's spending the weekend drinking cocoa with some people.'

'Cocoa?' Inga asked, raising an eyebrow.

'Yes. From Peru or Guatemala. It's what's called a spiritual journey, if I understand correctly. Særós called it a cocoa retreat, whatever that means,' Guðgeir said. 'To my mind, it sounds unlike Elsa Guðrún, but it seems that she's still struggling to be at home alone, and the twins are up in the north with their father.'

'She's still recovering from the trauma. It's understandable. It's the kind of ordeal that nobody should ever have to experience,' Inga said and her deep sympathy for Elsa Guðrún was plain. 'People search in different places, often unexpected ones, when other things don't help. This has to be harmless, surely.'

'You know about this?' Guðgeir asked, staring at his wife in astonishment. She never failed to take him by surprise, even though he knew that she was keenly aware of what was going on around her. He himself had heard this mentioned, but hadn't troubled to find out any more.

'You mean a cacao ceremony? Yes, I've heard about it, and even been invited to take part through my yoga group. People gather together, meditate, dance, do breathing exercises and other things, and they drink pure cacao from Guatemala,' Inga said, opening the fridge and putting the cheese and butter on the top shelf.

'What's wrong with the usual stuff, the sort we use in a chocolate cake?'

'Ach. Guðgeir. This is completely different to cocoa that comes from a supermarket in a tin. This has no additives and no sugar, just pure natural cacao, and it has a bitter taste. There's something in it that encourages you to open your heart,' Inga explained with a quizzical look on her face as she stacked crockery in the dishwasher. 'We ought to try it together.'

'So it's dope?' Guðgeir grumbled as he picked his mug from the dishwasher. 'I'm not finished. I'll have some more coffee.'

'No. There's a tiny amount of some natural substance in this cacao that gives a feeling of wellbeing. It's all quite innocent, as far as I know, and ruinously expensive. I don't recall how much a weekend was supposed to cost, but it's definitely not cheap,' Inga said.

'I can well believe it. There's always someone ready to pick the pockets of people who don't feel well,' Guðgeir said in disgust. 'It's not as if Elsa Guðrún is rolling in money. Police officers aren't paid a fortune, as you know.'

'Hey, calm down,' Inga said, a teasing glint in her eye. 'All right, so it's expensive, but let's say that Elsa Guðrún had bought herself some new clothes, had her hair done and a facial, and maybe more. Then she had gone out on the lash and had a good time... Would you have been disgusted by that?' she asked, catching his eye. 'No. I imagine you'd have said that it would do her good to go out, enjoy herself and forget her troubles. Wouldn't you?'

Guðgeir grunted and scratched a smooth cheek.

'When you put it like that, I can understand, but...' He drummed the table with his fingers as if to emphasise his thoughts. 'All the same, I can't stand people who take advantage of the misfortunes of others by selling some bullshit. I just can't be doing with it.'

35

Guðgeir was at the station early on Monday morning. Following the latest twist, he was troubled by the thought that he and Elsa Guðrún could have carried out a more careful investigation in the Westman Islands. Now he felt that they should have taken detailed statements from the four travellers, instead of just an informal conversation. He could see now that they should have paid more attention to checking movements in Herjólfsdalur that night, and they should have spoken to more people familiar with the area. All the same, he reminded himself that it was always easy to be wise after the event.

Guðgeir hung up his coat, fetched himself a cup of coffee and went over to Særós's office.

'Good morning. Are we meeting in here?' he asked, placing his cup on the table.

'Yes. Elsa Guðrún will be here any minute now, and Ísgerður is coming as well. Leifur said that he doesn't have anything new for us, so he'll give this meeting a miss,' Særós replied, sipping her green morning smoothie.

Guðgeir took a seat at the table, directly opposite Særós's weekly nugget of wisdom. Last week's axiom still hung there in 48-point type. ***Patience is bitter, but the fruits of patience are sweet.***

He saw it as a necessary reminder, but it was a surprise that it hadn't been changed. In all the years he and Særós had worked together, she had never forgotten. A new line of wisdom appeared every Friday, regardless of circumstances, and now it was Monday. He wondered if the world had stopped turning, or if Særós was taking her routine less seriously? Maybe she had fallen in love and her mind was on other things? Could that be? The thought was quickly snuffed out as Særós picked up a sheet of paper, took down the old one and pinned ***Treat everyone as if you'll never them again*** in its place.

Guðgeir squinted and tried to make sense of the words. What did that mean? He slid a hand into his inside jacket pocket and took out his glasses, even though he could read it perfectly well. He read it again, but still failed to figure out the meaning or the sentiment behind the words. He mulled over the context again, and glanced at Særós, who sat straight-backed at the table, preparing her notes. He coughed courteously, wanting to ask her what this was supposed to mean, but decided it was probably best to keep quiet.

Særós's axioms weren't up for discussion today and he forgot about it as Elsa Guðrún came in, looking cheerful. It seemed that her South American cacao weekend had done her good, as she looked rested and there was a glint in her dark blue eyes that he hadn't seen for a long time. As everyone did, she cast an eye at the week's axiom. Her eyes widened and she just managed to cover her mouth to stop herself laughing.

'I haven't a clue what that means,' she whispered to Guðgeir, grimacing.

'Nor me,' he replied under his breath, a quizzical look on his face, and he scratched his head. 'She must have been in a hurry...' he said, just as Ísgerður joined them. Her brown hair, flowing in soft waves over her shoulders, contrasted sharply with the angular lines of her face. The latest axiom didn't escape her notice and she looked at it on the wall for a moment, and appeared to find it no less perplexing than the other two. A questioning look on her face, she shrugged and said nothing. She slipped off the red leather jacket she wore over a plain, thin dress, hung it over the back of a chair and put her black briefcase on the table.

'Good morning, everyone,' Særós said, looking up from her laptop. 'Let's make a start.'

The next hour passed quickly. According to Ísgerður, Diljá had been running a temperature the previous evening, but that had since dropped to a normal level. All that troubled her now was a bad cold. Guðgeir was relieved to hear this, as he had been concerned that she had been released too early from hospital.

'She suffers badly from claustrophobia, and that has a more debilitating effect on her than the cold she picked up after her dunking in the river,' Ísgerður said seriously.

'Not much we can do about that,' Særós said, straight to the point. 'If she's on the right side of the law, then she'll be free before long.'

'Let's hope for the best,' Guðgeir said, before he began going again over the main points of the investigation up to now. The forensics team were going through the caravan and its entire contents once more. The examination had stopped after the discovery of the drugged sugar, but now things had changed and every square inch was being inspected.

'There's every likelihood that he was suffocated,' Ísgerður said with emphasis. 'I believe that your investigation should be carried out on that basis. That's my medical opinion, based on the information that has come from the forensic pathologist.'

'This changes everything,' Guðgeir said, catching the eye of first Særós and then Elsa Guðrún.

'It's most likely he was suffocated with a pillow or something like that, and that's what the forensics team need to be checking particularly carefully,' Ísgerður continued. 'But whether Diljá has the strength to suffocate him, I don't know. That depends how heavily drugged he was.' Ísgerður stood up and took her jacket from the chair. 'I have to go. We're ridiculously busy. Give me a call if you need any further information. See you,' she said, taking her briefcase and hurrying from the room.

'We need to concentrate on the group of friends,' Guðgeir said once the doctor had left. 'I did some searching online yesterday and talked to a few people to build up a clearer picture of each individual. Hold on a moment, it's coming,' he said, tapping at his keyboard until a picture of Ásmundur appeared on the screen on the wall. The man's face was noticeably chiselled, with a strong jaw and hair cut short. 'We'll start with him, and as you can see, I've already put together some notes.' Guðgeir switched the picture before standing up. 'He's in a relationship with Katrín, who believes he's still involved with Diljá. The two of them are both personal trainers and work at the same gym. Ásmundur claims to suffer from both hyperactivity and attention deficit disorder. There's a suspicion that he spent the night Ríkharður died with Diljá, and if that's the case, he could have been aware that she intended to drug her husband to make him sleep, so that the two of them could be together undisturbed. Ásmundur dropped out of college after a year and a half, as he was in trouble due to drug use. He has a criminal record for driving under the influence, and also for public disorder offences.'

'What was that for?' Elsa Guðrún asked with interest.

'He was caught scrawling graffiti on a wall and kicked a police officer. But that's more than twenty years ago,' Guðgeir explained. 'Ásmundur cleaned up his act, started doing some serious weightlifting, was highly successful, and then began to train others. He's qualified as a personal trainer. Over the last few years he has done well. He's not only trained physically but also puts emphasis on spiritual effort, and that kind of thing.'

'In what way?' Særós asked, looking dubious.

'This is what Ásmundur's and Diljá's manager said. I have to admit that I didn't go any further into that,' Guðgeir said, flashing a new picture onto the screen. 'This is Katrín, the woman he lives with.'

'That's the one with the dark blue nails and the diamond in

her nose,' Elsa Guðrún added, glancing at Særós, who had only seen pictures of the four of them, and read the reports.

'Exactly. She has an office job at the Association of Driving Instructors,' Guðgeir continued. 'She trained as a beautician and has also qualified as a bookkeeper. She and Ásmundur met at the gym and have lived together for some years. We have seen two sides of Katrín. There's the noticeably self-confident but rather shallow version, if I can put it like that, and there's the other side of her. We know she was aware of Ásmundur cheating on her with Diljá, and that she pretended not to know anything about it.'

'That's interesting,' Særós said, her brow furrowed in thought.

'Yes. Could be a defence mechanism against emotional pain. What troubles me most about her is how she was completely indifferent to Ríkharður's death,' Guðgeir said.

'Katrín is bigger and looks like she's stronger than Diljá. Physically, she could have done it, and if this is to do with Ásmundur's infidelity, then she knew that Ríkharður was alone in the caravan and in a vulnerable state,' Elsa Guðrún said. 'But why? What motive could Katrín have had to want him dead?'

'That's just it,' Guðgeir replied thoughtfully. 'But I found out yesterday that Katrín's father was once married to Ríkharður's sister Ingibjörg. It seems the divorce was a painful one, but whether that connects in any way to the murder is another question.'

'It's an interesting angle that's worth checking out,' Særós said, sitting back and crossing her legs. 'OK. Who's next?'

'Ingi Thór. It wasn't hard to find information about him. But it's debatable how accurate a picture this provides,' Guðgeir said as a picture of Ingi Thór appeared on the screen. His pale blue eyes stared straight at them from under beautifully long lashes, and his fair hair formed a frame around his face. He had high cheekbones and elegant lips.

'Good-looking guy,' Særós muttered to Elsa Guðrún.

'Some people just win the genetic lottery,' she whispered back with a smile. 'He's so cute.'

'Ingi Thór qualified as and works as a carpenter, but he's known on social media for some kind of spiritual awakening, if I understand correctly,' Guðgeir continued, pretending not to have heard their whispers.

'That again,' Særós said, shaking her head in surprise.

'Exactly. His name's all over the internet in connection with this,' Guðgeir said. 'As a couple they run some kind of ceremonies at their summer house, the place near Hekla where Diljá concealed herself. Ingi Thór and Eygló appear to be financially well off, although their tax returns don't exactly reflect that. They live in a decent detached house, have two fairly new cars and a summer house, and if their social media is anything to go by, they like to live pretty well.'

'Interesting,' Særós said, placing both hands flat on the table as she spoke.

'Of course, I don't know what type of ceremonies they hold, but I've just been to one of these cacao retreats,' Elsa Guðrún said. 'It's not cheap.'

'Really? You've been on one of these things?' Guðgeir asked with pretend surprise, and Elsa Guðrún nodded.

'Yes. And people pay in cash or else directly into an account, as I did,' she explained. 'Do you know what the cacao ceremony is all about, Guðgeir?'

'Me? Of course I know. Do you think I don't keep tabs on what's going on in the world of spiritual health?' he grinned. 'But what bugs me is seeing Ingi Thór and Eygló in some kind of guru role. When I was young, people like that were very different, more like Mahatma Gandhi or Mother Teresa. They lived frugally, worked with the poor and let their actions speak for themselves. But what was your experience of this cacao weekend?'

'Ach, it was all very different and I have mixed feelings about it,' Elsa Guðrún said. 'What got on my nerves was that people were expected to open themselves up completely about difficult life-changing events, to a couple of amateurs who were running this thing. I stayed away from that side of it, but heard that some people became deeply emotionally upset.'

'Well, I see,' Guðgeir said quietly, his tone unmistakably dismissive.

'What about Eygló?' Særós asked. 'Did you find out any more about her, Guðgeir?'

'Unfortunately, not so much,' he said, and switched to a new picture on the screen. In this her red hair was longer than when they had met in the Westman Islands, and she was without glasses. The photograph was clearly intended for advertising, as in it Eygló looked straight ahead, doing the splits and with her arms high in the air. She was dressed in a white singlet and pale, close-fitting yoga trousers.

'Is that the only picture you could find?' Særós asked with a smile.

'That's a yoga monkey pose,' Elsa Guðrún said. 'As far as I remember it was originally called Hanumanasana.'

'Is that so?' Guðgeir said, and quickly continued so as to prevent any further irrelevant conversation. 'She's married to Ingi Thór and they have two children, which we knew already. I understand that she's now focused completely on teaching yoga and has been for some time, and that she has a strong following. She even opened her own retreat a year ago and teaches a variety of yoga, breathing exercises, sound therapy, cold therapy, reiki and shamanism, and that's just counting up what I can remember. It's expensive, but despite that and the retreat being successful, word is that Eygló isn't great at paying her debts. Anyone who tries to call in a debt gets sent some spiritual platitudes and pictures of flowers.'

'It must all be on her website,' Elsa Guðrún said.

'There's no website,' Guðgeir replied, eyes on the red-haired woman in the picture. 'It's all word of mouth.'

'That's all interesting, but what's Eygló's background? What did she do before?' Særós asked.

'She previously worked in a shop in the Kringlan mall for

years,' Guðgeir said, drawing out his words. 'She suffered a significant trauma. Eygló is from the countryside and when she was sixteen, she and another girl accused the local priest of sexual harassment. A substantial proportion of the locals turned against them and supported the perpetrator. It was a major shock and Eygló moved to Reykjavík when she was very young. Later on it turned out that more young women had been harassed by the priest, so in all likelihood, Eygló was telling the truth.'

'That's terrible,' Elsa Guðrún said, clearly affected.

'One thing more to finish up,' Guðgeir said. 'What these five people all have in common is that they were all searching for something on a spiritual level, and all of them either had a difficult youth or had suffered a trauma of some kind, or both.'

'All of them?' Særós asked. 'Surely not Ingi Thór?'

'Oh, yes,' Guðgeir said. 'He lost his parents at a young age, and he and his brother were sent to a couple who looked after them. The man was a relative. It seems that his parents were lovely people, but the same couldn't be said of the couple they were sent to live with in the Westfjords.'

36

This room was an improvement on the cell where she had felt stifled, with the walls closing in on her. She had tried to explain that she suffered badly from claustrophobia, not just a touch of it, but practically off the scale. Nobody had taken any notice. She was a prisoner, a prisoner on remand who was allowed an hour of fresh air just once a day. She still hadn't met anyone other than the lawyer who had been assigned to her. He had visited her, but their conversation had been stilted and somehow they hadn't been able to make a connection. She had asked if it would be possible to open the cell door just while they talked, but that wasn't allowed so those conditions hadn't exactly helped. All the same, the old guy was very decent, but she sensed right away that he didn't understand her and it was going to be hopeless trying to explain her side of the story.

The room she was in now was bigger but, just like the cell, there was no window. Diljá pulled her feet up onto the chair and wrapped her arms around them. She shivered; she had picked up a filthy cold. She tugged the sleeves of her sweater down over her hands, her fingers gripping the bunched cloth. The lawyer told her politely that it would be better for her to sit straight in the chair, not hunched like a child. He was about to say something else when the door opened. There were two of them, the same ones who had questioned her before. There was the tall man with the dark complexion, Guðgeir or Guðmar, she couldn't remember exactly what he had said his name was. She had felt that he was agreeable, and had noticed that he was sensitive. There was no doubt about that, she felt it clearly, and she quickly figured out that he was also very clever. The last time they had spoken he had unerringly found a weak point in her account, and she could understand now how he had easily found her out. Up to then, everything she had said had been true and correct, but then she had wrecked her own credibility with a single lie. That couldn't be allowed to happen again. Would they believe her now if she were to tell the whole truth? She wasn't sure that they would.

The woman with the ponytail and the broad, open face was Elsa Guðrún, and Diljá immediately felt a connection to her. They had to be around the same age, although Elsa Guðrún was possibly a couple of years older. Diljá's feeling was that she would be more likely to believe her as there seemed to be a warmth to her. But it would be best to be cautious, so she wouldn't catch her out as Guðgeir had done. The pair of them were no doubt doing their jobs, but they had just one objective and that was to find her guilty as quickly as possible. The quicker they could do that, the sooner they could go back to unconcernedly mowing their lawns or barbecuing with their families, or whatever they did when they weren't at work. They would undoubtedly have forgotten Diljá Sigurðardóttir the moment their backs were turned. She was just one more case they had to deal with. The media would cover the verdict in a few words and she would be left to rot in prison, to her own eternal shame and that of her family.

Diljá felt her hands shaking and she gripped the cloth of her sweater between her fingers even harder to keep them still, but she followed the lawyer's advice, putting her feet on the floor and sitting up straight. There were the usual greetings, and they introduced themselves by name again, presumably for the benefit of the recording. So, the man was Guðgeir, and not Guðmar, as she had thought in her confusion. He placed his glasses case on the table in front of him and said something she couldn't make out to the lawyer whose name she couldn't remember, and who looked at her sternly. She looked back into his eyes. Yes, she would speak truthfully and correctly, regardless of whether or not they would take any notice of her words.

'I just wanted to make sure he slept. I never thought that he might die. You have to believe me. You must! Just this once!' The words tumbled out of her before either of them had a chance to open their mouths.

'All right. Tell us what you were doing during the night,' Elsa Guðrún said, looking at her intently.

'I was with Ásmundur. We went up to the highest peak above Herjólfsdalur. It's a long way,' Diljá said. She was determined to push the truth to its limits.

'In the middle of the night?' Guðgeir asked, appearing perplexed.

She felt that his eyes could drill holes right through her, which had the strange effect of making her doubt the veracity of her own words, even though she was telling the truth.

'It's August and there's still light at night, and we had head torches with us to be sure,' she explained cautiously.

'All right. And then what?' Guðgeir asked.

'We must have been up there for more than an hour. We looked out over the sea and talked for ages, meditated, and we danced,' Diljá said, and felt their disbelief reverberate around the room. The lawyer coughed, as if reproaching her.

'Did you keep an eye on the caravan?' Elsa Guðrún asked.

'No. I saw no reason to. I was sure that Ríkharður would sleep soundly,' she replied. 'Because of the drugs.'

'Why didn't you simply tell him that you wanted to climb the mountain during the night? Wouldn't that have been a more honest way to go about things?'

Guðgeir's dark eyes bored through her and she could sense the coldness in his voice. She understood clearly that what had made perfect sense to her a few days ago sounded ridiculous under these circumstances.

'He would never have understood,' she muttered. 'Not ever.'

'What did you and Ásmundur talk about?' Elsa Guðrún asked, a touch of warmth in her voice.

'About the trip,' she mumbled, fiddling with a thumbnail that had split.

'A trip for the two of you?' Guðgeir asked, picking his glasses up from the case.

'Yes. And maybe a few others who would come too,' Diljá replied, gnawing at the thumbnail.

'Who?' Elsa Guðrún asked.

'Ingi Thór and Eygló. They went with us the time before,' she said, and sniffed.

'But not Katrín?'

Diljá shook her head.

'No, she's not coming with us.'

'Why not?' Guðgeir asked, seeking eye contact, but she looked away.

'She doesn't understand,' Diljá replied. She wasn't able to continue, as she was suddenly shaken by a fit of sneezing. She clapped a hand over her mouth and nose. Her eyes filled with tears and her palm with mucus. The lawyer handed her a tissue and hand sanitiser. She wiped her face and cleaned her hands. She could feel the pressure growing in her temples, and suspected that she had sinusitis.

'What is there to understand?' Guðgeir asked, pushing the box of tissues towards her.

'Ach. Doesn't matter,' Diljá replied, taking her time to reach for a tissue, folding it carefully and blowing her nose. She felt it wouldn't be worth going any further down this route. It wouldn't work, as these two would never understand what she meant, and they could easily wreck something that was important to her, and she didn't have much left.

'Yes. It does matter. Where were you planning to go?' Guðgeir cajoled, his dark eyes fixed on hers.

'It doesn't matter because you'd never understand,' she muttered.

'Give us a chance and let's hear it,' Guðgeir said, taking the little white cloth from the case and starting to polish his glasses.

It's one of his tactics, Diljá thought, looking sideways at what he was doing. Or was it just a mannerism? Whatever it was, it strung out her nerves. Guðgeir folded the cloth precisely into four, unfolded it again, and then laid one half over the other. Then he polished each lens in turn with great care. She longed to ask him to stop doing this, but didn't. No, she wasn't going to humour him.

'Was this planned trip going to be expensive?' Elsa Guðrún asked after a moment's silence.

'Yes. Very,' Diljá said, her voice low. She drew her feet again up onto the chair and wrapped her arms around them. She tugged at the sleeves of her sweater, which pulled at the wide neckline. She had a strong feeling that she shouldn't say anything to these people about the big trip. What was precious to her was no importance to them.

'I can see you have a tattoo on your shoulder. Am I right in thinking it's a snake?' Elsa Guðrún asked in a mild tone, smiling.

'Yes,' Diljá mumbled.

'Is it big?' Elsa Guðrún asked, clearly interested.

'Not that big. It reaches a little way down my back,' she said, running her fingers over the snake's head.

'Does it have some personal meaning for you?'

'Yes, it's very personal to me. I can't talk about this now, but the snake protects me and gives me strength,' Diljá said sincerely, and to her surprise felt a strong intuition that this police woman appeared to know what she was talking about, because she looked deep into her eyes and there was sympathy in her gaze.

'It's good that you have a protector,' Elsa Guðrún said, and stood up. 'I suggest we take a quick break, and we leave the room for a moment, Guðgeir.'

He nodded, although there was a look of surprise on his face and he got slowly to his feet.

'We'll be back in a few minutes,' Elsa Guðrún said as they went through the door.

37

Elsa Guðrún strode along the corridor with Guðgeir following a few paces behind her until they reached the office. She sat at a computer and began to tap at the keyboard.

'Hold on. I need to look something up.'

'Is this going to take long?' Guðgeir asked impatiently. 'We were just starting to make some progress in there.'

'You know I was at a rather special place at the weekend,' Elsa Guðrún said, looking at him intently and her deep blue eyes glittering.

'Weren't you out drinking some kind of South American cocoa with a bunch of people?'

'I was. But this isn't ski chalet cocoa,' Elsa Guðrún explained. 'As you know, I haven't been as well emotionally as I would like to be, and an old friend recommended this type of weekend retreat, and in a moment of madness, I decided to go. To tell the truth, I found the whole thing a very odd experience, along with this pure cacao you're given to drink with some kind of ingredient that affects the central nervous system. The people running the retreat seemed to think this was something out of this world. It's supposed to open your heart, and all sorts of blah, blah, blah. People are encouraged to open up about traumatic experiences and all kinds of deeply personal stuff. When it got to that point, I wasn't sure about all this, and some of the things that went on there just didn't feel right.'

'And so what? What connection does this have to the

interrogation?' Guðgeir asked, genuinely impatient now that he was faced with this unexpected interruption.

'You remember when we said that what all five of them have in common is that they are searching for something spiritual, they had all had difficult early years or suffered a trauma?' Elsa Guðrún said and Guðgeir nodded. 'I have this in common with all of them,' she continued. 'Like practically everyone who took part in the cacao retreat.'

'Understood,' Guðgeir said, glancing at the clock.

'You remember Ásmundur's tattoo?' Elsa Guðrún asked quickly.

'The snake, yes. And Diljá has something similar?'

'That's it. And that's the heart of the matter. Look at this,' Elsa Guðrún said, pointing at the screen.

There were images of tattooed bodies and body parts. Guðgeir had left his glasses in the interview room, and he leaned close to see more clearly. These were colourful tattoos, snakes and serpents, with piercing eyes.

'What do you have in mind? What's the connection?' Guðgeir asked as he looked up from the screen. His interest had been sparked.

'When I got home I started doing some reading about this cacao, and found that there is an ingredient, in small amounts, which is a narcotic, and so I looked further and found all kinds of websites. When Diljá said something about the big trip they had all made, except Katrín, because back then Diljá and Ásmundur were a couple, then I started to understand...' Elsa Guðrún said, about to continue when Guðgeir interrupted.

'But I don't, and I'm losing the plot here,' he said in confusion.

'All right. You know what ayahuasca is?' she asked, unable to hide her own impatience.

'Well, I've heard something about it,' he said, his brow furrowed in thought. 'Some kind of rich people's dope?'

'Exactly. Ayahuasca contains an ingredient that's

hallucinogenic. The same ingredient is present in cacao, but in very small amounts. I'm certain that the four of them went to South America together, to Peru, Costa Rica or Guatemala, for one of these ayahuasca trips. You've heard about these holidays?'

Elsa Guðrún looked intently into his eyes.

'No. But I've heard of this kind of thing here in Iceland. How does this work, exactly?' Guðgeir asked.

'To be brief, it's a ceremony, normally conducted by a shaman or a person known as a mother. It's supposed to be a spiritual journey with the aim of working on emotional problems or damage that the person in question has suffered. They drink this ayahuasca, which is referred to as tea, and it's supposed to taste terrible. It's made from a plant that grows in the Amazon jungle, and it gets people high. That's to say, after they've thrown up and had raging diarrhoea for hours on end, or even days, which is supposed to be a cleansing so that the person can get in deeper touch with their spiritual self. In reality, the journey is a trip, as the tea contains all sorts of hallucinogenics, like DMT does. People see all kinds of visions, like old-fashioned hippies dropping LSD, and for some reason ayahuasca has much the same spiritual imagery. They talk about it as if it gives you some kind of supernatural powers. People genuinely believe that they are in touch with some higher power and that they are cleaning up their lives, when what they are experiencing is an acid trip. Ayahuasca has become very popular with a certain group of people here in Iceland.'

'And the snake? That tattoo, what about that?' Guðgeir asked, now both excited and fascinated. He was sure that Elsa Guðrún was on the right track. This was a connection he would never have been able to make.

'It's supposed to be a deity of some kind, and many people encounter a snake or a serpent during an ayahuasca trip,' Elsa Guðrún said. 'Or some other animal. You can find pictures of those tattoos online.'

'And the big trip that she and Ásmundur were planning up on a mountain top above Herjólfsdalur...' Guðgeir said, and Elsa Guðrún broke in to finish his sentence.

'Was going to be another trip to South America, and you can imagine how much something like that in the middle of a South American jungle is going to cost, considering the crazy price of a cacao weekend like the one I went on. When they take ayahuasca, they travel with seventy or eighty other people to some remote place for several days. Ceremonies take place every day, and people lie on mattresses and each one has a bucket for vomit and other bodily needs. That happens mostly during the first few days, while people believe they are purging themselves of evil spirits, like I told you just now.'

'And they make a fortune from these rich westerners who are desperately searching for fulfilment,' Guðgeir said, his expression hardening.

'Those are your words, not mine,' Elsa Guðrún said. 'So shall we go back and talk to Diljá again?'

38

It was unfortunate that Diljá had shifted in the chair by the time they returned and the snake could no longer be seen. Guðgeir was disappointed, as he would have liked to have been able to compare it against what he had seen on the computer screen. He nodded to the lawyer, whose expression made it clear that the long break was not appreciated.

'Could my client have some water?' he asked tersely.

'Of course,' Elsa Guðrún said, leaving the room again. Guðgeir said nothing, but took a seat and waited quietly for her to return. He sat with his hands tightly clenched, looking down at them in thought.

'Diljá also requests a larger cell,' the lawyer continued. 'She suffers badly from claustrophobia.'

'Unfortunately it's not possible to accommodate her, but the request is acknowledged,' Guðgeir replied and looked up as the door swung open.

'Here you go,' Elsa Guðrún said, handing Diljá a glass.

'Thanks.'

She gulped down the water; she had clearly been thirsty.

'So, let's pick up where we left off. We were discussing the ayahuasca snake,' Guðgeir said, his expression impassive. 'On the night in question you went up into the rocks above Herjólfsdalur for some spiritual reasons and to dream about another trip to South America. Did I understand you correctly?'

Diljá was obviously unsure how to react, glancing at each of them in turn, noticeably confused.

'How...? How...?' she stammered uncertainly.

'I've been on some of these cacao retreats,' Elsa Guðrún said, allowing herself a little exaggeration. 'Of course I get to hear a few things. I've also had to come to terms with an emotional trauma, and someone who meant well mentioned this possibility to me.'

'That's right,' Diljá said, sitting up straighter in her chair. Her large brown eyes were no longer as furtive as they had been.

'So could you explain all this for us a little more clearly?' Elsa Guðrún said softly. She rested her chin on her hands, elbows on the table. Every line of her face showed her keen interest.

Diljá glanced to the lawyer, who seemed just as keen to hear what she had to say to the two police officers. She hesitated, and haltingly began to speak, occasionally glancing at Elsa Guðrún as if seeking approval.

'I've always struggled. My life has been full of all sorts of problems. I've tried everything, done my best to find solutions to get myself out of the mess, and then I met Ásmundur in one of these groups. We were searching for... Ach. There's so much. Ingi and Eygló have been running these ceremonies in their summer house. We got to know them, and it grew from there. I was always skint, always saving to pay lawyers over the custody case, and the psychiatrists. The personal training course was expensive until I got a few clients of my own. Endless debts, payday loans, crazy interest. It was all shit and I was constantly running to stand still. But we managed to get an ayahuasca trip to Peru. Ásmundur helped me with that...' Diljá said, and fell silent, pushing her hair back behind her ears. Her face brightened and she seemed to gain a new confidence. 'It was a fantastic experience and it changed all our lives. I started doing better and things that had been so complicated were so much clearer, if you see what I mean. Then time passed after we came back from the trip and all four of us had a strong feeling that we needed to go again. I still need to get myself straightened out, and Ingi Thór, for instance, has had a difficult spiritual journey and he's been struggling because he's stuck in the same place he was before. It's vital for him to go back and finish what he started.'

'What trip are you talking about?' Guðgeir asked.

'Ayahuasca sends you where you need to be. Sometimes it's important to work out difficult stuff, and ayahuasca is a mirror on your life that can be hard and merciless,' Diljá said, speaking with the conviction of a true believer.

'I understand,' Guðgeir lied, as he understood practically nothing. 'Tell me where Ríkharður fitted into all this.'

'My mistake,' Diljá said, and her face fell.

'Yours?' Elsa Guðrún asked.

'Yeah. I was still struggling to pay off the overdraft after the trip to Peru, and all the other stuff. Then Covid came along and I was earning next to nothing. It wasn't long after we got to know each other that he started to help me financially. I really thought that I'd be able to stay with him for a few years, but I was being stifled...'

Diljá fell suddenly silent, a furtive look in her eyes.

'But you married him only a month ago,' Guðgeir pointed out in his own down-to-earth manner.

'That's true. And right away I felt like I was being suffocated,' Diljá said heavily. 'You have to believe me. He wasn't supposed to die. I'm no murderer. I was fond of Ríkharður, even though I couldn't stand to be with him any longer. I didn't wish him anything bad.'

Guðgeir and Elsa Guðrún exchanged glances. This was the moment to bring Diljá up to date, and to take careful note of her reactions.

'We have new results from the autopsy. According to these, Ríkharður's cause of death was suffocation,' Guðgeir said darkly.

Diljá gasped, and her surprise seemed to be genuine.

'What? How could that happen?' she wailed, her distress at

this new development unmistakable as she clasped both hands over her mouth and huddled in the chair.

'We don't know,' Elsa Guðrún said, watching her carefully.

'Then I'm free?' she asked, visibly relieved. 'Can I go home now?'

Guðgeir shook his head and gazed at her seriously.

'You're remanded in custody for a week, and you have to remain...'

'Under these circumstances, it's unlikely that will be extended.'

This time it was the lawyer, who had up to now sat in silence, interrupting Guðgeir.

'There's every likelihood that you'll be able to leave here after the weekend.'

'So I'll be cleared of everything?'

Diljá's eyes went to each of them in turn.

'No. You're not beyond suspicion, and there will undoubtedly be a penalty for doping your husband,' Guðgeir replied, a grim look on his face as he stared at her. 'But in the light of this latest information, I can tell you that someone gave you away. We had a tip-off from an unregistered number, but we'll find out soon enough who called. However, you could save us time and effort by telling the truth.' Guðgeir leaned forward, frowning and with his eyes fixed on Diljá. 'So now I want to know. Who knew you were there in the summer house?'

She sat motionless, as if in shock. Then her face darkened and her expression hardened.

'Ásmundur,' she said at last. 'Nobody else knew.'

39

Guðgeir powered through the water, taking breaths to left and right on alternate strokes, his legs pumping. He pushed off from the side of the pool again and again, and it wasn't until he had completed a dozen lengths that he felt he had cleansed his thoughts after the working day.

He took off his goggles, shook the water from his ears and got out of the pool. He was relieved to see that there were few people in the hottest of the hot tubs. Normally he enjoyed chatting there about anything and everything, but today he was in no mood for conversation. He needed to digest these new twists in the Heimaey case without being disturbed. He had experienced a great many strange things in his career and encountered the stranger side of what people could get up to, but this ayahuasca or whatever it was called that had become part of the investigation was something he hadn't come across before. A brief search online had taken him to interviews and podcasts about this stuff. He had speed-read through some of this, scanned articles and listened to people recounting their experiences, and he was still astonished that people from tiny Iceland were prepared to travel all the way to the jungles of South America to drink some muck that would give them a buzz.

Guðgeir let himself sink deep into the scalding water so that it covered his tired shoulders and lapped at his stiff neck. He took deep breaths of cold evening air and closed his eyes. What was the reason for this? Was it a need to find some higher plane of reason for this life or to worship at the ideal of something higher than man? Had the dismantling of the old belief systems resulted in an emptiness in the lives of modern people? A shortfall in spiritual health? He thought of his parents in the west of Iceland who had worked hard all their lives, and who on Sundays either went to church or listened to the service on the radio. Their values were clear and their aims were simple: to bring up their children well, have enough left to pay for their own funerals and to have no debts to anyone.

He and Inga had also worked hard in their younger years, although in a different fashion to his parents. Instead of going to church, Sundays had been spent working on their house, one of a new terrace, and Ólöf, then just a few months old, had been with them, playing as they worked. When Pétur Andri was born, he naturally became part of all this. The build took time, and it was a delight to see each step completed, and friends and relatives frequently pitched in to help. Of course there were tradesmen as well, but it was the contributions of the family that were most welcome. He and Inga had only ever been to church at particular times – Christmas, christenings and confirmations, weddings and funerals – but their childhood faith was still there and they had taught their children to say their prayers.

After moving in to the house, there had been a steady flow of guests, and they also often visited friends and relatives. Guðgeir couldn't remember any feelings of emptiness during those years. There had simply been too much to do, and he looked back on those days with longing. These days visitors were rarer and everything had become so much more formal. Despite all the technology designed to make life easier, everyone was so much busier.

His thoughts drifted from the emptiness of modern life to the accounts of those who had taken ayahuasca, recounting the vomiting and fearsome diarrhoea that were the precursors of visions. These young people seemed to believe firmly that these physical reactions were some sort of cleansing, that something bad or even downright evil was being expelled in this way, as they were prepared to drink this crap without having any idea what it might contain. This was something he found baffling.

Guðgeir felt his head swim slightly, which told him he had spent long enough in the scalding water. He stood up, waded to the steps and left the hot tub. He had become lost in his own thoughts and had spent too long in there.

He sat on a bench for a moment, and when he felt better, he took a cold shower and dressed in one of the outside cubicles. Walking away from the swimming pool afterwards, he felt a surge of renewed energy and wellbeing.

On the way home, he called Elsa Guðrún.

'So, what do you think of this new turn of events?' he asked eagerly.

'I've hardly had time to think about it,' she replied. 'I've been busy collecting the boys from the airport. We're just going to the car now, and they're pretty lively after being spoiled up north, to put it mildly.'

'Understood. I'll see you tomorrow,' Guðgeir said, and ended the call.

Instead of going home, he took the opportunity to drive out to Grótta to think things over in solitude. Once he was there, he gave in to the temptation to take a short walk along the shore. There were few people about and the stillness was broken only by the murmur of waves and the calls of birds pecking for food in the shingle. It was a clear evening and he could make out the plume of rising smoke from the Fagradalsfjall eruption in one direction and the white peak of Snæfellsjökull in the other. Walking back, he could clearly see the buildings of Akranes across the bay, although Esja's blue-green slopes naturally drew the eye more than anything else. He took a seat on a bench made from coarse trunks of driftwood, looking out over the sea.

New angles to the case had certainly opened up today, but

there were other aspects of this that also deserved to be investigated. Guðgeir took out his phone and looked up the number for Ríkharður's sister Ingibjörg. There was no reply. He tried again, with the same result, so he sent a text message, before standing up and going to the car.

Inga and Ólöf were deep in conversation on the sofa when he came home, while his little namesake slept in the cot in his and Inga's bedroom. Guðgeir waved to them, and went straight to see his grandson, who had stretched out on the duvet, his cheeks rosy after a day in the fresh air. He slept soundly, totally relaxed and trusting. Guðgeir smiled and reached out to touch his silky hair. What future lay ahead of this little child? What would the world look like when he was the same age as Diljá? Would Guðgeir Jökull feel a need to search for answers to life's conundrums in some South American jungle by taking hallucinogenic drugs?

His phone emitted a low ping, as Ingibjörg replied to his message. She could meet him at eight in the morning at her home, because she had to be at work no later than nine-thirty.

That's fine, he thought to himself as he sent an immediate reply. The sooner he could talk to her, the better.

'Guðgeir!' Inga called out to him. 'Can you come here? We need a word with you.'

He laid a gentle finger on the boy's cheek, and left the room.

'Don't you want to stay here tonight?' he asked Ólöf. 'Guðgeir Jökull is so fast asleep it's a shame to wake him up.'

'No thanks, Dad. It's best if we go home. I'll carry him out to the car and he won't wake up. No problem.'

'All right, sweetheart. Up to you,' he said, with a twinge of disappointment. He had been looking forward to waking up with the little boy in the morning. 'What did you want to talk to me about?'

'Well, his father is arriving in Iceland tomorrow and asked if he could stay with us for a couple of days, and I said yes. I just wanted to let you know.'

Guðgeir felt a stab of unease. Why did Smári have to show

up right now, just as Ólöf was doing so well? Just as she had been getting over their relationship coming to an end. The little lad was doing so well, and Ólöf was making great progress in her legal studies. Couldn't the man just stay in Spain and leave them in peace? Guðgeir sighed, and did his best to force a smile.

'Sounds good,' he said, his voice neutral, as he caught Inga's eye. As far as he could make out, she had no objections to the arrangement. He felt that sometimes she could be too positive.

'Does Smári have to stay with you and Guðgeir Jökull? Doesn't he have friends or relatives who could help him out with a place to stay?'

'It'll be just a couple of weeks, and then he'll move to a rented place not far from us,' Ólöf explained.

'OK, but is that certain? Has he signed a rental agreement?' Guðgeir asked, his expression hardening. Why the hell did Smári always have to cause upset and trouble wherever he went?

'Yes, of course he has! What's the matter with you, Dad?' she asked sharply, catching his eye and holding it firmly.

40

Guðgeir set off early the following morning for Grafarvogur, determined to not be even a minute late for the meeting with Ingibjörg. Fortunately, most of the weight of traffic was in the other direction, so there were no serious delays on the way. It was still a few minutes to eight when he turned in to a district of apartment blocks that all looked more or less the same. He searched for the right number and saw a face framed by long black hair appear for a moment at a window as he parked in a space outside the right block.

'Good morning. Guðgeir Fransson, from the police,' he said.

'Hello, come in,' Ingibjörg said, after opening the door as soon he rang the bell. 'Vilhjálmur and Lára would have liked to have been here as well, but since their father died they have both had to take so much time off that I couldn't ask them to...'

'I understand,' Guðgeir said, interrupting to end the flow of apology.

'They'll need to be away from work for a few more days when it comes to the funeral, as you can understand,' Ingibjörg continued. 'Whenever that is.'

'That should all become clear in the next few days,' Guðgeir said.

She showed him to an overfull living room. He had the strong feeling that she must have moved from somewhere much larger to live in this apartment that appeared to be slightly too small. Maybe Ingibjörg had to cram all her belongings in here, unless she suffered from a compulsive shopping condition and was unable to stop herself. The predominant colour was black, although a white vase with stripes in many colours stood out from its place on a black sideboard. Candlesticks of the same brand – Guðgeir couldn't remember the name, but knew it was a popular one – stood on three lines of shelves, along with heavier candles placed in holders and by mirrors. Two tall, ornate lamps gleamed from where they stood among feathers, reindeer horns and other items.

A long black table with a mirrored top and two black sofas covered in an array of cushions of all shapes and sizes took up most of the floor space and at the end of the living room was a kitchenette, also outfitted in black. Guðgeir picked his way through the maze of furniture and ornaments. It was an ordeal for a man of his height not to knock into anything. He sat on a corner of one of the sofas, his shins close up to the coffee table.

'Can I offer you anything? Coffee, tea? Water?' Ingibjörg asked, white teeth glinting behind plump scarlet lips. It was clear that this woman paid serious attention to her appearance and made an effort to look her best. He sensed that there was a sadness that was an integral part of her. He declined, explaining that breakfast hadn't been that long ago. Besides, he couldn't see how a coffee cup would fit onto the overfull table before him.

'Well, then. What can I do for you?' she asked, a sharp note in her voice as she pushed a few cushions aside to make space to sit, and was immediately on her feet again. 'Should I let some fresh air in? I'm at work so much that I'm hardly ever at home, and there are no windows on the other side, no air flow, you see.'

Without waiting for an answer, she pulled open a door leading to a small area of decking with a fence around it. As far as Guðgeir could see, that was also packed with furniture, statues and plants. He was relieved as the fresh air filled the dim apartment and the morning sun flooded in. He could breathe more easily, and realised that he had suffered a touch of claustrophobia. He thought of Diljá in her cell.

Ingibjörg returned, smoothed down her snug-fitting top and tucked her dark hair behind her ears.

'How is the family coping?' Guðgeir asked.

'Not bad, all things considered,' Ingibjörg sighed. 'It's a relief to know that wretched girl is behind bars. Has she confessed?'

'No,' Guðgeir replied.

'She will, sooner or later,' Ingibjörg snapped.

'Her custody comes to an end at midday tomorrow and it won't be extended,' Guðgeir said, carefully watching for any reaction this news might trigger.

'And why not?' she demanded, visibly surprised. 'You can't let her go free.'

'We have new information and no longer see any reason to hold her.'

'But Diljá poisoned him!' Ingibjörg protested, her voice rising.

'Where did you hear that?' Guðgeir responded.

'Everyone knows that!' she retorted.

Guðgeir decided to leave it there.

'You mentioned coffee just now. Maybe I could do with a cup after all,' he said with a friendly smile. It seemed the right thing to do to allow her an opportunity to let her nerves settle before they went any further.

Without a word, she stood up and went over to the kitchenette. He stayed where he was, gazing out of the window that was shaded with dark blinds, pondering how to continue the conversation. The windowsills were just as crowded as every other surface in this apartment. But instead of flower vases, candlesticks and ornaments, there were rows of framed pictures. Guðgeir put on his glasses and leaned closer. There was Ríkharður with his children and a blonde woman with them. He glanced up and saw that Ingibjörg was busy brewing coffee in a cup.

'Ordinary coffee or espresso? Or I could do a latte?' she called out over the roar of the machine.

'A latte would be lovely,' he said, confident that it would take her longer to prepare. As far as he could see, the blonde woman in the photo was Ingibjörg herself, just a younger and more normal-looking version of her.

'Thank you,' he said with a warm smile as she handed him a glass of milky coffee. He had no appetite for it, but sipped it for courtesy's sake. Ingibjörg again took a seat on the sofa by the window. Her synthetic leather trousers squeaked against the genuine leather of the sofa.

'Your brother's children have lost their father and that's an ordeal in itself,' Guðgeir said sympathetically. 'But for it to happen in this manner is even more of a shock... How about you? Do you have someone you can talk to?'

'The priest was fine,' she said.

'Were you close, you and your brother?'

'My brother Ríkharður has always been at my side and always supported me in every way. Right up until...'

She fell silent, unable to hide her bitterness.

'Until he met Diljá?' Guðgeir said, finishing her words for her.

'Yes. She was simply looking for a sugar daddy, someone to pay her way. As far as I'm concerned, Diljá is nothing more than a slut, plus she's off her head. This isn't just my opinion, in case you were wondering.'

'And Ríkharður? If that was the situation, don't you think he would have seen through her?' Guðgeir asked, moving aside a porcelain pineapple so that he could put down the glass.

Ingibjörg shook her head and snorted in derision.

'The smartest men, like him, can be unbelievably stupid when it comes to things like this.'

'Was there a similar situation with your own divorce?' Guðgeir asked and saw Ingibjörg's face immediately tighten.

'I don't see how my personal affairs are related to my

brother's death,' she said, picking up a phone that lay on the sofa beside her. 'It's getting late and I have to get to work.'

Guðgeir pretended he hadn't heard her.

'In fact, your personal affairs don't have any significant bearing, but I understand that your former husband is the father of one of the group who were there in the Westman Islands.'

'I heard that as well. But I have no contact with Katrín. She was already practically grown up when I got to know her father.'

'Is it long since the divorce?'

'Five years and it's only now that I'm getting back on my feet. He had fixed things so that I emerged from that marriage practically destitute. Since then I've been trying hard not to have to pay the debts he racked up,' she said, her expression calm, but her voice as cold as ice.

'Well, I won't keep you any longer. I have to get to work as well,' Guðgeir said lightly, as if he had just dropped by for a coffee with an old friend, and the call had nothing to do with work. 'I just wanted to keep you informed about the custody. It's not something that the close family should just hear about or read in the media. I'll leave it to you to inform Lára and Vilhjálmur.'

'I'll do that, of course,' Ingibjörg said, softening. 'Thanks for stopping by. It may sound strange, but it was lovely to see you.'

She smiled.

'Speaking of them, how did Lára and Diljá get on?'

'Ach. Not well. My brother was a strong personality who could be forceful and this girl was nowhere near being a good match for him, to say the least,' Ingibjörg said, shaking her head so that her black hair shimmered.

'Were you alone when you heard the news?' Guðgeir asked, making an effort to come across as concerned.

'Maybe not completely alone,' she said. 'I stayed at Hotel Rangá that weekend. I had a gift voucher from work, you see,' she said with a smile, as if needing to provide an explanation for how she had been able to stay somewhere so expensive.

'It's not far from Hotel Rangá to the Landeyjarhöfn terminal,' Guðgeir said. 'It's remarkable what coincidences life can throw our way.'

'Exactly. I noticed there was a lot of police traffic as I was driving home that Sunday. I was almost back in town when the call came and I still don't understand how I managed to get all the way home without causing an accident.'

41

The atmosphere at the station was unusually quiet. Guðgeir nodded right and left as he made his way to his office, where he hung his jacket on the back of his chair. This sent a signal that he wasn't far away. Then he sauntered over to find Leifur. There were still no DNA results from the samples taken from the pillows and pillowcases in the caravan, but Leifur was able to give him the encouraging news that further samples had been found on the duvet cover.

'Four hairs,' Leifur said. 'They're fair and I'd expect the person to have wavy hair.'

'How long?' Guðgeir asked.

'Not that long. Twelve to seventeen centimetres, but that doesn't necessarily mean anything. This individual could have longer hair, as there are always shorter hairs among them on every scalp, and these could also have been cut shorter.'

'These aren't from Diljá. She has dark hair,' Guðgeir said. 'And they aren't from Ríkharður.'

'That's true. It's unlikely, but they might not be from the killer, whoever that is. They could belong to the salesman who sold Ríkharður the caravan, or one of the other staff there. Then there's also the possibility that it could have been open for people to view. In that case, these could belong to anyone, but it'll become clearer when we get the DNA results.'

After speaking to Leifur, Guðgeir made some calls from his desk, and it was confirmed that the hair samples were unlikely to have come from the broker who sold the caravan. It had never got as far as their showroom, in addition to which none of the bedclothes had been provided with it and the mattresses had been supplied still in their factory covering for the new owners to remove.

Guðgeir's next move had been to visit Diljá in her cell. This time she was brighter and willingly answered all his questions. She recalled that she and Ríkharður had stopped at Selfoss on the way to the Landeyjarhöfn terminal to buy duvets, pillows and bedclothes. They had made the beds there, and left the packaging in the shop's bin. Their four friends had done no more than put their heads around the door, without coming inside.

He stood up from his computer to fetch a large pad he kept in the locker. Sometimes he found it easier to make the connections in a case with a pencil and paper than by using some computer programme. He tore out one sheet and used a red biro to write Ríkharður's name in the middle and drew a circle around it.

Wavy fair hair was something that fitted just one of the group of friends – Ingi Thór, the mysterious builder with the social media following who also presided over ceremonies of some kind in his summer house. Guðgeir added his name to the sheet of paper, joining it to Ríkharður's with a line of dots. Then he went back to his computer to search online. He spent some time reading about ayahuasca, and found that its effects were not always positive, and that some people had faced terrible incidents from their past under its influence, without being able to resolve them. These people were left in a worse state than before. During her statement, Diljá had said that Ingi Thór's ayahuasca experience had been difficult, and he had not been able to move on from it. That made it vital for him to try another such trip. But how did this connect to Ríkharður the doctor? Was there something dubious in his past? Could he have had some connection to ayahuasca?

Guðgeir made a note on another sheet of paper and wanted

to draw a line between Ingi Thór and Ríkharður, but had to settle for another dotted line. Then he decided to add Ingibjörg's name to the list. Her divorce from Katrín's father had been described as more than difficult and complex, it might even be described as brutal; according to what he had been told Ingibjörg's bitterness towards her former husband was crystal clear. She had done nothing to hold back concerning her opinion of Diljá, the woman who had taken her brother from her.

'My brother Ríkharður has always been at my side and always supported me in every way. Right up until...' Ingibjörg had said. Guðgeir took the cap off the biro, and drew another broken line, this time connecting the siblings. Ingibjörg claimed to have spent the night Ríkharður died at Hotel Rangá. Guðgeir reached for the phone.

'She was travelling alone and spent the night in a double room,' said the man who picked up the phone. 'I was on reception myself and remember her clearly.'

'Can you see how she paid her bill?' Guðgeir said.

'Yes. She had a gift voucher, with dinner and breakfast included. I don't see anything else on her bill.'

'Was this a fair-haired woman?' Guðgeir asked.

'No. She had very dark hair. Well, obviously dyed black, you know?'

Guðgeir decided that was enough. He put Lára's name next to Ingibjörg's. Then he added Katrín to the cast of characters. He recalled her perfectly straight hair and long, blue nails. He wondered why she made an effort to come across as stupider than she really was. Had she something to hide? He joined her name to Ríkharður's with another dotted line.

Then he texted Elsa Guðrún.

Is it easy to straighten wavy hair?

The answer came back right away.

Easiest thing in the world. You just use straighteners. Why?

Just wondering, still waiting for results, Guðgeir tapped in.

Gotcha, Elsa Guðrún replied, adding a symbol showing a

yellow face with one eye closed and a red tongue sticking out.

He had no idea what the symbol was supposed to mean and had no time to spend finding out, so replied with a thumbs up.

Guðgeir sat for some time over the sheet of paper, rolling the pen between his fingers, removing the cap and replacing it, and staring at the list of names. Then he again read through all of the statements they had taken in the Westman Islands. Finally, he took his jacket from the back of the chair, and went out to let Elsa Guðrún know that he needed to go out for a while.

'Going to spend some time in the sun?' she said, and winked.

'Just a little while. Won't be long,' he said, and was gone.

42

Ingi Thór's workshop was on a long-established industrial estate and it took Guðgeir a while to find it, hidden away behind other buildings. It was only when he reached a wide gate behind the old paint factory that he noticed the ITI Carpentry sign. Next to it was a half-completed summer chalet, and a man in work trousers and grey shirt was busy on the roof. His back was to Guðgeir, but the fair hair that brushed his broad shoulders was familiar.

'Good morning,' Guðgeir called out, taking off his sunglasses, and Ingi Thór was clearly startled to see who had come to see him, as the ladder he was standing on wobbled alarmingly. 'Take care... I didn't mean to take you by surprise,' he said, taking care to sound jovial. 'Is this a bad time?'

'Now? No, not at all,' Ingi Thór replied. 'I was about to take a break.'

He clambered carefully down the steps, which gave Guðgeir time to take in the python's head baring its teeth on his arm.

'I was passing, and it seemed a good idea to drop by and ask a few questions. Nothing formal. Just a few gaps in your statement in the Westman Islands that need to be filled in. That looks a real beast,' he added, gesturing with his folded sunglasses at the man's tattoo.

'Ha! Yeah,' Ingi Thór said, his hand going instinctively to his arm. 'I set this guy on people who don't pay their bills,' he said with a forced laugh.

'You're mostly building chalets?'

'Yes, it's a big part of our work, but we do all kinds of things,' Ingi Thór replied, putting down his hammer and running his hands through his wavy hair. 'We'll do pretty much any job. Do you have some work you need doing?'

'Me? No,' Guðgeir smiled. 'We're in a fairly new place and everything's in order, and no plans for a summer house. The reason for this is that there's something I need to check. We weren't quite precise enough about timing when we spoke to you in the Westman Islands.'

'Really? We weren't?' Ingi Thór asked in surprise.

'Diljá and Ríkharður left the restaurant before you, and the rest of you stayed there for a while?'

'Yes, but only for a short while. We paid the bill and all that pretty quickly,' he said, gazing at the ladder as if he had other things on his mind than chatting.

'I see. Did Diljá pay their bill?'

'No, they left without paying. Ríkharður was in no state to do anything, and Diljá had her hands full getting him out. I paid their share of the bill and was going to get them to pay me back on the Sunday,' Ingi Thór said. His answer was quick and accurate, as when they had spoken to him before.

'So I guess you haven't been reimbursed?'

'No, of course not,' he said, and his expression made it plain that he thought the question ridiculous.

'Since Ríkharður was in such a state, it didn't occur to you to help Diljá get him to bed?' Guðgeir asked.

Ingi Thór looked uncertain, as if unsure of how to reply.

'Well, actually, no. Diljá was driving ... so it seemed a sort of personal matter.'

'Personal?'

'I mean, when people go way over the top and embarrass themselves, you don't want to add to their embarrassment, do you? It would have been humiliating for Ríkharður the next day if we had made anything of it,' he said, speaking slowly.

'So the four of you walked over to the hotel. The girls went to sleep and you and Ásmundur sat in the bar?'

'Yes, but only for a very short time.'

'What time was that?'

'It was almost eleven. It's not even a bar as such, just a part of the restaurant that's connected to the hotel,' he explained, and he seemed to be avoiding eye contact, glancing to each side, and at the chalet he had been working on.

'Yes, I saw that. Was there anyone else there?' Guðgeir asked.

'No. It was practically closed. The guy behind the bar was putting things away. He served us a drink and he did his stuff while we sat and chatted.'

'Exactly. And we know now that Ásmundur told you that he was going to meet Diljá during the night, and asked you to lie to Katrín that the two of you had been together, if she were to ask,' Guðgeir said. 'You forgot to mention that in your statement.'

Ingi Thór blanched, but quickly recovered.

'Hey, there's no need to make a big deal of it. I made a mistake. I mean, I was in a state of shock over there in the Westman Islands.'

'Weighing that up isn't your job,' Guðgeir said. 'It didn't occur to you that by keeping this quiet you could be hindering an investigation? I hope you realise there are laws about that kind of thing?'

'Can't we ratchet down the tough cop stuff?' Ingi Thór said, lifting his hands as if he were an actor in a film showing he was unarmed. 'I mean when we were in the Islands nobody mentioned murder. It wasn't an interrogation. You made that clear, you and the woman who was with you.'

'So that was why you decided to gloss over the infidelity?'

'It's no big deal, you understand? They just wanted to spend time outside, experience Heimaey and the nature at night time ... I mean, Ríkharður was on a totally different wavelength to the rest of us, and a lot older,' Ingi Thór said.

'Are you telling me that this wasn't a case of normal, old-fashioned infidelity between Diljá and Ásmundur? Why the secrecy, if they were just friends?'

'Hey, yeah. They were a couple at one time, so there might have been something like that going on. What do I know? In any case, he went out to meet her and I went up to the room to go to sleep, just like Eygló and I told you.'

'That'll do,' Guðgeir said, making as if to leave. 'I just needed to get the timing confirmed.'

Ingi Thór's relief was plain.

'No problem, pal. I hope it all works out,' he said, taking a step back.

'Thanks,' Guðgeir said. 'While I remember, I saw somewhere that you were brought up in the Westfjords? That's a coincidence. My family came from the Strands, and I lived in the West for a few years as a child.'

A shadow passed across Ingi Thór's face.

'I'm not from there,' he said firmly. 'Lived near Ísafjörður for a few years.'

'It's a beautiful part of the country.'

'Can't say I noticed,' he said, going over to the ladder and picking up his hammer.

'I won't keep you. Are you working here alone?' Guðgeir, as if he hadn't heard.

'No, there are three of us. The others nipped out,' Ingi Thór replied, clearly disgruntled.

'OK, the chalet looks great,' Guðgeir said, waving a hand as he walked away.

Ingi Thór's phone pinged just as Guðgeir was getting into his car.

'Hey! Hold on!' Guðgeir heard him call out. 'I've just had a request to come and provide you with a DNA sample. What the hell's that all about?'

43

Neither Særós nor Elsa Guðrún were there when Guðgeir got back to the station. He added some notes to the active shared case file and then went over to the coffee room for the skyr with blueberries that had been waiting for him in the fridge. He had just resumed his seat and had sent a message to Leifur asking him to request that the other three of the group of friends provide DNA samples, when Elsa Guðrún hurried in.

'I need a word,' she panted.

'Where have you been?' he asked, wondering what was going on.

'Ach. I needed to sort the boys out. It's an inset day at school, which is a headache for me.'

'Life can get complicated for a single parent,' Guðgeir said, his thoughts going to Ólöf.

'You mean an independent parent,' Elsa Guðrún said, the dimples appearing in her cheeks as she corrected him. 'Yes, it's a puzzle getting all the pieces together, but that's not what I need to talk to you about. There was something I was thinking over as I was driving to Kópavogur and back.'

'Don't you want to sit down?' Guðgeir asked. 'You're gasping for breath.'

'Yes, thanks,' she said, pulling a chair closer and dropping into it. The pause wasn't a long one, and the words tumbled out of her even faster as she got her breath back. 'Look, Guðgeir. I was thinking over how people's attitudes and behaviour towards me changed after the assault. It's almost two years ago, and I feel there are still people who think I'm going to shatter into a thousand pieces if they put one foot wrong.'

'That's certainly because everyone wishes you well,' Guðgeir said quickly. He wanted to give her an encouraging pat on the shoulder, but refrained.

'Well, I don't doubt that people mean well. But sometimes it bugs me. The thing is, I just want to be Elsa Guðrún again, you see? I don't want to be seen by others as Elsa Guðrún the rape victim.'

'I don't think that anyone...' Guðgeir began, and stopped, realising that he might be somehow making light of the ordeal she had endured.

'I find it difficult when people around me are walking on eggshells, acting as if I'm some delicate flower, which I'm definitely not. I mean, hello? I'm a police officer,' she said, her voice rising and she raised her hands in the air to give her words emphasis.

'In that case I'll take care not to... Thanks for the tip,' Guðgeir said, sincerely hoping that it wasn't his behaviour that she was referring to.

'That's fine. But it's Diljá I wanted to talk about, not me,' Elsa Guðrún said, to Guðgeir's great relief. 'When did we first hear that she had suffered from mental health problems?'

He didn't need to think for long.

'It was during the statements session on Sunday. The same day that Ríkharður was found in the caravan, and it was Ingi Thór who mentioned it,' he said, drumming the table with his fingertips.

'Exactly. What I'm driving at is that we focused very quickly on the assumption that Diljá was guilty, and I think our own prejudices played a part in that. Maybe she hasn't enjoyed the complete confidence of others after she was diagnosed as a teenager. In people's minds she has always been crazy Diljá instead of simply Diljá. I mean, aren't we too hasty in labelling people and putting them in a box? We act as if we take a hundred per cent notice of them and their lives, but that knowledge is always there in the background and we base everything they do on that.'

Elsa Guðrún fell silent, arms folded as she waited for Guðgeir's reaction.

'I'm not sure that we aren't getting ahead of ourselves here,' he said cautiously, and felt that he was on the defensive. 'Let's not forget that Diljá fled the scene, and that brought suspicion on her right away, so it was natural that we would assume some level of guilt on her part, and I can remind you that her innocence hasn't been proved yet. She administered narcotics to Ríkharður, and for that matter she could have suffocated him as well or been party to the crime. The question remains, if she's innocent, why did she run for it?'

'Maybe because of her illness? Perhaps because she has so often encountered disbelief and her self-esteem is on really low? Do you see?' Elsa Guðrún looked at him intently, and when no answer was forthcoming, she continued. 'If that's the case, then we will soon have wasted a whole week. For that matter, the real killer could have left the country by now.'

44

What remained of that day was uneventful, but on his way home from work Guðgeir thought over the conversation with Elsa Guðrún and found that it had shaken him up, not least at a personal level. He had never seen himself as someone who harboured prejudices, he thought of himself as an open, broad-minded individual. But how did he see others? Why had he been so upset to hear that Smári, the father of Ólöf's child, was about to return to Iceland? And why had he maintained such a low opinion of this young man? Deep inside, Guðgeir knew the answer. He had always known it, but had dressed up his opinion of Smári as something different, more acceptable. The unvarnished truth of it was that he didn't think he was up to his daughter's level, that he wasn't good enough for her. He felt that Ólöf could have done better, and that she was both cleverer and a better person than Smári. That was the simple reality of it and his suppressed opinion had coloured their relationship right from the outset, while Inga and Smári had immediately formed a good relationship. Guðgeir sighed. *The truth always hurts,* he thought to himself, recalling that Inga had at one point told him that he needed to get to know Smári better.

'It takes two to tango,' she had told him. 'Try doing something together in which Smári has an interest.'

More than likely he should have followed her advice and got to know the young man on his terms rather than on his own. While Guðgeir knew that he hadn't behaved badly towards him, he wondered if Smári sensed that his father-in-law thought he wasn't good enough. Ólöf must have picked up on his thoughts.

Guðgeir felt uncomfortable at the thought and resolved to make a real effort when Smári returned to Iceland. If the young people were to rekindle their relationship, then he would make every effort to connect with Smári properly, to be encouraging and to have faith in the boy.

Turning into the swimming pool car park, Guðgeir felt that this ruthless self-examination had done him good. Now he needed to swim for half an hour, get a good night's sleep and turn up for work in the morning refreshed. He reached across to the back seat for his sports bag, but there was nothing there. His trunks, towel, shampoo, comb and deodorant had all been left behind at home, and he wasn't keen to rent a pair of trunks. The last time, they had been on the small side and showing up poolside like that had been an uncomfortable experience.

But he needed to clear his mind with some fresh air and decided to take a walk through Laugardalur. He locked the car and set off. Instead of relaxing and enjoying the outdoors, however, he found himself thinking about work. The Heimaey case wouldn't let go of him. Diljá would be questioned again tomorrow morning and he needed time to think over what would be the best way to approach her this time. It was vital to form a connection and to somehow win her trust, but Diljá was visibly suspicious of anything to do with authority. She undoubtedly had her own reasons for that, but she was hiding something. He could sense it. Yes, he was certain of it. He mulled over every possible aspect of the case as he walked. He tried to visualise every moment from the point at which he and Elsa Guðrún had arrived in front of the caravan in Herjólfsdalur. If Diljá hadn't murdered Ríkharður, then who had, and why? He thought again through the group of friends. He considered each one, their words and their demeanour. Ásmundur and Ingi Thór had both known of the drugs that

Ríkharður had unwittingly taken, and also that he was helpless in the caravan. Ingi Thór had long fair hair that matched what had been found at the scene, but Ásmundur had been the one who had called from an unregistered phone to let the police know about Diljá's hiding place. Why had he done that? Were the two of them both guilty? Then there was Katrín and her connection to Ingibjörg, with her long black hair that was in reality blonde. Did she have some connection to all this, or maybe her niece, Ríkharður's daughter Lára? There was no doubt that both of them were angry and jealous, but murder? No, that was going too far. Guðgeir's train of thought was abruptly broken when he practically walked into a woman who had a long-haired white dog on a lead.

'Sorry? What did you say?' she asked, holding on to the lead as the dog scratched with its hind legs in a hopeless attempt to hide its own turds.

'Me?' he replied, still deep in his own thoughts. 'Nothing. I didn't say a word.'

'Really? I thought you were telling me off for not picking up dogshit,' the woman said, a grey bag fluttering in her hand. 'I was just about to do it.'

'No, not at all. I wasn't even aware of you. Completely in another world, I'm afraid. Talking to myself,' Guðgeir explained awkwardly, shifting uncomfortably.

'I see. So you were talking to a specialist, in that case,' the woman said cheerfully. She slipped the bag over her hand and picked up the dog's offering. Then she rolled it back over her hand and tied it in a secure knot.

'Well, yes!' Guðgeir agreed and laughed. 'I suppose so,' he said to himself once the woman had moved on and couldn't hear him.

He felt for his phone, and saw that it was late enough for him to be on his way home. As he sat in the car, a little breathless after the brisk walk, Inga's words came back to him. What had she said the other evening? That going by her own experience, everyone had something they wanted to keep hidden away, every single person. Only the circumstances vary. This wasn't exactly some new revelation, but he decided that in this case, these were words that he needed to keep clear in his mind.

45

Despite having good reason to be optimistic, Diljá looked obviously despondent when she was brought to the interview room the next morning. She sat slumped in a chair, her hair uncombed, her eyes red, with black shadows beneath them. Elsa Guðrún felt a stab of alarm as she could not fail to see Diljá's misery, so she started by asking her how she felt, and if she had been able to sleep.

'No. I can't stay locked up in that cell. I'll die if I have to be in there any longer,' Diljá said through gritted teeth. 'You can't do this to me and I'll see to it that the police are prosecuted for inhuman treatment of a remand prisoner.'

'You won't be there long,' Guðgeir said gently, running a hand over the stubble on his chin. 'But there are still things that we need to clear up. When you told us about the ayahuasca trip to Peru, you mentioned that the spiritual journey, I mean after you had drunk the so-called tea, had been difficult for Ingi Thór and afterwards he had struggled with some problems. Is that right?'

'Yeah. More or less.'

'So he feels he needs to go again?' Elsa Guðrún said with an encouraging smile.

'Yes. He has to go so he can finish it,' Diljá said.

'Do you feel that you have anything that needs to be concluded?' Guðgeir asked.

'Not just me. We all want to go back, but for Ingi Thór it's a necessity.'

'Why's that?'

'To become free. It's not something I can explain. You'll have to talk to him about his problems,' Diljá said, rubbing her nose with the back of her hand.

'We'll do that, and you can go now,' Guðgeir said, getting to his feet.

'Go?'

She stared at them in turn, her astonishment unmistakeable.

'Yes. You're free to go,' Elsa Guðrún said.

'Don't I have to finish the time on remand...?' Diljá said, her words fading away, and it was as if a veil had been pulled from her face as she brightened suddenly. 'I can go now? Home?'

Guðgeir nodded and opened the door.

'Be my guest,' he said. 'But please bear in mind that although you're free to go now, that doesn't mean that your innocence has been proved and don't forget that you can expect a prosecution.'

'Don't worry. I'll forget nothing,' she replied, but her ice-cold expression was unable to hide the relief in her voice.

They sat in silence for a while after Diljá and the lawyer had departed. Guðgeir put his hands behind his head and sighed.

'What now?' Elsa Guðrún finally asked.

'We bring Ingi Thór in to make a statement as soon as possible. In the meantime we need to establish every possible connection between him and Ríkharður. Let's start with him, and then we can bring Ásmundur in.'

'Diljá said that Ingi Thór needs to complete something,' Elsa Guðrún recalled. 'Otherwise, what? Could be become dangerous, or ...?'

She spread her hands in question.

'It's possible,' Guðgeir said. 'To my mind, the connection lies with the deaths of his parents or the people who took in him and his brother.'

'It seems they weren't the pleasantest people,' Elsa Guðrún said.

'That's exactly it,' Guðgeir said with a frown.

46

When Diljá had been released, they met Særós. Guðgeir hung his jacket on the back of the chair. Then he stretched his shoulders so that they felt right before he sat down. He was noticing stress symptoms, and knew that these were because of his frustration over the progress of the case.

'There are far too many loose ends in this case,' Særós said, sounding impatient. 'You should definitely call Ingi Thór and Ásmundur in, but my feeling is that the connections are too loose. In reality, we can say that we don't have anything to go on, nothing on either of them. According to Leifur, there was hardly a footprint to be found in the caravan, or else there were so many overlapping in a small space that they couldn't be made out clearly. That means that everything hinges on the work being done on these few hair samples found in the bedclothes. If nothing comes out of that, then I don't know where to turn next. On top of that, we don't have a single witness with anything of any value to tell us,' Særós said, and stood up, pacing the floor and rolling her shoulders. Every movement made her pale blue silk blouse ripple.

'Is it your opinion that we should hold off taking statements until we have the DNA results?' Guðgeir asked.

'No. But tread carefully,' Særós said, weighing her words.

'That goes without saying,' Guðgeir replied. 'Ingi Thór has been requested to be here this afternoon and I was thinking of meeting Ríkharður's son or daughter first. Preferably both of them. That could give us something more go on before we talk to him.'

'Have you been in touch with them?' Særós asked, her shoulders now relaxed.

'I sent the son a message but haven't heard back,' Guðgeir said, checking his phone.

'Their names are Vilhjálmur and Lára. I met them the day their father was found,' Særós said. 'Considering the circumstances, I found the son to be remarkably calm, but there was no mistaking that the daughter was very unhappy with Diljá, and she was naturally deeply upset. It'll be interesting to get your take on them.'

'Shall I come as well?' Elsa Guðrún asked.

'Sure. We're concentrating on this case,' Guðgeir replied. He took his jacket from the back of the chair. The axiom of the week caught his attention; ***Treat everyone as if you'll never them again***. 'Aren't there some loose ends there?' he asked, pointing at the wall. Elsa Guðrún rolled her eyes and Guðgeir could see that she was holding back her laughter.

Særós stopped what she was doing and stood with her hands on her hips as she stared at the wall.

'You're right,' she said in amazement, as if surprised at herself. 'That's totally incomprehensible. Absolute rubbish!'

Vilhjálmur Ríkharðsson replied to say that he was at his father's house and could meet them at one o'clock. That was cutting it fine, as Ingi Thór was due to be at the station at three. They pulled up outside the large detached house on the Reykjavík outskirts. In fact, all of the houses in the district were much the same size and shape, the streets were freshly laid and the pavements still being finished. There were white concrete walls around Ríkharður's house, and the only thing that gave it any colour were the cast concrete pots with a few pink flowers among the white ones.

'It's so cold and impersonal,' Elsa Guðrún said with a shudder. 'I couldn't live in this.'

'Maybe Ríkharður planned to smarten things up,' Guðgeir

said, his finger on the buzzer. The door opened almost immediately.

'Hello, come in, please. I'm Vilhjálmur,' the tall young man said. He looked to be in outstanding physical condition, practically like an athlete, and his mousy fair hair was pulled up in a bun on the top of his head. 'My sister isn't in town at the moment, but will be back tomorrow. Let's go in the living room.'

Paperwork that had been sorted into piles had been arranged on the vast coffee table and the large grey-green corner sofa was stacked with boxes and clothes.

'You've been busy,' Guðgeir said, looking around.

'Yes. It's no bad thing to have something to do. I'm a professional footballer and live overseas, but I've been stuck here for a while. First there was coronavirus, and then I had an injury.'

'I thought I recognised you,' Elsa Guðrún said, in a vain attempt to conceal her ignorance of football.

'No problem,' he said with a wan smile. 'It's only now that we are able to start organising the funeral. As you know, that wasn't possible before.'

'Understood, it can be difficult,' Elsa Guðrún said. 'Organising everything often helps those concerned get through the first weeks.'

'Sure,' Vilhjálmur said, and fell silent. He seemed to have exhausted his capacity for courteous small talk, and wanted to know what had brought them, as he didn't ask them to take a seat.

'Well,' Guðgeir said, clearing his throat. 'The autopsy results indicate that the drugs weren't the cause of your father's death. He was suffocated, most likely with a pillow or something similar, as no marks were found on his throat or elsewhere on his body. Diljá has been released from custody as there is no proof of guilt on her part.'

Vilhjálmur looked shaken, and dropped into a chair. He buried his face in his hands and his broad shoulders shook. He sat that way for a moment before looking up again at them.

'Poor Dad,' he groaned, brushing away a tear that had run down his cheek. 'I hope he didn't wake up while this happened. This is terrible. Just a complete nightmare.'

'True,' Elsa Guðrún agreed sympathetically and Guðgeir nodded.

'Who could have done this to him?' Vilhjálmur asked, staring into space as if in a trance.

'That's what we need to find out. Do you know of anyone who bore your father a grudge?' Guðgeir asked, his face grave.

'What do you mean?' Vilhjálmur appeared to have not understood the question.

'If anyone would have wanted to do him harm?' Elsa Guðrún explained.

Vilhjálmur got stiffly to his feet and began to flick through one of the piles of paperwork.

'I found this by chance, and was wondering whether to show it to you,' he said heavily, placing a couple of sheets of paper on the table.

The letters were all from the Directorate of Health. Vilhjálmur passed the letters to them, one at a time. Elsa Guðrún and Guðgeir immersed themselves in the letters, flipping through them and speed-reading. Each letter concerned complaints and court actions that the Directorate had received, all relating to Ríkharður's work. Their eyes met. This shone a whole new light on the case.

'This was all in one place,' Vilhjálmur said in a dull voice, picking up a brown A4 envelope. 'As you can see, the dates of the letters vary. This came as an unpleasant surprise, and I haven't yet told my sister Lára about it. I imagine it'll have to wait for a while as I don't think she'll cope with another shock. She has been in a bad way.'

'There are no names. Only case numbers,' Guðgeir said, the paperwork in his hands. 'Can we take this with us?'

'Of course,' Vilhjálmur said. 'When I found these papers, I remembered something else that you ought to know about.

About six months ago, when Dad had just moved in here, stones were thrown at the living room window and his tyres were slashed. Dad called the police and blood was found on the decking by the living room. They took samples for analysis, but the upshot was that Dad absolutely didn't want them to pursue the case.'

'Really? Why?' Elsa Guðrún asked. 'What was the obstacle?'

'Lára and I couldn't understand it. We told him again and again that he ought to make sure the investigation was kept alive, but he wouldn't have it. You know what I mean, it was as if some stalker was after him. But Dad said he couldn't be bothered with it, and in addition, it could be dangerous to involve the police too much. He said that kind of thing just enrages nutcases like that,' Vilhjálmur said. 'He was absolutely determined.'

'Nutcases? Plural?' Guðgeir said.

'Something like that. I don't remember his exact words.'

'When was this? Can you be precise?'

Vilhjálmur paused in thought.

'Maybe not even that long ago. It could have been March or April. Yes, I think so. I'm sorry, I'm really not thinking straight after what you told me just now. I mean, who does this kind of thing?'

'It's completely understandable. It's a tough piece of news to take on board, and you've had enough to cope with already,' Elsa Guðrún said. 'Do you want to inform your sister, or shall we do it?'

'I'll talk to her,' Vilhjálmur replied, noticeably subdued.

'Thank you for all this,' Guðgeir said and got to his feet. 'And please get in touch right away if there's anything relating to this stalker that comes to mind. Yes, and while I remember, my colleague Særós mentioned that you had acted as if you hadn't known about your father's marriage when she called just after his death, when she met you, your sister and your aunt. But now we know that you and Ásmundur were witnesses at the wedding. Why did you tell an untruth?'

Vilhjálmur's expression was deeply awkward.

'I can't really explain it,' he stammered. 'It's the way I am. I normally just say what I think is going to cause the least trouble. Dad and Diljá wanted to keep it to themselves to start with... You see...'

An apologetic smile spread across his face, and his eyes asked for their approval.

47

As soon as they got to the car, Guðgeir opened the envelope and took pictures of each letter, which he sent to Særós with a request that as the department's senior officer, she should contact the Directorate of Health. He also sent a message to Erna, Ríkharður's former wife, who replied immediately. When they finally set off, the air was becoming heavy and occasional drops of rain were falling.

'Do you expect the Data Protection Authority will kick up a fuss?' Elsa Guðrún asked as she clipped her seat belt into place. 'This is information that we need to get as soon as possible, and this is a completely new angle on the case.'

'Let's hope not,' Guðgeir muttered, deep in thought. 'I'm wondering if we should postpone the statement session with Ingi Thór.'

'No, I don't think we should. If the Directorate of Health drags their feet coming up with answers, we could still be making a mistake somewhere else in the investigation,' Elsa Guðrún said.

'All right. Let's stick to the plan. Are you OK to talk to Ingi Thór? If you have someone with you, Særós or Víðir Jón, maybe...' Guðgeir said, his words coming to a halt as he saw the surprise on Elsa Guðrún's face. She clearly didn't understand this change of direction.

'Really? Where are you going with this?' she asked, unimpressed.

'I get the feeling we've concentrated too closely on the

ayahuasca angle. It's as if we've already decided that something happened during the trip to Peru that led to Ríkharður's death. I'm not convinced we've been on the right track and I'm going to take a closer look and see if there's any bad shit to be found.'

'Bad shit?' Elsa Guðrún asked in bemusement. 'You're not talking about dope?'

'No, nothing like that. I'm talking about something shitty in Ríkharður's past that connects to his murder,' Guðgeir said, switching the windscreen wipers to sweep faster as they could now barely cope with the rain. 'I'll drop you off at the station and have to nip out for a little while. With any luck I'll be back in time for the statement session.'

Elsa Guðrún nodded, but said nothing. They both stared in silence out through the windscreen for the rest of the journey.

'Don't forget the envelope, and put it inside your coat so it stays dry,' Guðgeir said as the car came to a halt outside the station. Elsa Guðrún reached for it on the back seat. 'It'll be fine,' he said. 'I'll be back soon.'

'Thanks. See you,' she said shortly, and was gone.

He watched as she hurried in out of the rain before he set off. Elsa Guðrún's reply had been uncharacteristically short, which was unlike her, just as it had been for her to be silent for so long. Was she upset with him? He decided it was more likely that she had been mentally preparing herself for Ingi Thór's statement, which was why she had been unusually taciturn. That seemed the most likely explanation to him, although it occurred to him that she had taken badly his comment about the investigation's focus on ayahuasca. Elsa Guðrún had been the one who had taken them down that route. On the other hand, her silence could simply be because she felt that he could have told her where his thinking was going; something that he had simply forgotten or overlooked. Guðgeir stopped at a red light and drummed his fingers on the wheel while he waited.

Ach, he told himself. Best to not brood on something so silly.

Elsa Guðrún had never been one to sulk or take things personally, but maybe the ordeal had left her more sensitive in that respect? That was where the answer had to lie, and he reproached himself for having been inconsiderate. But he also felt a touch of irritation. The nature of the job was that there wasn't much space for delicate flowers and people in their position had to be strong all round.

He shook his head and stared into the traffic that was becoming progressively slower. There was a red light ahead, and as it flashed yellow before turning green, Guðgeir realised that this was precisely what Elsa Guðrún had been explaining to him earlier. She was not the violence that had been done to her, but it was nevertheless part of her story. He felt relieved. Of course, Elsa Guðrún's mind must have been on the statement that she had suddenly been expected to take, and nothing else was wrong. Her concerns were totally understandable, as new angles on the case had appeared in the last few hours. He pushed these uncomfortable thoughts to one side, and concentrated on driving the shortest distance that would take him to Erna Daníelsdóttir.

The rain was coming down hard and in the distance he heard a heavy noise, like a roll of thunder. Shoulders hunched, he ran from the car park to the doorway, from where he scanned the sky but saw no lightning. He shook off the worst of the water, and rang the bell. As before, she responded by calling out to him to come inside.

'No need to take your shoes off,' she instructed as he opened the door.

'It's chucking it down outside,' he called back.

'Doesn't matter,' Erna replied. Guðgeir kept his shoes on, but wiped them carefully on the mat before going into the living room. She sat in front of the television. It was switched on but the sound was off.

'Hello. I'd suggest an intercom for the front door,' he said. 'Leaving the front door unlocked isn't exactly secure.'

'Well, I don't know. It helps to have a little tension in your life, doesn't it? Not that I frighten easily,' Erna said with a heart-warming smile. She was fair-haired, with a curl that formed over her forehead, so there must be wavy hair on her head, Guðgeir thought, and immediately dismissed such a far-fetched train of thought. How on earth would the wheelchair-bound Erna have been able to get to a caravan in the Westman Islands? I must be off my head, he told himself, and developing a prejudice against people with fair hair?

'Would you like coffee?' Erna asked.

'Thanks, but no. I'm in a hurry.'

'Ah, that's fine.'

'Fine?' he said in surprise, raising an eyebrow.

'I can't be bothered to make coffee, and I was just trying to be polite,' she said, and they both laughed. Guðgeir felt a growing liking for this outspoken woman. 'But please sit down,' she added. 'It's uncomfortable when...'

'When people have to look down on you,' Guðgeir said. 'I know.'

'Exactly,' Erna laughed. 'What brings you here? I'm really busy right now watching TV on my own.'

Guðgeir moved aside a couple of books that lay on the sofa so he could sit down. His attention was drawn again to how pleasantly colourful and varied her surroundings were, while also being tasteful. Wherever you looked, there was something that pleased the eye or attracted interest.

'When I came to see you the other day, you mentioned that Ríkharður had no tolerance for any kind of failing in his personal life, that he wanted perfection, even if it was just on the surface,' Guðgeir said, his expression becoming serious.

'Yes, that's the way it was,' Erna said, as direct and to the point as before. 'He was a terrible perfectionist, but not in a way that held him back, as happens with some people who never get anywhere in life for fear of making the kind of mistake that only a perfectionist would notice. No, Ríkharður wasn't that type. Instead, everything facing him...' Erna paused and made quote marks in the air with her fingers. 'Had to outwardly be perfect. Our children suffered for this. Their appearance had to be impeccable, they had to have top marks and preferably had to be outstanding at pretty much everything, but he was less interested, and sometimes completely uninterested, in their emotional wellbeing. Anything along the lines of problems or difficulties was unpleasant in his view, and wasn't to be discussed under any circumstances. So if he didn't see a problem, and it wasn't mentioned, then it didn't exist. That was his outlook on life. I wasn't as extreme, but admit that up to the accident, I thought in a similar way. It was pivotal for our marriage and it changed all my opinions. Yes, my outlook on life used to be very different.'

'The new wife, Diljá, is far from perfect,' Guðgeir said. 'She has certainly had challenges she has had to face.'

'Maybe he didn't know the whole story. But we should also bear in mind that Ríkharður was past fifty and had dropped his standards. From the pictures I've seen, she has looks on her side. She's the sporty type he always fell for, the type I once was. He'll have enjoyed being seen with such a beautiful young woman,' Erna said, her tone disdainful but not caustic. 'Showing the boys that he still had it.'

'Not unlikely,' Guðgeir agreed, and his eye went to a recent family photo on a shelf next to the television, of the handsome mother with her two grown-up children sitting each side of her.

'But I'd bet both legs that he asked her a few times to talk less,' Erna said with a hoot of laughter so ice-cold that Guðgeir wasn't sure whether he should echo it. He decided against it.

'Sure you don't want coffee? It's no problem to make some. I was joking just now,' she said, sending a warm smile his way.

'No, thanks. Unfortunately I don't have much time,' Guðgeir replied. 'I came to ask if you knew whether or not Ríkharður had ever made any professional mistakes?'

The question obviously took Erna by surprise. Her expression turned serious, her brow furrowed and she sighed.

'Do you know of any instances?' he asked.

She didn't answer right away, but gazed out of the window. There was a large garden outside that had to be a communal area for the whole building. A widening puddle had formed at the end of the slide.

'Autumn rain, isn't that what it's called?' she said. 'Plenty of it and often.'

'Yes, I think so. But we can hope that summer can last a little longer,' Guðgeir replied, waiting patiently for an answer to his question. He sensed that she was coping with an inner turmoil and was uncertain what to do.

'Look,' she said, her face grave. 'Ríkharður wasn't the kind of doctor who called up his patients to check how they were coping after an operation. He could be extraordinarily insensitive towards other people.'

Erna fell silent. She unlocked the brakes of her wheelchair and went to the kitchen area at the far end of the room. She picked up a notepad and a pen.

'Come over here,' she said and he hurried over to her. 'This doctor isn't going to thank me for this,' she said, handing him a slip of paper. 'But try to talk to him.'

48

Ingi Thór was still being interviewed for his statement when Guðgeir got back to the station. He decided against interrupting and went to his desk. He started by checking the police log, using 'smashed windows' and 'slashed tyres' as keywords. While he waited for results, he turned over in his fingers the slip of paper Erna had given him. There was a phone number on it, and there was something familiar about the doctor's name, but he couldn't quite place it. He searched online, found a picture of him and recognised the face, not that this told him much, so he decided to call Inga.

'Am I interrupting, my love?' he asked, stretching out his long legs as he spoke.

'I have a couple of minutes before I have to be in a meeting,' she replied.

'Do you know a doctor called Einar Baldvin Thórhallsson?'

'Hold on. I need to find a picture of him.'

'OK,' he said, and took the opportunity to fish out a pack of Opals from his pocket. He had just popped two of the liquorice sweets onto his tongue when she came back with an answer.

'He's a doctor who's prominent in the media. He writes articles and appears regularly on the radio. As far as I know, this guy is on the level.'

There was a tap on the half-ajar door and Elsa Guðrún peered inside. Særós was behind her. Guðgeir beckoned them both inside.

'Thanks, love,' he said quickly. 'See you at home later, bye.'

He pressed the red button and turned to his colleagues. 'So how did it go with Ingi Thór?'

'Elsa Guðrún pushed him hard and asked a lot about his parents' illness and the time he spent with foster carers,' Særós said, taking a seat in front of Guðgeir's desk.

'And?'

He looked over at Elsa Guðrún who stood uncertainly in the doorway.

'He's very secretive and it wasn't easy to drag much out of him. But he admitted to having had a difficult experience during the ayahuasca trip to Peru. He said that he saw his own life replayed to him like a movie and that he wasn't able to run away or shield himself behind any excuses, but saw himself in a mercilessly detailed mirror, to use his own words. He said that it had been a very tough experience to see himself stripped bare like that and that he was still struggling to come to terms with it.'

'He repeated again and again that he would have to return to Peru,' Særós said. 'He's obsessed with it.'

'It was all rather unusual, to put it mildly. But Ingi Thór was adamant that there are no links between them and Ríkharður. He stated that he knew nothing of the man before he took up with Diljá,' Elsa Guðrún said. 'I'm going to get on with the statement and you can look through it when I'm done. Shall I shut the door?'

'Yes, please,' Guðgeir said. He put his hands to the back of his neck and massaged a sore spot. 'I think it's clear that we're not going to make progress in this direction unless we get a positive match from the DNA analysis on those hairs,' he said to Særós.

She nodded her agreement.

'Where did you go just now?'

'First to meet Ríkharður's son Vilhjálmur. His sister is out of town. Then I went to meet their mother. To cut a long story short, I found out that in March or April this year there was damage done to some of Ríkharður's property and that his personality was dominated by a strong perfectionist trait...' he said – about to add that his perfectionism was of a different type to hers, but stopping himself in time.

'So it's unlikely that he would ever have admitted to a professional error of judgement,' Særós said.

'That's what occurs to me,' Guðgeir said. He leaned his chair back and clasped his hands behind his neck.

'Then I hope that the Directorate of Health comes up with a response as soon as possible,' Særós said. 'I'll chivvy them along. This is information that we need urgently.'

'Very much so,' Guðgeir agreed, and glanced at his screen, where his keyword search was starting to produce results. 'I'm searching for information on the wilful damage that Vilhjálmur mentioned, and he's correct,' he said. 'Look.' Guðgeir adjusted the screen so that Særós could see it clearly. 'Ríkharður called the police, there's a witness who reported seeing a fair-haired man in good physical condition and at least one metre eighty in height run from Ríkharður's house, stop by his car, take out a knife and slash the tyres.'

'Was this witness a neighbour?' Særós asked, moving back from the screen.

'No, a postman on an electric scooter. He wasn't able to describe the man any better than that, which made no difference as Ríkharður didn't want to pursue the matter,' Guðgeir said, massaging his right shoulder with his left hand. He could feel the muscles across his shoulders and leading up to his head were inflamed.

'The description fits Ingi Thór,' Særós said and watched Guðgeir thoughtfully. 'If your shoulder muscles are inflamed, then you shouldn't swim breaststroke, only crawl. Yes, and make sure you do stretch exercises for your shoulders every day. Roll them both ways and stretch properly. The same as you see me doing.'

'I'll start right away,' Guðgeir said, not bothering to tell her that crawl had been his preferred stroke for many years, and he never failed to do shoulder stretches every single day. 'I'll speak to Egill, the officer who attended the scene. Maybe he can add to what we already know.'

There was a tap at the door, and it opened. Leifur walked in and stopped in the middle of the room, tugging up his trousers that were a size too large for him.

'Well,' he said. 'We have a result on the hairs and they don't match any of the group of friends.'

49

Einar Baldvin Thórhallsson turned out to be elusive. He worked mainly at the National Hospital, but also ran his own practice where he received patients one day a week. After a long wait with a robotic voice informing him at regular intervals that he was number eleven in the queue, Guðgeir gave up and headed for the car. It was already late in the day and he didn't want to risk not being able to get through to him. The traffic was getting thicker but now most of the flow was going in the direction Guðgeir wanted to go. He felt it was running too slowly, and he glanced repeatedly at his watch, hoping that the doctor would continue to see patients well into the evening. By the time he reached the junction of Reykjanesbraut and Stekkjarbakki, the traffic was practically gridlocked, and it looked like there was an accident somewhere ahead. He sighed in disappointment. If he couldn't get up to the doctor's practice at Mjódd, then he would just have to put up with it. Instead, he would have to track the man down at his home this evening, or the next morning. Guðgeir drummed his fingers on the wheel in sheer frustration and tried to figure out what was happening further along the road. The queue of cars wasn't moving at all. He picked up his phone and called Leifur.

'I took a screenshot of the statement concerning the damage at Ríkharður's home,' he said. 'Could I ask you to talk to the officer who attended the scene? I'm tied up with something else and won't have time today. I'm mainly interested to know if there were any biological samples or any evidence, maybe fingerprints, from the scene.'

'Leave it to me,' Leifur assured him in his booming bass voice.

'And will you let me know as soon as you find anything out? It doesn't matter what time of the day or night,' Guðgeir said, and ended the call as the knot of traffic seemed to be about to unravel and the car behind was sounding its horn at him. A few metres further on, the traffic came to a halt again. He took the opportunity to send the screenshot to Leifur. Once he had done that, the knot of traffic untangled itself, and he was able to turn into the car park at Mjódd a few minutes before the medical practice was due to close. He parked in the first available space, and had to jog some distance to reach the entrance. It was still open. He ignored the lift, instead rushing up the stairs and through a door where a solidly built woman with cropped grey hair barred his way.

'We're closed,' she said, with a discouraging scowl. Guðgeir could see that all the lights inside had been switched off. A young man edged past the woman and headed out, nodding a goodbye as he went.

'Einar Baldvin Thórhallsson,' Guðgeir puffed. 'It's vital that I speak to him.'

'Did you have an appointment today? If you couldn't make it, then you'll just have to call tomorrow to make a new one,' she said in one long rush of words and with a tired look of courteous apology.

'No. I'm from the police and have a few urgent questions for him. Has Einar gone home?' Guðgeir asked, trying to sound calm. The woman peered at him in suspicion. 'Hold on, I should have a police ID somewhere.'

He felt in his inside jacket pockets for the wallet and was relieved that it was where it should be. This was something that he was increasingly forgetting and leaving on his desk or at home, as everything he needed to do his usual work was in his phone – with the exception of his warrant card. He fished it out of his wallet and held it up.

'This is like in an American cop show,' he said with a smile that she didn't return.

'He's in room 23. I think he's still there,' she said. 'I'll take you there,' she added, a hint of suspicion still in her voice.

The door of the room stood open, and Einar sat, a thin-haired man with hunched shoulders, at a computer. Guðgeir wondered if he shouldn't be retired by now.

'Are you waiting for me?' he asked, his question directed to the woman when he noticed them. 'I need to stay a little longer. I'll lock up, so you don't need to wait.'

'From the police,' the woman said, jerking her head towards Guðgeir. The doctor's surprise was unmistakeable.

'Really? What brings you here?' he asked, taking off his glasses, the lenses grimy.

'My name's Guðgeir Fransson and I need answers relating to the death of Ríkh...'

He got no further as the doctor smartly interrupted.

'Anna, I'll set the alarms and lock up. Thanks for everything today and I'll see you next week.'

'All right. I'll be on my way, then,' Anna said, although this seemed to not be to her liking. 'You'll lock up,' she added, glancing at them in turn.

'Of course. Don't worry,' Einar assured her. 'You can be off home, Anna.'

He said nothing more until her footsteps could be heard receding along the corridor and a distant door banged.

'Well, won't you take a seat?' he said. 'So you want to ask about Ríkharður? That was so sudden. Are you any closer to knowing what happened?'

'We know that he was murdered,' Guðgeir said and sat down in a chair by the desk.

'Yes, I'd heard something about that. Deeply sad,' Einar said heavily. 'May I ask who suggested you should speak to me?'

'Erna Daníelsdóttir, although she said you wouldn't be best pleased.'

'Well, then. She said that? But did it all the same. She must have concluded that you need this information, and I trust her judgement. What do you want to know?'

The doctor leaned back in his seat, wringing his hands as if he were waiting for awkward questions from a patient.

'I want to know if Ríkharður had made any professional mistakes,' Guðgeir said.

'Every doctor does that. Something we have in common is that we all have something on our consciences, something that could have been done better. We're ordinary people, not superhuman, and science isn't infallible either,' Einar said, an inner tolerance showing through in his manner. His hands were clasped together, his thumbs turning slow circles around each other.

'I'm not referring to minor errors,' Guðgeir said. 'But something major, something that could have taken away someone's life, in literal and figurative terms.'

'Precisely. I understand,' Einar said, his expression grave as his thumbs spun faster around each other and his voice hardened. 'The answer is quite simply yes. Ríkharður was not sufficiently conscientious in his work, he did not monitor his patients particularly well. There were frequent complaints about him, and it's my opinion that he should have been struck off.'

50

Guðgeir called Leifur as he walked out of the building. Waiting for him to pick up, he watched the stream of people coming out of the supermarket that was part of the same commercial complex as the medical centre, bags in their hands or pushing shopping trolleys ahead of them. He made a mental note to call Inga and let her know he wouldn't be home for dinner.

'Did you get hold of him?' he asked as soon as the phone was answered.

'Yes.'

'Any samples?' Guðgeir asked, preparing himself mentally for disappointment, as it was rare that this kind of investigative work would be undertaken for a relatively minor crime.

'Listen, yes! There's some evidence because the perpetrator cut himself when he smashed the living room window and left a trail of blood. Some samples were taken, but there was no further action as the victim didn't want to pursue the matter,' Leifur said.

Guðgeir felt his heart beat faster.

'We need an analysis to compare to the hairs from the caravan.'

'Is that what you want to do? Aren't you stretching things a little too far?' Leifur asked, his tone sincere.

''I'm practically certain that I'm not, and I need these results as soon as possible. Would you make this a priority, Leifur? And give me the address and phone number of our colleague who took the statement? I need to talk to him.'

Guðgeir waited in the car until the information from Leifur came through, which was just as well because the officer's home wasn't far from Mjódd. He punched in the address and drove up to the Selja district.

Egill's home was in a blue and white terraced house at the end of a cul-de-sac. Guðgeir rang the bell and glanced around as he waited. The area was very smart, and it occurred to him that maybe he and Inga ought to sell their new, modern apartment in a block and look for just such a modest, cosy place as this where they could walk straight out into the garden. Inga had often mentioned that she would like to try her hand at growing varieties of roses.

A girl of around ten opened the door.

'Is Egill here?' Guðgeir asked.

'Are you selling something?' the girl replied.

'No. We work together,' he said with a smile.

'You're a cop?'

'Yes.'

'Dad!' she called out with all the power she could muster, without taking her eyes off Guðgeir. When there was no response, she turned and yelled into the house, even louder. 'Dad! Dad!'

She waited for a reply, but when there was none, she informed Guðgeir, dropping her voice back to a normal level, that her father had most likely gone to the shop to get something for dinner.

'All right, I'll wait,' Guðgeir said. Another girl of about the same age appeared behind Egill's daughter. She looked at the caller with wide eyes, exploring her nose with a finger, while listening to the conversation.

'This is my friend and we're playing,' the daughter explained. 'You can wait outside but you can't come in. Strangers aren't allowed inside the house.'

'That makes perfect sense,' Guðgeir said with a smile. 'You can go on playing and I'll wait in the car.'

'All right,' they chorused, and pushed the door shut.

Guðgeir didn't need to wait long. A small white car pulled up in the drive and a bony man wearing sunglasses got out. He went to the back of the car and opened the boot, then tucked a pack of toilet rolls under one arm and picked up a shopping bag in each hand. This left him struggling to close the boot of the car, which refused to click into place. Guðgeir came to his rescue.

'Hello, Egill, can I help you with that?' he asked, pushing it shut for him. 'I'm Guðgeir Fransson from CID.'

'Of course I know who you are. You're pretty well known,' Egill replied. He put the shopping bags down, and pushed his sunglasses up to his forehead. 'Leifur from Forensics spoke to me earlier today about the case this spring that you're interested in. Unfortunately, we don't have any names, as the case was closed almost as soon as it had begun.'

'That's right. But I'm more interested in the victim, Ríkharður Magnússon. Do you remember if there was a reason why he didn't want the case to be pursued?'

'I've been trying to recall the details and found a few notes I made at the time. Ríkharður's manner put me in mind of someone who had been the victim of a stalker. It was as if he had some idea who was behind it, and pulled back for that reason. Know what I mean? He might have been concerned about something worse happening next. But of course that's just speculation on my part,' Egill said. He was about to say something more when his daughter tiptoed down the drive on stockinged feet.

'Did you buy something nice to eat, Dad?' she asked. Her eyes were alive and she gave him a gap-toothed smile. 'Can Tinna stay for dinner?'

'We'll see, but I bought stuff that's good and healthy. Go on in, my love. I'll be right with you.' He lifted the two bags and turned back to Guðgeir. 'To be honest, that's about all I could recall.'

'Weren't you about to say something before your daughter came out? What was that?'

'Ach, nothing much. But I have a recollection of Ríkharður swearing under his breath something about the Westman Islands. "Bloody Islanders" or something like that.'

Guðgeir stared.

'He said that?'

'As far as I recall. But like I said, this was a few months ago.'

'Thanks,' Guðgeir said. 'That's a great help.'

He could see Egill standing with shopping bags in his hands, watching him as he drove away. This had been a very worthwhile visit, and now he urgently needed to get hold of Diljá. He was fairly sure that she would have gone to her mother, and he called the station to check he had the right address. When it was confirmed, he took a sharp turn and headed in the direction of Pálína's home. At the first set of lights, he paused and thought again. Diljá had no liking for him, and with good reason. Supposing she refused to talk to him after everything that had gone on? Now that she had been released from custody, she had no obligation to answer any questions. The slightest error could wreck everything and nothing could be allowed to go wrong now. Guðgeir thought no further, and called Elsa Guðrún.

'*Hæ*. How are you fixed?' he asked. He could hear cheerful music playing in the background.

'Clearing up after dinner and the boys are playing football outside,' she said, and Guðgeir could make out from her tone of voice that the interruption wasn't welcome.

'I know you're not on duty, but is there any chance you could get away for an hour or so?' he asked gently.

'What for?'

'To call on Diljá and ask her to go over in detail everything that happened on that Saturday evening,' he replied.

'One more time?'

'Yes,' Guðgeir replied firmly.

'Just the evening? Not the day?'

'That's it. From when they left the caravan in Herjólfsdalur for the aperitif at the hotel, and everything that happened after that. Every single thing. This has to be very precise, if you know what I mean,' he explained quickly.

'Sure, but why don't you go? Isn't that a better option since you know what you're looking for?' Elsa Guðrún asked, and there was no mistaking that she would prefer to be without this unexpected assignment.

'No. You connect much better with her. She responds much more positively to you than to me, you must have noticed,' Guðgeir said with conviction.

'All right, but what am I supposed to do with the boys?'

There was a note of resignation in her voice.

'Is there anyone who can keep an eye on them? The people upstairs?' Guðgeir suggested.

'No. I don't like to do that. It just feels wrong.'

'In that case I'll be there for a kickabout in a few minutes,' Guðgeir said, signalling left to make a U-turn for the road that would take him to Kópavogur.

51

He was worn out by the time Elsa Guðrún returned. The group had grown considerably after the twins had shouted around half the neighbourhood that there was a guy from the police playing football in their garden. What had been a relaxed kickabout with the boys had turned into something more serious and a real effort on his part had been required to keep pace with them. He was relieved to see approaching freedom in the form of Elsa Guðrún's car pulling up outside the building.

'Ten more minutes!' she called out to her sons before turning to Guðgeir. 'I recorded the conversation and sent it to you.'

'Thank you. You're an absolute life-saver. How was she?' he asked anxiously.

'Pretty down,' Elsa Guðrún replied, lips pursed. 'The atmosphere at Ríkharður's place is so poisonous that she couldn't go there. There's all kinds of stuff that needs to be settled between her and Ríkharður's children.'

'That's hardly a surprise,' Guðgeir said.

'No, of course not. But now Diljá is sleeping on the sofa in her mother's eighth-floor flat. The claustrophobia she was suffering from before is worse than ever and she can't use the lift. On top of that, the owner of the gym where she had clients called and said he doesn't want her back any time soon. According to him, her presence could adversely affect the gym's reputation.' Elsa Guðrún shook her head and sighed.

'Shall I go on?'

'Ach, no,' Guðgeir said. 'That'll do. But she was co-operative?'

'All things considered, I reckon she was. I hope you find what you're looking for in the recording,' she said.

'That makes two of us,' he said from the doorway. 'Thanks again. Kindest regards to your two balls of fire. It's pretty obvious where that energy comes from.'

'North country super-genes,' Elsa Guðrún grinned. 'See you at work tomorrow.'

He waved to the boys as he drove away, but didn't go far. As soon as he was out of sight around the corner, he turned off the engine and switched on the recording. He was so excited that he could hear his own heartbeat pounding in his ears. He listened to Diljá's account, which was perfectly in line with her previous narrative, except for one thing. He spooled back and listened again.

'She was so long getting one glass of whisky that my nerves were completely on edge,' he heard Diljá say.

'Why was that?' Elsa Guðrún asked.

'I was terrified the medication would kick in too hard before we went over to Magni for dinner,' Diljá replied.

She. Diljá had said she. There was no doubt about it. Guðgeir went through his notes and found Ásmundur's phone number, called it and there was no reply. Glancing at the clock, he saw that it was almost eight-thirty. He drove along Breiðholtsbraut, calling the number again and again, but with no reply. He decided to try calling at the gym, as Ásmundur could still be at work.

'He's in the middle of a session in the gym,' said the young woman at reception. 'We close at ten, and I don't know when he'll be finished. Can I take a message?'

'No, thanks. Can you call him?'

'He's with a client,' the girl said, as if shocked at Guðgeir's lack of understanding.

'Yes, I know. But this is incredibly urgent and a very

personal matter,' he explained, emphasising every word.

'It's something serious?' she asked, and seemed confused about what to do next.

'It's a family matter,' he conceded, as he didn't want Ásmundur to be excluded from his work at the gym as Diljá had been.

'Oh!' the girl said, a hand to her mouth. 'Has someone died?' Guðgeir said nothing, but held her with his serious gaze. 'I'll fetch him. Wait there,' she gabbled and left at a run.

Ásmundur appeared after a few minutes.

'It's you,' he said, appearing at first to be relieved, before a look of concern clouded his face.

'Let's go outside,' said Guðgeir, who could see that the girl was listening in to what they were saying. 'There's a bench outside. Do you want to get a jacket?'

'No. I'm fine,' Ásmundur said, following Guðgeir out into the cool evening air. 'What's this all about?' he demanded once they were sitting on the bench.

'You don't need to be worried. I just want you to try and remember who served you at the hotel bar before you went over to Magni on that Saturday evening in the Westman Islands. Can you remember that?' Guðgeir asked. 'That would be a big help.'

Ásmundur leaned forward and held his head in his hands. Guðgeir could see the serpent's colourful tail writhe from beneath one sleeve, and red-orange tongues of flame stretch up to his neck.

'Er...,' Ásmundur said as he looked up. 'My memory's not great, but I'm pretty sure it was a woman, on the young side and as far as a can remember, she was blonde.'

'Good,' Guðgeir said. 'And do you remember who was serving at the bar later that evening? That was after you came back from the restaurant, and when you and Ingi Thór went to the bar for a drink before it closed.'

Ásmundur again put his hands to his head, elbows planted on his knees.

'I... How should I...? Look, we all had a massive shock the next day when all you cops turned up. I already told you I have hyperactivity and attention deficit disorder...'

'Try to remember. You undoubtedly remember more than you think. Don't decide in advance that you're forgetful,' Guðgeir said encouragingly.

'I didn't even think about who was at the bar. I was talking to Ingi Thór and wondering if Diljá would get away from Ríkharður,' Ásmundur muttered, massaging the tattooed snake on his arm.

'Just say if it was a man or a woman. That'll be enough,' Guðgeir said. 'Do you remember that?'

'It was a man,' Ásmundur said quickly, sitting up straight. 'Definitely a man.'

'Absolutely sure of that?' Guðgeir asked, sensing the tension rising inside him. He took deep breaths and did his best to conceal his emotions. If this was correct, then the solution could be in sight.

'A hundred per cent!' Ásmundur said, pleased to have been able to help.

'Could you describe him?' Guðgeir asked.

'You'd have to ask Ingi Thór about that. I don't remember that sort of stuff. But maybe you've already spoken to him?'

'Not yet. But you've been a great help,' Guðgeir said with genuine sincerity.

'OK. Hey, I have to get back inside. My client's waiting.'

'Just one more question,' Guðgeir said. 'Then you're free of me. Why did you give the anonymous tip-off letting us know where Diljá was hiding?'

'Did she tell you that?'

'Yes. But we would have found that out anyway sooner or later,' Guðgeir replied.

'Ach. I was just being a complete idiot. I was on edge, and then I didn't know if she had given Ríkharður a few too many sleeping pills.'

'I see,' Guðgeir said.

'Hey, I have to go.'

Ásmundur jumped to his feet.

'Yes, thanks. And I hope it all works out for you,' Guðgeir said as he hurried over to his car. He had decided that this was enough for now. But all the same, he made a call to Ingi Thór to cross-check what Ásmundur had told him. Guðgeir decided that the man's memory wasn't so poor after all.

'You're sure it was a man?' Guðgeir asked a second time.

'Yes,' Ingi Thór replied, without hesitation. 'Absolutely.'

'I'm going to send you three pictures. I want you to look at them carefully and not show them to anyone else. Then call me right back,' Guðgeir instructed before ending the call.

He didn't have long to wait.

'The one in the middle,' Ingi Thór said with decision.

'Absolutely sure?' Guðgeir asked, feeling his heart beat faster.

'Hundred per cent sure. I remember him clearly,' Ingi Thór replied.

Guðgeir thanked him and ended the call. He tapped the wheel thoughtfully a few times as he stared out into the warm summer evening. Then he called Særós and Leifur.

52

It felt as if this night would never end. He switched from one side to the other at intervals and tried every strategy he knew to force himself to sleep. Inga surfaced from sleep for a moment, and asked him to lie still and relax. She instantly fell asleep again, while he lay motionless and wide awake. At four in the morning he downloaded an app of relaxing music. After listening for half an hour to the sound of lapping waves and pan pipes, he gave up and switched on the bedside lamp. Inga didn't move, despite the light, and he picked up a novel he had bought recently. He read a few pages and found that book so interesting that he was more alert instead of sleepy. He put it aside, switching off the lamp. He tried to concentrate on anything other than work, instead focusing on arranging furniture inside an empty apartment, which someone had told him was effective against insomnia. But it didn't help, as his thoughts constantly went back to the caravan in Herjólfsdalur or to Ríkharður's house. He visualised the masked man with a sharp knife slashing the tyres of the dark grey jeep, before padding to the floor-to-ceiling living room window and smashing a gloved hand through the glass. Blood seeped through the glove and the man ran, escaping from Guðgeir's sight like a flickering shadow. He followed around the corner at a run, but the figure escaped around the next one and the next...

He was jerked from sleep with a gasp. His heart hammered and he glanced around in confusion. He shut his eyes, imagining he was still in the nightmare, but quickly opened them again. Inga's side of the bed was empty, and he could hear the sound of running water coming from the shower. He picked up his phone from the bedside table and saw that it was twenty past eight. The emails were already piling up. It was obvious that Særós and Leifur had been at work early and were sharing the latest information. Guðgeir ran a hand over his forehead and eyes. Then he opened the first message from Leifur and took a deep breath as he read through its contents. This confirmed a match between the hairs found in the caravan in Herjólfsdalur and the blood samples collected in Reykjavík on 13th March. Guðgeir let the phone drop onto the duvet and stared up at the ceiling. His theory had been correct. He picked up the phone and opened the first message from Særós. Yes, he had been quite right. The Directorate of Health had released the names of those who had sought to sue. There were two, and both had been resident in the Westman Islands.

53

There was just a gentle breeze blowing as their flight took off from Reykjavík. It was a small aircraft, with a mere dozen passengers. Guðgeir had a window seat and he watched as the city's houses became smaller as the horizon expanded. This was a bright late summer's day and there was something warm about the green patches between the multi-coloured clusters of houses. Earlier that morning he had read the report from the Directorate of Health, after which he, Særós and Elsa Guðrún held an online meeting with Lilja Thóra Hallsdóttir, the Commissioner of Police in the Westman Islands.

Lilja had been stunned by the news, as in a small community almost everyone is connected somehow in one way or another. She apologised and switched off her camera for a few minutes while she composed herself. When her face reappeared on the screen, the public servant in her had gained the upper hand.

The aircraft climbed into the sky and before long all that Guðgeir could see were clouds and the occasional gleam of sunshine through them. He leaned back in his seat and closed his eyes, relieved that he could rest his mind for a while before getting to grips with what awaited them. It wasn't a long rest. Only fifteen minutes later the aircraft was descending. Just before touchdown in the Westman Islands he glimpsed Stórhöfði and Herjólfsdalur, less than half an hour after take-off from Reykjavík. Guðgeir slung the strap of his bag over his shoulder and went down the couple of steps leading to the tarmac. The wind was blowing harder in the Westman Islands and his jacket flapped. He stopped to button it up. Tall and pale, with his skin stretched over the bones of his face, Elías waited by the terminal building. He greeted Guðgeir with a serious look on his face.

'This isn't easy for us,' he said with a deep sigh, his thin lips pursed tight.

'No. I can imagine,' Guðgeir said.

'We'll start by fetching the Commissioner. She didn't want to start any unnecessary rumours by coming here.'

'Understandably,' Guðgeir agreed.

'News travels like wildfire here,' Elías explained.

'I know.'

They walked together to the car, and it took only a few minutes to drive to the police station. This was close to the higher end of the town, and at the end of the street the steep rock faces leading into Herjólfsdalur could be seen. Their arrival at the white-painted police station coincided with that of Commissioner Lilja Thóra Hallsdóttir, a woman of around forty with brown eyes and dark hair drawn back in a ponytail. Her looks were reminiscent of Diljá's, and Guðgeir could only reflect on how differently life had treated these two women. Lilja Thóra's police uniform and determined demeanour were the clearest indicators of this. Guðgeir opened the car window.

'His house is just around the corner,' Lilja Thóra said and her sadness was plain to see on her face.

'This must be a shock for all of you here. I mean, those who know,' Guðgeir said.

'You can just imagine!' Lilja Thóra's lips trembled and she shook her head as she spoke, as if unable to believe what had taken place. 'Our mothers were good friends and our fathers sailed together on a trawler. I had heard that he kept to himself after what happened, but I never went to see him. I always meant to, was always on the way, but never even called. He works a lot and... I don't know. I should have been in touch, should have dropped by or given him a call. Then maybe he wouldn't have...'

'Don't blame yourself. It doesn't do any good,' Guðgeir said. 'We could all do better for our neighbours. So shouldn't we make a move?'

'He's not at work, so let's start at his place,' Elías said.

They drove the short distance that would have been covered just as quickly on foot. Another police car followed close behind them. The red-painted, two-storey house looked deserted and there was nobody to be seen at the windows as the three of them walked up the drive. A battered doorbell hung loose on a length of wire by the wooden door. Elías pressed the button. Nothing could be heard. He tried again without any result, and it was obvious that the bell wasn't working. Lilja Thóra knocked, three hard blows on the door. They waited and nothing happened.

'Can he get away from here?' Guðgeir asked softly.

'He can't go anywhere. Neither the ferry nor the airport will let him past. The harbour's being watched, and so are all the small boats. We've already made sure of that,' the Commissioner said, knocking again, even harder. 'I don't know what to do if he doesn't answer. We can't enter the property without a warrant.'

'Oh,' Guðgeir said, his hand on the door handle. 'It's not locked,' he said in surprise.

'Well, we don't tend to lock doors around here,' Elías said. 'And it looks like the door's not even closed properly.'

Guðgeir caught Lilja Thóra's eye, and saw that they were in agreement. Sometimes necessity has to take precedence over legal niceties and he trusted himself completely to justify his actions if he had to answer later to Særós. He opened the door and went inside. A little bowl of keys stood on a shelf next to a row of coat hooks. One was clearly a house key, another for a bike lock, but there was no car key to be seen. That didn't mean anything, as it could well be that the man didn't own a car. You hardly needed one in a place where work and everything else were so close by. Guðgeir went silently into a neat living room and from there to a dining room and kitchen. There was nobody to be seen.

'Hello?' he called out softly. 'Anyone home?'

There was no reply.

A spiral staircase went from the living room down to the floor below and Guðgeir hesitated before putting a foot on the first step. What if the man was off his head, waiting for him down there? Maybe it was worth calling out the Special Unit? He didn't even have pepper spray or a taser on him. He instinctively held tight to the bannister, trying not to put his full weight on the steps, so as to avoid making any unnecessary sound. The stairs led to a space with a carpeted floor, with four doors leading off from it.

Guðgeir felt his heart pound as the first opened with a faint squeal of hinges onto a roomy bedroom where a large double bed faced him, along with bedside tables and an armchair. Some expensive curtains hung at the windows and ornate frames stood on the bedside tables, displaying pictures of a couple, or some of just the woman alone. The largest showed her standing on Eldfell, her arms spread wide to embrace the whole world. This was a healthy young woman with her life ahead of her.

A single duvet and some pillows lay on one side of the bed. A bedspread lay on the other side. Guðgeir knew why. He closed the bedroom door gingerly opened the next door. There was nobody there, nor in the bathroom, nor the washroom behind the fourth door. Guðgeir hurried back upstairs.

'Nobody here,' he reported once he was back on the street.

'I know,' Lilja Thóra said quickly. 'Back to the car. I received a report to say he just turned in to Hraunbúðir. Come on, quick! Elías, you drive.'

'Where the hell does the man think he's going?' Elías muttered as he drove down the street. His vast hands gripped the wheel, making it look smaller than it was, his face as if carved in stone and his pale skin more taut than ever.

'Where's Hraunbúðir?' Guðgeir asked.

'A little further uptown. His mother's a resident there,' Elías said, putting his foot down.

'It's the care home for the elderly,' Lilja Thóra explained and Guðgeir noticed that her lips shook and her face was pale. She was clearly dreading what was to come. They all sat in silence for the little while it took to get there.

'He drives a small blue jeep,' Lilja Thóra said as they turned in to Hraunbúðir, directing her words to Guðgeir. 'And it looks to me like it's parked over there.'

They pulled up beside the blue car and Guðgeir could feel the wind tugging at his jacket as he opened the door to get out, and he shivered. Without a word, the three of them went up to the timber-clad building.

54

Höskuldur stood at his mother's bedside. His back was to them as he held one of her gaunt hands ribbed with prominent veins, in both of his. Locks of hair that had once been as fair as his flowed over the pillow and her blue eyes shone with affection for her son.

Seeing him standing there was deeply moving. The man who had lost so much that humanity had abandoned him for a while.

Lilja Thóra had gone over the personal side of the case that was laid out in the paperwork supplied by the Directorate of Health during that morning's online meeting. Höskuldur's wife Unnur had travelled to Reykjavík for an operation to address an ailment that caused her considerable discomfort. The doctor, Ríkharður Magnússon, had failed to inform her of the potential risks or of alternative treatment options. He had casually described the operation as a minor procedure. Ríkharður had assured Unnur that she would be her usual self after a few days, or at most, a couple of weeks. On the morning of the operation she had been extremely anxious and once she was on the operating table her distress was such that she could hardly breathe and announced loudly that she no longer wished to go through with the operation. Then she heard Ríkharður give the instruction for an anaesthetic to be administered, and after that she remembered no more.

A few days later Unnur returned to the Westman Islands. She was in poor health, both physically and mentally. She was depressed and prone to violent nightmares, at the same time as being plagued by infections and other side effects. The imbalance between treatment and medication made her condition even worse, and so this vivacious and energetic woman became an invalid, in constant pain and unable to work. She sent emails to Ríkharður that he at first failed to reply to, and when he finally messaged her back, his reply was condescending, making light of her ill-health. Soon afterwards he responded again by prescribing tranquillisers and pointing in the direction of a psychiatrist he felt might be able to help her. Unnur had suffered a breakdown. She responded furiously to Ríkharður, which did not help at all.

Höskuldur had done his best to support his wife and to help her through the paperwork that was central to bringing a misconduct case, but the pressure of running the hotel on his own was a heavy burden. Unnur claimed that Ríkharður Magnússon had paid her no attention when she described her illness before and after the operation. Instead of responding immediately, he had disregarded everything she had to say, with the result that her quality of life was close to zero. She had sent both complaints and a formal grievance to the Directorate of Health, but dealing with her requests was constantly delayed. After more than a year of pain and constant disappointment, she fell into deep depression. One evening when Höskuldur came home after a double shift, he found his wife dead in their bed. Unnur had given up on life. From that moment on, Höskuldur had become a shadow of the man he had once been.

'Many of us here in the Westman Islands are familiar with this tragedy,' Lilja Thóra had said during the meeting. 'But for me, and no doubt for most people, it's beyond belief that Höskuldur, such a good man, could be capable of such violence.'

'We have emails that he sent to Ríkharður, and, to put it mildly, they aren't pretty. His anger is there to see in black and white, and it's clear that his hatred for the doctor had been growing by the day since Unnur's death. Ríkharður had done his best to erase all these messages and it wasn't easy to retrieve them. Like I said, they aren't pleasant reading,' Guðgeir said.

'This is dreadful news,' Lilja Thóra sighed.

'Forensics found a few hairs in the caravan that matched bloodstains at Ríkharður's house after a failed break-in and damage to a car in his ownership. Ríkharður refused to allow it to be followed up. These samples also matched a sample taken from a drunk driver who was stopped for breaking a speed limit a couple of months back not far from Ríkharður's house,' Særós had explained, as she requested that the Westman Islands police make necessary arrangements.

55

The three of them stood in the doorway. Guðgeir saw from the corner of his eye police officers clearing the corridor and lobby of the care home. Everything happened so quietly that the silence was almost unreal. Höskuldur still held his mother's hand and there was no indication that he was aware of them, although he could hardly fail to have noticed. He had to have sensed their presence.

He had twice been prevented from committing murder, first by a postman on an electric scooter, and then by the police after he had drunk enough to give himself the courage to drive to Ríkharður's house. The third time was under very different circumstances. That evening he had been clearing up at the hotel bar and heard the two men talking over a drink. Hearing the doctor's name mentioned, he had listened carefully. They mentioned tranquillising drugs and sleeping pills and someone called Diljá who was going to sneak out during the night. When he had realised they were talking about Ríkharður, the man he hated more than he had ever imagined he could possibly hate, he knew that the moment had come.

He had so often dreamed of revenge, and now fate had handed him an opportunity on a silver platter. Could it be a simple coincidence? No, it was clear that fate had taken a hand. Höskuldur listened to everything they said as he finished up. Then he closed the bar and drove home. His house wasn't far from Herjólfsdalur, and he left the car, taking his bike instead and leaving it by the turf cottage that had been built for the delectation of the tourists. He stayed there in the doorway and waited for Diljá to leave. It wasn't long before he saw her go, walking briskly towards the cliffs. Once she was a reasonable distance away, he ran to the caravan. He slipped inside the awning, cautiously opened the door and went inside. Ríkharður was snoring loudly. Höskuldur approached and picked up a pillow.

Guðgeir could see the events in his mind's eye. Now he watched the hotel owner, who had so cheerfully received him and Elsa Guðrún only two weeks ago, as he stood hunched at his mother's bedside. Höskuldur glanced over his shoulder and when he saw who was there, he shifted to obscure her view of them.

'Give me a moment,' he said in a low voice and reached out to touch her lined face. 'I'm all she has left.'

'Who are you talking to?' the old lady asked in a weak voice.

'Nobody,' he said, and his voice shook. 'Mum, listen. I have to go away and won't be able to come and see you for a while. But Lilja Thóra will drop by and see you. That's your friend Rósa's daughter. She's in the police now... You remember her, don't you? She'll come and see you.'

He stooped forward, stroked her thin, silver-grey hair and kissed his mother's forehead. Then he turned and walked towards those who waited for him.